I0715611

Praise for the Series:

The Nine

"Gripping paranormal series starter whose heroine boldly flips the script." —*BookLife*

"Murder, intrigue, and romance mix in this inventive…fantasy series opener." —*Kirkus*

"A white-knuckled ride through a brilliantly-imagined world from start to finish."
—Jen Marie Hawkins, *The Language of Cherries*

"A secret society. Young adults with enhanced 'abilities.' Some romance. Some murder. A lot of intrigue and who is to be trusted… I can't wait for the next book!" —*The Sassy Bookworm*

"With superb world building and visual storytelling this was an enchanting read that I found myself not able to put down, and when it was done I was sad and excited for the possibilities of the next installments. I will definitely be reading all of the books in this series and can't wait to get my hands on the next one."
—*Ann's Bibliotherapy*

THE NINE:
To the Nines

KES TRESTER

OWL HOLLOW PRESS

Owl Hollow Press, LLC, Springville, UT 84663

This book is a work of fiction. Names, characters, places, and incidents are products of the author's imagination. Any resemblance to actual people, living or dead, or to businesses, companies, events, institutions, or locales is completely coincidental.

The Nine: To the Nines
Copyright © 2024 by Kes Trester

All rights reserved. No part of this publication may be reproduced, distributed or transmitted in any form or by any means, without prior written permission.

Library of Congress Cataloging-in-Publication Data
The Nine: To the Nines / K. Trester. — First edition.

Summary:
With her back against the wall, Blake will do anything, risk everything, to divine fiends from enemies as she races to uncover the truth behind Scarlett's disappearance.

Cover: Pocket Hollow Designs

ISBN 978-1-958109-73-1 (paperback)
ISBN 978-1-958109-74-8 (e-book)

*For Luke and Jordan
with love*

The Nine Gifts

Elementalists: Those who influence the natural elements

Empaths: Those who read or influence emotions in others

Enchanters: Those who influence thoughts, memories, and actions of others

Evanescents: Those who channel living energy

Materialists: Those who conjure from the material world

Phantomists: Those who commune with the nether world

Telekinetics: Those who move objects with their minds

Telepaths: Those who hear the thoughts of others

Voyants: Those who discern the future and/or the past

...

Sentinels: Those who are immune to the Nine Gifts

Change is the Only Constant

My father, a sentinel, was immune to the supernatural influences of the mind. He was safe from enchanters altering his memories or controlling his movements. Telepaths couldn't penetrate his mind, nor could empaths interpret his moods. Not even a powerful clairvoyant like me could catch a glimpse of his past or future. It was how I'd grown up ignorant of The Nine, a secret and ancient society founded to protect people like us.

He'd known how miserable my childhood was after word got out I could predict traumatic events in my classmates' lives, but he'd let me think I was some freak. When The Nine discovered my existence and upended my life, and even when I'd started to develop telekinetic and empathic powers, he'd chosen to remain silent. When the truth of his ability and connection to The Nine finally came to light last week, I'd driven three hundred miles up the coast to demand answers.

I fidgeted at the kitchen table as he placed a fresh pod into the machine that produced a multitude of coffee beverages at the touch of a button. My parents' ranch house kitchen in Central California had changed little since I was a kid, the white beams overhead and the hardwood floors underfoot a crisp backdrop to slate blue cabinetry. A bank of windows crowning the porcelain farm sink displayed the darkening sky, but inside, hanging light fixtures of polished tin banished the dusk. It would still be at least an hour before my mom could escape her responsibilities as a family physician and head home.

My sister and I waited in the breakfast nook, my fingers drumming on the plank table in anxious anticipation. A moment later, she slapped her hand over mine.

"Chill out," Jordan said with a scowl.

"Sorry." I'd learned too much about The Nine's governing body—their thirst for power and the divisions within—to be at ease. Dad's official status was that of a Shadow Nine, an off-the-grid designation, but Chancellor Henry Thorne had known damn well where to find my family.

Unable to stall any longer, my father brought his steaming cup to the table and settled into the chair across from mine. Chico, a small rescue dog of indeterminate pedigree, jumped into his lap. His little black nose twitched, ever hopeful something edible would come his way.

"I've given this a lot of thought," Dad said, using a finger to slide his wire-rimmed spectacles back into place. He was on winter break from his job as a history professor at a private college and had neglected to shave that morning or even brush his salt-and-pepper curls. "The best way for me to explain why I stayed silent is for you to see how it all went down."

My brows drew together in confusion. He had to know only the most powerful sentinels could purposely suspend their inborn shielding and invite a voyant into their memories. Mr. Silver, the Prime Sentinel and The Nine's top cop, had once opened his mind to me in a bid to establish mutual trust; the harrowing moment his younger brother Rafe lost control of his new-found telekinesis would stay with me forever. My dad's file, which I'd surreptitiously accessed on my recent visit to Alder House, listed him only as a sentinel, and an unranked one at that.

That's when it clicked, and the revelation did little to lessen the feeling of betrayal. "You're a Class One sentinel, aren't you? Is there *anything* in your record that's not a lie?"

His expression tightened with chagrin. "I'm stronger than my file may have let on." He laid his hand on the table, palm up. "Find out the rest for yourself."

Jordan observed the byplay with fascination. At sixteen, she'd surprised us all with a burst of telepathic power, so whatever our dad had done in the past would affect her as well.

Slowly extending my own hand until it hovered over his, I regarded the man who had become a stranger in some respects. My trust in him had been absolute, my faith unshakable, but his sin of omission had left me questioning what other devastating secrets might be lurking in the underbrush, waiting to sink their fangs into my throat.

Stress pinched the crow's feet at the corners of his eyes into deep grooves, and shadows lurked within their hazel depths. Gray had continued its unrelenting march through his hair since I'd seen him last, making him look old for the very first time.

"This is going to change everything, isn't it?" I asked.

"Yes," he said.

I placed my hand on his.

Past Is Prologue

The steady beat of drums echoed in my ears as a seemingly endless chain of people snaked their way along a dark, forested path. Flaming torches gripped in upraised fists set shadows dancing among the surrounding woods. My mind conjured up a story my dad had once told me of Celtic druids and their rituals of human sacrifice, and for an irrational moment I wondered if I'd overshot the mark and somehow landed in a long ago century.

My fears were calmed by the site of Alder House, The Nine's ancestral headquarters, in the far distance. The English country estate was lit up like a homing beacon, the steady glow of electric lights an anchor to modern times.

The first glimpse of my father was a shock. I'd never much considered his appearance beyond sinewy arms that could carry a seemingly endless number of grocery bags, or flushed cheeks after he dissolved into laughter over one of his own silly jokes, but Luke Wilder at thirty was a good-looking man. Dressed in black from his overcoat to his pants, his short hair was the same rich brown as my sister's, though it was unlikely either she or I had been born yet.

He marched at the side of a woman in a royal blue cloak, her face obscured by a hood. The smooth planes of his own features were arranged in a rare expression of discontent.

"Would you stop being such a worry wart?" the woman gently chided, her voice bearing traces of Southeast Asian origins. She raised her gaze to his, revealing deep, penetrating eyes and an ageless beauty undiminished by the passage of fifty or sixty years.

"Would you please start taking this challenge seriously, Mitsuko?" he shot back.

Her proud bearing went positively rigid as she stared down her nose at her companion, an impressive feat considering she was several inches shorter than him.

"Pardon, Chancellor," he said, not seeming cowed in the least. "I don't trust any of your opponents to act with honor."

"Which is why I have you to protect me, sentinel," she responded easily, all rancor at his impertinence forgiven. "We will not allow the future of The Nine to be decided by people who care more about wielding power than using it wisely."

"I vow no harm shall come to you." His gaze returned to the path in front of them. "I just wish your optimism was a little more contagious."

The trail abruptly ended at the mouth of a huge clearing ringed by trees. As the crowd poured through the break in the foliage, the inky blackness of the sky began to fade. Within a minute or two, streaks of purple overhead revealed wooden bleachers set in a semi-circle around a portion of the grounds the size of a football field. As soon as the last straggler emerged from the forest, more bleachers appeared—the work of materialists, I presumed—until they completely encircled the crowd. There was no mode of entry, nor any means of escape.

Torches were tossed in a pile at the center of the clearing, creating a haphazard bonfire, before most people found seats on padded benches. One raised section stood out from the others, and nine people in regent's robes moved to claim their places.

My father remained on the field. He joined a lineup of men and women similarly dressed in black—presumably fellow sentinels—while another group, uniformly outfitted in gold jackets and matching pants, mirrored them in a row of their own. The chancellor and three others swathed in blue cloaks gathered near the center, as did another foursome cloaked in red, their features likewise concealed. In the middle of it all stood a sleek wooden pole at least sixty-feet tall and crowned with a battered silver goblet glinting dully in rays cast by the rising sun.

A lone woman, wearing a knee-length coat in winter white and matching fur-trimmed boots, marched onto the field and gestured for silence. The audience complied.

"People of The Nine," she called out, her pack-a-day smoker's voice betraying Middle Eastern roots. "I am Tara Viziri, a Class One phantomist and three-time patron, and it is my honor to preside over a most momentous event: a challenge for the chancellorship."

The response ranged from enthusiastic to subdued. The stakes were much higher than those of deciding a regent's seat, as my boyfriend, Nicholas Thorne, and I had recently endured. That event had been more blood sport than political contest, though considering how divided the regents were on the future direction of The Nine, I feared it might be a portent of things to come.

This contest would decide who set the tone for the union of Nines, how threats to its people would be addressed, and what policies would be introduced, preserved, or discarded. It placed a lot of power into the hands of one individual.

"Defending her position as sitting chancellor is Mitsuko Hayashi," Tara announced, eliciting widespread cheers. The chancellor lowered her hood, revealing dark hair streaked with ribbons of gray. She smiled serenely before the master of ceremonies continued. "As stated in our bylaws, both the challenger and defender may designate up to three supporters to fight at their side. To aid in her defense, Chancellor Hayashi has chosen telekinetic Hadiza Ibrahim of Cairo, materialist Beatriz Santos of Lisbon, and elementalist Sutton Sinclair of Santa Carla, California."

I blinked in surprise as the younger version of real estate developer Sutton Sinclair dropped his hood. I knew him as a powerfully built man in his sixties, and while his close cropped blond hair was not yet gray nor had he come to adopt the pair of oversized eyeglasses that would shield hooded eyes, it was apparent he'd changed little since this day.

"It is now time to meet our challenger and his supporters," Tara continued. "Challenging Chancellor Hayashi for leadership of The Nine is Henry Thorne of London."

My head whipped around as Nicholas's father, the chancellor in my time, shrugged off his hood. The applause was not as robust as it was for Chancellor Hayashi, but it didn't put a dent in his arrogant stance. He was in his prime, the battle to hold together the fraying edges of the ancient society not yet waged. He shared Nicholas's height, angular face, and broad shoulders, but his features were more sharply defined, as if ambition had whittled away any softness he may have once possessed.

Was this the day he seized power, or had he been compelled to throw down the gauntlet more than once? I didn't know enough about the rules of contesting the right to be chancellor to determine if such a thing were even possible.

"Supporting Mr. Thorne on the field is Solenn da Silva, an enchanter from French Guiana, materialist Danila Kovalenko of Bucharest, Romania, and evanescent George Thorne, also from London."

The DNA was strong in the Thorne family, and I pegged George Thorne as Henry's brother. He wasn't as handsome as Nicholas, nor as hardened as Henry, but was instead the version of a thirty-something Thorne male who'd stayed too long at the party. The skin on his face was puffy and sallow; long, dark hair aged him rather than making him appear youthful; and his self-satisfied smirk made my own lips turn down in distaste.

"The Chancellor's Cup"—Tara pointed to the goblet perched atop the towering pole—"was one of Lady Alder's most prized possessions. She carried it with her when she fled from those who would have burned her as a witch, and it remains an everlasting symbol of both power and freedom to this day.

"The rules of the challenge are simple," she continued. "The first team to take possession of the cup without the use of paranormal intervention wins. If it is dislodged by any means other than human hand, the responsible team will immediately forfeit the day."

It seemed a rather arbitrary means of electing a leader, but then so did voting for a president based on empty promises.

"Additionally," she said, "in a test of leadership ability, only Chancellor Hayashi or Mr. Thorne may act autonomously. Other participants must wait for a command before engaging. Then and only then will sentinels retract their shielding to allow such orders to be carried out. Violating this rule will result in that team member's expulsion."

She gestured to those dressed in gold. "Evanescents will erect a transparent shield to protect our spectators, while each team member will be guarded by their assigned sentinel to prevent interference from outside the field of play. Overseeing the safety of challenger Thorne is Ashwin Trivedi."

Ashwin stepped out of the line of sentinels and bowed his head in acknowledgement. I'd met the older version of Henry's personal sentinel on my recent visit to Alder House, but this Ashwin had yet to sport his distinctive beard and mustache. His bare face revealed rounded cheeks, full lips, and freckled brown skin.

Tara continued. "For this event only, Chancellor Hayashi's former personal bodyguard has been reinstated, so she will be guarded by our Prime Sentinel."

My father stepped forward.

The Prime Sentinel

I was a voyeur, an eavesdropper during my visions, not present in the flesh. If I were, my knees would have folded as the blood rushed to my head.

My father had been the Prime Sentinel.

How had he gone from one of the most powerful and respected positions within The Nine to a history professor at a quiet, Central Coast college? Moreover, how did he end up classified as a Shadow Nine—an outlier—whose whereabouts were supposedly unknown?

While the two competing teams took positions on opposite ends of the field, a woman with the lanky beauty of a runway model approached my dad. I snapped to attention, wondering if here was the moment that led to his exile.

They stood shoulder to shoulder so she too could observe the activity on the field. After a few moments, she said, "The chancellor is most fortunate to have the Prime as her sentinel today."

Not taking his eyes off Mitsuko, he gave a barely perceptible nod to acknowledge the compliment. "Mrs. Thorne, is it not?"

"Sabrina," she corrected.

I sucked in a breath. It was Nicholas's mother, or she soon would be. She wore her copper hair long and parted down the middle, her face devoid of any makeup that might mar her freshness. It was a stark departure from the vision Nicholas had shared with me of the day he'd discovered her lifeless body when he was twelve years old. The killer had dumped her on the driveway outside the family home, the gold coin left in her hand marking her as a victim of the New Order, a radical faction within The Nine. They were determined to emerge from obscurity as imposed on the society's people since the rule of Henry the Eighth, to openly take what they believed was their rightful place as political, corporate, and spiritual leaders. People who stood in their way had a habit of turning up dead, though The Nine's current leadership was holding fast against them. For now.

"I hope we can be friends once my husband is chancellor," Sabrina added.

"You are quite confident in your team's abilities," he observed.

"I am quite confident in my husband's ability to win. Tell me, what happens if only one candidate for chancellor survives the challenge?"

He paled slightly, the only outward sign of how her question disturbed him. "As long as the death is accidental, the survivor will be named chancellor, but that hasn't happened in over two hundred years."

"Isn't that interesting?" she said, though it was more of a statement than a question.

He finally looked away from his charge to focus on her. "Is there something I should know?"

"My family is descended from Erik The Red and his son, Leif Erikson," she said, seemingly out of nowhere. "It was before we even knew what Nines were, but considering the Viking Code of Honor is also known as the Nine Noble Virtues, I would guess my ancestors weren't mere humans."

My father's brow furrowed, probably as confused by the turn in the conversation as I was.

"The point is," she went on, "we have always lived by the Viking Code. In particular, that the best victory is a clean victory."

He let that sink in a moment. "And you think that will happen today? A clear and decisive victory?"

She turned her attention back to Henry and his teammates. They were in the process of handing their cloaks off to an attendant, revealing close-fitted athletic jackets and matching pants in the same red hue.

"I'm saying a clean victory is in the best interests of all concerned. Wouldn't you agree?"

"I would think having a chancellor who demonstrates the highest caliber of honor and leadership would be in the best interests of all concerned." His lips thinned along with his patience. "Wouldn't you agree?"

She smiled. "I do love how righteous all you Prime Sentinels are. You could have a place with us if you're willing to use that virtue to your advantage." Shooting him a final glance, she left to go find her seat.

The woman made me uneasy, and not just because she seemed to assume the current chancellor would not survive the challenge. It had been my assumption Nicholas had inherited his moral compass and sense of decency from his mother, but it appeared I'd been mistaken.

My dad shook off the pall of apprehension Sabrina left in her wake and refocused on the proceedings. The evanescents were now strategically arrayed around the field's perimeter, and

Tara Viziri had mounted the regents' platform. She took command of the scene once more.

"Evanescents," she called. "Erect the barrier!"

The air suddenly crackled with electricity. A translucent barricade made of pure energy grew from the floor of the arena. The newly risen sun caught the shield's edges and angles, shooting splinters of light around the clearing like the mirror ball on The Lower Eight's disco night. The shield became transparent as borders met and gaps sealed.

"People of The Nine," she said, gripping the railing in front of her. "Just as a throne is only a chair covered in velvet, the chancellorship is only as strong as those who protect and believe in it. It is more honorable to earn leadership than to be born to it, so therefore..." She raised a fist in a show of strength and power. "We fight for it!" She basked in the cheers until they quieted enough for her to add, "Let us not forget: the power of the one..."

"...is the power of the many!" a thousand voices roared in response.

The competitors formed a loose ring around the pole, and the sentinels tensed.

"Let the challenge begin!"

Death at Dawn

"**S**utton and Hadiza—now!" Mitsuko commanded.

The blue team's elementalist ran full tilt toward the pole while their telekinetic, Hadiza—a young woman with dark, sparkling eyes peering out from a rounded face capped by a halo of tight, black curls—threw up her hand with the same delight as if she were catching Mardi Gras beads in the French Quarter. Her gesture propelled Sutton into the air. In just a few seconds, he would close the distance to the top of the pole and claim the prize. The match would be over almost before it began, and the crowd gasped at what could possibly be an immediate win.

"Danila! Make it rain!" Henry responded, and the teenage materialist, pink-haired and with multiple facial piercings, jumped into action. Spiked metal spheres the size of golf balls started pelting Sutton, not a surprising choice of weapon for a girl whose face was decorated with plenty of its own hardware.

Sutton curled in upon himself, but he howled as dark patches of blood sprouted from the back and arms of his fitted blue jacket.

"Shield him, Beatriz," the chancellor ordered, sending her own team's materialist into battle mode. "Hold him steady, Hadiza."

Beatriz, a bony woman in her early forties with a hard set to her mouth, waved her hand. A steel shield bloomed over Sutton's head and protected him from the deadly storm. As soon the bombardment was diverted, he straightened, his focus once again intent on the goblet. Hadiza continued his upward trajectory, though more slowly this time, as Beatriz's face scrunched with concentration to move his cover at the same pace.

George Thorne paced like a pit bull on a chain. "Put me in, Henry!"

"Destroy the shield, George!" The words were barely out of his mouth when his evanescent brother flicked open a hand as if releasing a ball. Several fingers of lightning struck the shield, one after another. Sutton covered his head, and Beatriz broke out in a sweat.

"I can't hold on!" the materialist cried.

"Bring him down, Hadiza," Mitsuko commanded. A moment later, Sutton was back on the ground, and both the shield and electrical strikes disappeared.

"Time to climb, Danila," Henry urged his own materialist as the red team launched their first assault. A spiral staircase began to encircle the pole from the bottom up like a fairytale beanstalk growing from a single pod. Danila hit the first tread at full speed. She circled the shaft twice before Mitsuko decided her next defensive move.

"Beatriz," she called out. "Keep her from reaching the top. Sutton, block her retreat."

Perhaps the blue team's materialist was inspired by the old Indiana Jones movie, because a large boulder materialized on the staircase near the top of the pole. It began to roll, gaining speed as it whipped around the curves. At the same time, Sutton simply glanced at the base of the stairs, and it was immediately engulfed in flames. Danila froze in her tracks, unsure which way to turn.

Henry, eyes on his imperiled teammate, raised his hands as if anticipating catching a ball. Instead, as he turned his palms to the flames, water cannoned from his hands. Seeing her salvation, Danila retreated from the path of the oncoming boulder as steam from the vanquished fire clouded the air, but her reprieve was short-lived. With a look of grim determination, Mitsuko waved her own hand, and a translucent tiger burst from the mist to bound up the stairs. As with all creatures created by evanescents, it sparkled with the energy used to created it.

The audience screamed in horror and delight while I looked on in terror. It was no different than gladiators killing or being killed for the entertainment of Caesar in the days of ancient Rome.

With only a split second to go before she was either crushed or electrocuted, the materialist dove over the railing. It was a thirty-foot drop to the ground, but a trampoline winked into existence, and Danila landed with a bounce. No one batted an eye at the materialist's unauthorized use of powers to save herself, and the challenge continued.

Mitsuko pivoted to the blue team. "Rope and pulley, everyone!"

Beatriz gestured toward the pole, and a pulley wheel appeared at the very top. A heartbeat later, a coil of rope looped over the wheel and unfurled with lengths dropping to the ground on either side. Hadiza twirled a finger, and one side of the rope slithered into a tightly knotted loop. The materialist dashed over to fit her foot into the loop before Sutton grabbed the other end with his powerful hands and pulled. Beatriz soared, one arm raised like a superhero in flight, and the audience roared its approval.

"Solenn!" Henry barked at his enchanter, a woman with a dark complexion and a broad, flaring nose that reminded me of a bust I'd once seen of Queen Hatshepsut. "Make him drop the rope."

She bowed her head with a regal nod, and suddenly Sutton was no longer in control of his own actions. He let out a frustrated growl as his hands relaxed their grip on the rope. Beatriz lunged for it, catching it just before she would have plummeted to the ground. Hand over hand, she grimaced with the effort to pull herself upward.

"Cut the rope, George," Henry said in the same offhand manner as if asking his brother to pass the salt.

George grinned. "With pleasure, Henry."

A semi-transparent hawk winged into existence, its curved talons outstretched and ready to do damage. Before it could reach its target, Mitsuko conjured a dragon with the same telltale translucence. It swooped over the heads of the delighted crowd before zeroing in on the hawk.

Beatriz glanced over her shoulder to see what had provoked the rumble of excited voices from the bleachers. Her mouth opened in a silent scream when she spied both creatures bearing down on her. I understood her fear. My car had passed through the belly of one such electrical beast, and it had fried every circuit into oblivion. What would happen to a human?

The crowd screamed as the dragon dropped protectively in front of Beatriz with wings outstretched, and the hawk sheared off to avoid a collision. George glared at the chancellor, but her eyes were locked on preparing her dragon's next move. Henry decided it for the both of them.

"Stand down, George," he said, whipping his arm as if throwing a curveball. The result was a whirlpool of air spinning so fast, Beatriz was forced to stop climbing and simply cling to the pole lest she be blown off. The hawk had already evaporated, but the dragon became a tumbling mass of wings and sparkles as it got caught in the tiny tornado. With an angry toss of her head, Mitsuko's creation joined the hawk in oblivion.

Henry turned his attention to the hapless materialist still clinging to the rope. Beatriz screamed as the winds bore down, her feet lifting into the air until her body was horizontal to the ground. Unable to hold on any longer, she lost her grip and tumbled through the air.

"Hadiza! Save her!" the chancellor bellowed.

The telekinetic cupped her palms, arresting her teammate's fall before lowering her gently to the ground.

"Lift me like when we were kids," George called to his brother as he ran toward the windstorm still kicking up dust and debris. Henry hesitated, but George didn't pause in his stride. Doubt registered on Henry's face, but he redirected the winds until they roiled beneath his sibling's feet.

George grinned triumphantly as he rose into the air. Mitsuko resurrected her dragon and set it on course to intercept Henry's brother.

"Back off, Thorne, or I will block him," Mitsuko warned Henry as George closed the distance to the Chancellor's Cup.

George lifted his arm, intent on snatching the goblet—and victory.

Henry's eyes darted between his brother and the chancellor. Maybe he thought Mitsuko lacked the guts to act on her threat, or perhaps his brother's safety was secondary to his boundless ambition. Whatever the reason, he was paralyzed with indecision, but the chancellor suffered no such hesitation.

Both George and the dragon reached the goblet at the same moment. As the man prepared to seize his prize, the creature shielded the cup with an outstretched wing. Whether he banked on being immune to a fellow evanescent's creation or was too close to victory to care, George plunged his hand through the dragon's wing. Instantly his fingers froze in the shape of a claw, his body stiffening as if cast in bronze.

"No!" Henry shrieked as George slowly tipped over and fell headfirst toward the ground. "Save him, Danila!"

The order came a moment too late. George landed with a thud, a cloud of dust churning up to obscure his crumpled form. The crowd fell silent.

"Time!" Tara cried from the platform.

My father ran onto the field, presumably taking up the mantle of Prime for a moment. His stricken expression conveyed he already knew what he'd find as he knelt next to the still figure. Henry reached his brother's side a few seconds later, his eyes wide in a fervent mixture of hope and dread. Sabrina came up behind her husband but remained outside of the immediate circle, as if that would allow her to remain untouched by the raw emotions threatening to spill forth.

The Prime laid two fingers on George's neck, twisted at a sickening angle, and pressed into the man's carotid. A few moments later, he met Henry's panicked gaze and shook his head. A burble of hushed voices rolled through the bleachers as the news of the George's death spread.

Henry stumbled away and into the arms of his wife. He buried his face against her shoulder, his body shaking. Two more sentinels trotted out to load the body onto a stretcher, and as they retreated, Tara asked, "Does the challenger wish to withdraw?"

"No!" Henry's guttural cry echoed across the field, silencing the murmuring masses. He tore away from his wife, dashed the tears from his cheeks, and directed a furious glare at Mitsuko. "We are not done here."

"Very well," Tara said, her eyes darting uneasily to the regents seated on the platform. When none of them met her gaze, she soldiered on. "Red and blue teams, resume your starting positions." The remaining combatants moved to comply, Henry sidling up to his enchanter and whispering in her ear as they went. My father cast them both a frown as he retreated to the sidelines.

"Let the challenge continue!" Tara announced.

Mitsuko wasted no time. She ran to the pole. "Lift me up, Hadiza!"

The telekinetic bit her lower lip, visibly straining with the effort. She'd already expended a tremendous amount of energy, so instead of soaring as Sutton had at the beginning of the match, Mitsuko rose much more slowly.

"I can't hang on much longer!" Hadiza yelled, just before the invisible force lifting Mitsuko gave out. The chancellor threw her arms around the pole and hung on, saving herself from a terrifying drop.

She didn't hesitate with her next command. "Beatriz, give me hand holds!"

Metal rungs sprang up under the chancellor's hands, extending all the way to the top.

Henry stood unmoving, his reddened eyes glued to his opponent as she climbed ever closer to winning the challenge. What happened next occurred in such rapid succession, it left me stunned.

Henry appeared to brush something from his shoulder.

My father flinched as if he'd been shocked.

"Now, Solenn!" Henry yelled to his enchanter as he flexed a hand. The entire pole went up in flames.

Mitsuko screamed as the fire consumed her, but she couldn't, or wouldn't, save herself by releasing her grip on the rungs.

Sutton fired a stream of water at her, heedless of acting without orders, but it was too late. Mitsuko fell from the pole, caught in a net Beatriz conjured.

Dad shook off whatever had caused him to lose focus and tore onto the field, his eyes wide with horror while Henry extinguished the fire. The chancellor's skin was blackened, and what remained of her clothes were a wet and smoldering ruin. The entire audience seemed to hold their collective breath as Dad dropped down beside his charge. With a trembling hand, he probed her neck for a pulse. After several frantic seconds, his chin dropped to his chest in defeat. Shocked murmurs from the crowd filled the morning air.

The master of ceremonies had remained on the platform looking on in disbelief, but finally she found her tongue. "With the accidental death of Mitsuko Hayashi, I declare Henry Thorne the new chancellor."

There were a few cheers, but mostly the onlookers remained silent. It was quiet enough to hear Henry's muttered protest. "Not yet. Not until the cup is mine."

He stamped his foot on the ground like a frustrated toddler, but his action was no petulant gesture. The ground began to shake. Squeals erupted from the bleachers, though the mild tremor would barely have warranted rising from the sofa in California. It was strong enough, however, to cause the cup atop the smoldering pole to tip.

Henry raised his arm, and the chalice landed neatly in his hand. He gazed at it for a long moment before holding up his prize for all to see.

"*Now* I am chancellor," he announced.

Web of Thornes

The family kitchen swam back into view. Since my visions never lasted more than a fraction of a second—despite sometimes feeling like I'd been gone for hours—nothing had changed. On the surface, at least.

Jordan leaned forward. "Well? Are we still mad at Dad?"

I took a long, shuddering breath, fighting back tears. I'd been angry with my father for almost a week, resentful at having the right to chart my own course taken from me. His silence had kept me from learning who I was and knowing others like me, and most importantly, from developing the necessary skills to protect myself. My temper still simmered, but now it was compounded with confusion over what I'd just witnessed, and uncertainty of whether my animosity was on solid ground.

Dad set Chico on the floor and came around the table to sit next to me. "I know how you feel about Nicholas Thorne, and I will forever regret not telling you the truth about his father sooner."

A bark of bitter laughter tore from my throat. I'd been so focused on my dad, I hadn't yet considered how Henry's deeds might impact Nicholas or our relationship. My feelings for him were so intense it was like a physical ache at times, but equally strong were the walls around his heart. He sometimes made decisions based on keeping me at a safe distance, even if we both suffered as a result. The way he'd ghosted me when faced with a deadly challenge for the regent's seat had taught me that.

I'd never be sure if Dad reached for me or if I fell into his arms, but suddenly we clung to each other as my inner turmoil boiled over.

"I'm so sorry," he crooned, stroking my hair while my shoulders heaved. "I've made so many mistakes, but it was only to keep us safe."

After a minute I pulled back and dragged a sleeve across my wet cheeks. "Henry Thorne got away with murder, didn't he?"

He didn't answer right away, his gaze fogging over as he once again recalled the fateful sequence of events. "There was a moment, right before Mitsuko died, when it felt as if someone tried to *burrow* into my head. I don't know how else to describe it, but somehow I was distracted at the exact moment Henry put his enchanter in play. I think Solenn forced Mitsuko to keep her grip on the pole, but I'm still not sure how he did it."

I did. Sentinels were accustomed to being immune from all paranormal influences, but I knew differently. "I once tried to force a memory from a sentinel. All I got were a few hazy images, but more importantly, we both felt a bit of a shock, and her powers faltered." I let that sink in before delivering the final punch. "Henry was in league with a voyant, and touching his shoulder was the signal."

Chico jumped between us and reclaimed his rightful spot on my father's lap. Absently stroking the dog, he considered the implications of this new information before he spoke. "It's a good theory, and maybe it fits what happened that day, but the only voyant in attendance was Megan Thayer, the voyant regent at the time. Not only were all the regents personally guarded to prevent undue influence, but Megan was one of Mitsuko's staunchest allies."

My brows furrowed. "How can you be so sure no other voyant was there?"

"Part of the Prime's duties includes knowing the name and ability of every Nine who walks through the door at Alder House. I can promise you none of the other seven registered voyants at that time were in England."

I filed that away to think about later. There were more important questions needing answers.

"What's going on?" my sister asked. "Who's Mitsuko?"

My mind was so busy puzzling out the events of twenty years ago I barely heard her. "Dad, I still don't understand how you went from being the Prime to hiding out here."

"Wait—what?" Jordan interjected. "Dad was the Prime?"

He shifted uneasily in his chair, and Chico shot him an inquisitive look. "I was a hotheaded fool. I should have bided my time, used my position to investigate what went wrong. Instead, I confronted Thorne later that night and accused him of cheating—and murder."

"If one of you doesn't start explaining what you're talking about," Jordan said through gritted teeth, "I'm going to start announcing everyone's darkest secrets from now until Christmas."

I looked to my dad. It was his story to tell, which he proceeded to do in a just-the-facts kind of way. He omitted the conversation with Sabrina Thorne, and I wondered if he'd forgotten the small part she'd played all those years ago. That was the thing about visions—they were much more reliable than mere memory.

"I had no proof of Thorne's treachery, and he knew it," he concluded. "He was also smart enough to realize it was dangerous to keep me around as Prime, so we came to an agreement."

My stomach roiled at the idea of my father selling his integrity. "What could he have possibly offered to make you compromise your beliefs?"

"Your mother's life." He let the stunned silence settle for a few moments before continuing. "We were engaged to be married, and I hadn't yet shared that part of my life with her. She thought I was an international consultant who traveled a lot, but since she was in her first year of residency, she didn't have the bandwidth to ask too many questions."

I sat back in my chair, at a complete loss for words. With everything I now knew about paranormal abilities being an inherited trait, how could he not warn his fiancée that any children they might have could be freaks of nature?

"That was a douchey thing to do," my sister said, having arrived at the same conclusion.

"I'm not proud of my actions, but I was afraid of losing her if she didn't believe me, or losing her if she did. Thorne took advantage of my weakness."

I pursed my lips. "How exactly?"

He lifted his chin and forced his eyes to meet mine. "He gave me two choices. I could put a quick end to the speculation surrounding Mitsuko's death by accepting blame and agreeing to go live a normal life with the woman I loved far away from any Nines. Or I could stir up trouble with allegations I likely couldn't prove, divide our people, and be framed for my fiancée's murder." His shoulders slumped. "You know your mom. She would never have abandoned her patients to go hide somewhere while I fought to bring Mitsuko's killers to justice. It felt like I had no choice."

"How could anyone believe you were responsible for the chancellor's death?" Jordan was affronted on his behalf.

A twist of pain tightened his features. "Some did. Others, mostly friends and fellow sentinels, tried to defend me, but how could they when I couldn't explain it myself? Since neither

Mitsuko nor I were there to stand up for ourselves, the story of that day has somehow taken on a life of its own."

I pushed back my chair and stalked to the windows, distractedly noting the Christmas lights decorating our front yard had flicked on. Dad loved his automatic timers.

Was it fair to cling to the fantasy about what might have been if I'd known there were others like me? If I'd been in my dad's position, would I have handled it differently? Admittedly, the answer was rather muddled.

"Does Mom know everything now?" Jordan asked.

When he didn't answer right away, I turned to face him. "She doesn't, does she? It's why you never told me about The Nine, and why you always said not to tell her about my visions."

"She knows," he responded, his calmness at odds with my own snappishness. "She's forgiven me for not revealing it sooner. I didn't tell you about The Nine because I was afraid you would seek them out, and I didn't want Thorne anywhere near you." He caressed the dog's golden ears as he reflected on his choices. "What I didn't count on was how he kept tabs on us. I held up my end of the bargain, and I stupidly thought he would do the same, but now here you are, entangled in a web of Thornes."

The last of my temper fizzled out. He'd made the best of an impossible situation, and his biggest mistake had been trusting a deceitful man.

I returned to the table and plopped down in my seat. "What happens now?"

He drew in a deep breath. "I'll do what I should have done twenty years ago. I'll tell the Prime everything I know… and hope he or she has the courage I lacked to bring the chancellor to justice."

Mr. Silver, the current Prime Sentinel, was a man of integrity who would take my father's claims seriously, but what would happen if Henry Thorne got wind he was the subject of an inquiry? I suspected he'd find a way to shut it down, no matter who or what he had to bury along

with it. It made me wonder what other chaos he'd sown in his quest for power.

Then there was Nicholas. To learn that our families were mired in a brew of death and

destruction years in the making felt like the unraveling of our already tenuous connection. Did he know his father had somehow engineered the murder of the previous chancellor? Would he forgive me if I forced Henry to atone for his sins?

I blinked with bewilderment as my common sense caught up with my outrage. It wasn't my job to take on the chancellor nor to mete out punishment. Why should I risk my safety and that of my family to expose Henry's crimes? Why chance throwing away what Nicholas and I had together? Despite all this, the words on my tongue would not be silenced.

"I'll help," I said.

A Warning

Business at Jitters, the coffeehouse where I worked as a barista, was slow. We were a week into the new year, and people were probably trying to stick to resolutions such as drinking less coffee or eating fewer sweets. Whatever the reason, my bib apron (today it read *No Matter The Question, The Answer Is Always Coffee*) was still spotless as my befuddled boss, Al Vanderbeek, and I spent a few moments considering the startling transformation of my co-worker, Cindy.

She'd dumped her unfaithful boyfriend right before Christmas. They'd been together since high school, which was now a few years in her past, and she'd allowed Todd's obsession with horror movies to dictate her personal style. Until this week, I'd never seen her without heavy, goth-style makeup, hair the color of a raven's wing, and clothes that would do a vampire proud.

The only makeup this version of Cindy sported was tinted lip gloss. Her short, newly brown hair sparkled with a variety of jeweled clips, the pink sweater set she wore would fit right in at a country club tea, and the swarm of bats tattooed across her chest was in the process of being reworked into a flock of bluebirds.

"That *is* Cindy, right?" Al whispered, observing her through blue-tinted eyeglasses as she wiped down tables. Having come of age during San Francisco's Summer of Love, he'd seen plenty of change, but apparently none so startling as his employee's metamorphosis from Queen of The Dead to sorority princess.

"That's what happens when you lose a hundred and thirty pounds overnight," I said with a snicker. Todd had been tall but gangly.

"Gee whiz, you don't have to whisper," Cindy said with a breezy smile as she attacked a sticky spot on the table nearest the coffee bar. She'd always sprinkled her sentences with throwback expressions, but they worked a lot better now that she dressed like a 1950s housewife. "I know y'all are talking about me, but I finally feel like the outside matches the inside, and that's what matters."

"I totally agree, and you look great," I rushed to say. "Please don't take this the wrong way, but why did you let Todd tell you how to look all this time?"

She paused in her cleaning, her eyes bright with unshed tears. "I thought it would make him love me."

Al's nostrils flared with indignation. "If a man tells you to be a different girl, then you tell him to go out and find that different girl for himself."

Cindy and I both stared at him in surprise. Who knew a feminist heart beat within his comfortably rounded body?

He preened under our scrutiny. "What? I've seen *The View*. I know a few things."

The front door opened, and a welcome face appeared. Marina Novak, a local real estate agent and Class One double telepath, strolled up to the counter. A creamy blouse peeked out from beneath her heather gray pantsuit, her ever present strand of pearls glowing richly against the olive skin of her throat. At the same moment, Al retreated into his office. Marina was an outrageous flirt, and the happily married man wriggled like an eel in a net whenever she trained her mischievous brown eyes on him.

The last time we'd met she'd warned me of a ghostly presence that seemed to be tracking my every move. On the way to confront the only phantomist of my acquaintance, Jessie McCabe, about spying on me, I'd unwittingly repaid her kindness by putting her nephew in the line of fire. It was my fault he'd been attacked on a dark and isolated road by a ruthless evanescent.

Don't give it another thought, she thought, using our private form of telepathic communication. *Peter was glad to help, and now he has an exciting story to tell.*

He'd almost died in the act of defending my sister and me, but I appreciated her willingness to overlook it.

Aloud she said, "Good to see you, Blake. Did you have a pleasant holiday?"

"Yeah, it was great." *I also discovered a few old secrets that would set your hair on fire, but that'll have to wait for another time.* "What can I get for you?"

"Just a half-caf Americano," she said with a dispirited sigh. "It seems no one wants to buy a house while waiting for their December credit card bills to arrive." She silently added, *Have you seen Jessie lately?*

In addition to his ability to commune with the dead, Jessie was the owner of an exclusive nightclub for Nines. Over the past several months we'd forged a friendship of sorts—despite a mutual attraction I pretended didn't exist.

No, I responded. *I've been staying close to home.*

As I prepared her order, my thoughts strayed to Scarlett, my best friend and roommate. While my new telekinetic abilities didn't seem to bother her too much, she hadn't taken the news of my rising empathic powers well. This past week had seen a softening in her reserve. We'd spent the last several days as we used to do on school breaks: playing Rummikub, baking cookies, and watching every rom-com on Netflix. Her boyfriend, Warren, was at the apartment more often than not, but he never complained of being a third wheel, no matter how awful the movie we'd chosen turned out to be.

Marina, of course, overheard every thought, and when I set her beverage on the counter, a warm smile shaped her lips. *I'm a big fan of sisters before misters, but you may want to drop by The Lower 8 when you have a minute.*

I paused in the middle of ringing up her coffee. Jessie had recently escaped a trumped up murder charge, though the detective on the case was less than convinced of his innocence.

The police aren't after him again, are they? I thought with dread.

She tipped her head in a gesture that conveyed she had other concerns, her chin-length bob swinging with the movement. *Jessie's met someone.*

My entire body went cold. It had only been two weeks since I last saw him. How could he have fallen for someone in less time than it took the yogurt in my fridge to expire? He had every right to do whatever he wanted with whomever he wished, of course, and I was with Nicholas. Still, it didn't mean I had to like it.

"Is there a problem with the register?" Cindy had slipped behind the counter to grab a fresh towel.

My fingers hovered over the keys, and I was startled into motion. "Oh, no, it's fine."

Marina slid a five dollar bill across the counter. *If it makes you feel any better, I don't think she's right for him. There's something off about her, but I can't quite put my finger on it.*

I counted out her change and shrugged as nonchalantly as possible. *Why should I care who Jessie's dating?*

There was no question Marina heard every embarrassing thought as I had them, but she graciously pretended she hadn't. She scooped up the coins and dropped them in the tip jar before leveling her gaze at me. *Because Jessie is your friend.* "Thanks for the coffee. I'll see you soon."

I considered her words while cleaning one of the cappuccino machines. Whoever Jessie chose to spend time with was his business, but I supposed it couldn't hurt to drop by the club after work. Marina was a fair-minded person, so if she had reservations about the girlfriend, I should at least meet her.

Wiping leftover milk off the steam wand, a sudden sensation of movement under my hands made me jump. Dropping the towel, a scream lodged in my throat at the sight of a snake protruding from the coffee machine in place of the wand. My horrified gaze met the creature's cold, pitiless one as its black, forked tongue tasted the air. Some distant part of my brain argued this couldn't be real, but I knew enough about Nines and their dangerous games to tell the little voice inside me to STFU. The snake's yellowed scales flared at its throat, promising dire consequences should I be foolish enough to tangle with the cobra.

"Are you okay?" Cindy asked, jolting me from my trance. As my eyes locked once again on the threat, only a sparkling steam wand jutted benignly from the machine. The snake was gone.

I whirled around. My frantic gaze swept across the bank of windows fronting the parking lot and landed on a shadowy figure just outside. Swathed in a dark hoodie, a baseball hat, and dark glasses, the person's only revealing feature was his mouth. Teeth flashed as his lips curved into a malicious smile.

Shoving past a mystified Cindy, I raced around the bar and dodged the obstacle course of tables and chairs on the way out the door. Reaching the sidewalk, I panted with leftover fear and adrenalin as I pivoted in a frantic search for my assailant, but he was gone. There were a number of cars in the parking lot in which he could be hiding, or maybe he was fast enough to have escaped around the side of the building, but I didn't pursue him.

I didn't want a public confrontation with another Nine, and my guess was neither did he.

It had only been a few days since my father had set the wheels of justice in motion by telling Mr. Silver everything he knew and suspected about the death of Mitsuko Hayashi. According to the Prime, their phone call was conducted on a secure line, but today's visitor made me wonder if somebody had found a way to eavesdrop. Was the snake a sign of things to come if my father didn't retract his statement?

I'd also tried logging into The Nine's database to see what could be found about the voyants of twenty years ago, but I hadn't made it past the home page, let alone into the archives. Maybe someone had learned of my attempted break in and decided to derail my curiosity.

In light of those things, I had to view the serpent as a warning, but who had sent the message?

Stay With Me

Clothes I'd tried on and rejected littered my bed. It was a weeknight so almost anything would be fine for a visit to The Lower 8, but all my usual favorites were suddenly outdated or worn out. One pullover was so stained and pilled I opened my bedroom window and tossed it into the shrubbery outside. I'd retrieve it tomorrow, but the peevish act lessened the urge to set my closet ablaze.

Finally, I settled on a cute pair of dark jeans and an off-the-shoulder sweater my sister had given me for Christmas. I let my long blonde hair fall in loose waves and added a touch of makeup to combat the ghostly pallor earned from spending too much time indoors.

My phone rang as I pulled a pair of chunky-heeled boots out of the closet. It was Nicholas, and a whisper of uncertainty curled through my mind. We'd spoken almost every day since we'd parted at Alder House, but other than saying I'd forgiven my dad for concealing his connection to The Nine, I hadn't told him about our fathers' shared past. I'd rationalized it a dozen different ways, from fear of my words reaching unfriendly ears to Nicholas angrily cutting me off without hearing the whole story. I told myself the best way to combat those concerns was to tell him face to face—my silence had nothing to do with the way my heart pounded and my throat closed when I imagined how he might react to my accusations.

A quick calculation told me it was four in the morning in the UK. No one called at that time with good news.

"What's wrong?" I blurted, plopping down on my bed and giving him my full attention.

"The world has to be coming to an end for me to call?" He did his best to inject some levity into his voice, but there was no hiding the hoarseness, most likely due to exhaustion and overuse.

"I didn't mean it that way." My heart went out to him.

He'd been the telekinetic regent for less than a month, and already the demands on his time and energy were staggering. Not only was he overseeing the apprehension and punishment of a surprising number of rogue telekinetics—it was almost as if the criminal element among them was testing his resolve—but voyant regent Zoya Khitrova, who'd backed the losing horse in Nicholas's challenge for regent, peevishly attempted to block every policy decision he made. If he voted one way in a regents' meeting, she was sure to cast a ballot in the opposite direction. The wheels of progress were grinding to a halt, and the atmosphere in their gatherings had never been more tense.

"What's keeping you up?" I asked.

Ice clinked in a glass as he sipped. "Good news for a change. I would have called earlier, but this is the first chance I've had a minute to myself. Henry wants me to open the American League playoff of the Palmarium games."

I pulled on one of my boots and wondered what else might be on his father's agenda. "That sounds, uh, fun."

A rough chuckle escaped his throat. "You have no idea what Palmarium is, do you?"

"I know it's a game," I joked.

"It's the only game worth watching if you're a Nine, and this one will decide which team goes to the championship. People will be coming in from all over the world. There's also an exhibition game the night before, and both happen to be taking place in Los Angeles."

My face split into a grin. The metropolitan city was only an hour's drive south of Santa Carla. Butterflies fluttered within my ribcage at the thought of seeing Nicholas again regardless of what else came with it.

"When?" I asked.

"I'll be flying in Friday night." Two days away. "Can you meet me there?"

The spring semester didn't start for another ten days, so I'd volunteered for every shift Al would give me. My parents helped me out with rent, tuition, and books, but everything else came out of my paycheck. The responsible thing would be to stay home and work.

Then again, with so many Nines gathered, it presented a golden opportunity to seek out people who might have been there the day Henry murdered Mitsuko. Maybe seeing the event from another viewpoint could shed light on who had distracted my father. Besides, Cindy would jump at the opportunity to cover my weekend hours because moving out of Todd's apartment had taken every penny she had.

"I'll be there," I practically purred into the phone.

"I have a suite at To The Nines," he said. "It's the second oldest sanctuary club in the States. Back in the day, a lot of movie stars were Nines. Stories about the parties they hosted there are legendary."

"And now?" I prodded, eager as the next girl to see a famous face.

"You'll have to find out for yourself," he said with a laugh. As his amusement ebbed, it became apparent he had something else on his mind. "Blake?"

"Hmmm?"

"Will you, uh, stay with me?"

We'd spent only one night together, and I loved that he didn't presume he was owed another.

"I don't know, Mr. Thorne," I said teasingly. "Will there be only one bed?"

"I'm afraid so. The rooms with double beds are all sold out," he said, getting into the spirit of our little game.

"In the whole city?" I drawled.

"Big convention in town. Huge. It's the, uh, platonic best friends conference."

I laughed. "Oh good. I'll let Scarlett know. She'll be *so* excited to attend." He joined in the laughter. It was no secret my roommate was not his biggest fan.

"A car will pick you up late Friday afternoon. The driver will text you with the exact time." His voice turned husky. "I can't wait to see you."

"Me too. Now get some sleep and dream of me."

Flirting with a gorgeous guy who could have almost anyone he wanted went a long way to taming the possessive feelings Jessie's new girlfriend stirred up in me. In fact, I felt downright benevolent by the time I knocked on the front door of The Lower 8.

The rectangular portal in the door slid open. It was just large enough to reveal a glimpse of Suki's dark eyes before the sentinel banged it shut and opened the door. A tight black dress encased her willowy figure from throat to ankle, and her straight dark hair flowed to her waist like a lazy river at midnight. Her only ornamentation were silver hoop earrings almost big enough to perch a parakeet on.

"Hi Suki," I greeted her. "Quiet night?"

It was just the two of us in the antechamber that served as the gateway to the club, and judging by The Lower 8's half empty parking lot, it appeared Jitters wasn't the only business suffering from the new year blues. The dull thud of music bled through the walls, but at a more subdued volume than usual.

She smirked. "It was, but now that you're here, I fully expect all hell to break loose."

"Ha ha." It was true I'd found a dead body outside the building last month, and it was also me who'd uncovered a killer among us not too long before that, but it wasn't like I went around looking for trouble.

"Don't worry," she assured me. "It's cowboy night, so some moron will probably do it for you."

"Cowboy night?" The theme seemed a bit generic for The Lower 8.

"I don't know." She airily waved away the question. "Guys in hats, whiskey drinks on special, and the Old West rides again. Yeehaw."

She retreated behind the hostess stand and fished a red plastic bracelet from a discreet drawer. As she snapped it onto my wrist, tagging me as under the legal drinking age, she said, "As much of a headache as you can sometimes be, I can't let you go inside without telling you Jessie is with someone tonight."

Thanks to Marina's advance notice, I was able to maintain a placid expression, but it was still really decent of the sentinel to warn me. Suki and I weren't exactly friends, but my recent involvement in clearing Jessie's name had definitely moved us closer in that direction.

"Do we like her?" There were several members of Jessie's staff who weren't shy about expressing their opinions about his personal life, and I hoped Suki was among them.

"She seems nice enough, and of course she's very pretty…" She trailed off, but it was obvious she had more to say, and it wasn't necessarily glowing.

"And?" I felt like a gossipy neighbor leaning over the back-yard fence.

She glanced up through her lashes. "She's an enchanter, but there's something else about her power she's keeping hidden."

Any sentinel strong enough to guard the entrance to a sanctuary club could ferret out most secrets when it came to a Nine's paranormal abilities, so her observation intrigued me.

"Have you told Jessie this?"

She clicked her tongue, as if the answer was obvious. "I'd like to keep my job, thank you very much."

"Could she be a multi?" If so, I understood her impulse to keep it quiet. With more power came a brighter spotlight, one that brought the attention of those who coveted, exploited, or were simply jealous of what they couldn't have.

"Ask Layla. She thinks the girl is up to something too."

Layla headed up the waitstaff and had no respect for personal boundaries, especially where her friends were concerned. I tried—and failed—not to find pleasure in hearing for the second time that Miss Wonderful might not be so wonderful after all, which made me a terrible person. In a bid to rectify that, I decided that just because Jessie didn't like my boyfriend didn't mean I had to hate his girlfriend.

"Thanks for the heads up," I said. "I'll let you know what I find out."

Jessie's Girl

The Lower 8 had become a pool hall for the evening. Tables covered in green baize covered half the dance floor, and dartboards hung on a wall usually reserved for booths. A handful of couples twirled to the twang of Southern rock while the explosive crack of billiard balls in play punctuated the air.

I paused at the top of the club's sweeping staircase, anticipating the usual tidal wave of overwhelming energy, but with less than a hundred people in the place, it was more like a splash. Nicholas's former girlfriend, Julia Martin, told me I'd eventually grow immune to the paranormal onslaught, and I wondered if my near constant exposure to Nines had hastened the process. It couldn't come soon enough for me.

Descending the central staircase designed to see and be seen, I froze halfway down at the crash of an overturned table mingled with the explosion of breaking glass. Near the bar, two young men in cowboy hats lunged at each other, scattering bystanders. The larger of the two gripped the front of his opponent's shirt and cocked a fist, but before the blow could land, his entire body spun in the opposite direction, forcing him to release his adversary.

As the man shook off his surprise, Ricardo, the club's evanescent bouncer with a knack for invisibility, materialized between the two combatants. He held a quelling hand up to each of them, and considering those hands were attached to arms rippling with bands of muscle, it gave both fighters pause.

Ricardo spoke too quietly for his words to carry, but whatever he said earned begrudging nods from the two men. They each dropped a wad of cash on the bar before being escorted to the stairs. I stepped aside as they trudged by, the bouncer giving me a neighborly nod in passing. As Suki said, it seemed to be business as usual on cowboy night.

Layla greeted me when I reached the bottom step. Like the rest of the women on staff that night, she wore denim shorts and a flannel shirt tied at the waist. Wisps of dark, spiky hair escaped the brim of her cowboy hat.

"Hey, Blake, welcome to Honkytonk Night." The diminutive waitress's eyes sparkled with mischief. "Are you looking for Jessie?" She wasn't normally a shit-stirrer, but the new woman in her boss's life had obviously done something to rattle her enough that the bar fight was already an afterthought.

I gave her a knowing smile. "I've heard about his girlfriend, Layla, and I'm fine with it, if that's what you're asking. I'll be too busy meeting Nicholas in Los Angeles on Friday to give it much thought."

Her mouth turned down in a pout. "You too? Half the town is going to the game."

"You should come too," I urged before shifting gears. "I actually did drop by to see Jessie. Is he around?" Even if Suki hadn't already confirmed his presence, he took his stewardship of The Lower 8 seriously and was rarely absent when the doors were open.

Layla tipped her head toward the wall of dartboards. "He's teaching that woman how to play with sharp objects, not that she doesn't already know how."

From this vantage point, it was easy to pick him out of the crowd. He wore the requisite cowboy hat, and the rest of his clothes—a white cotton button down and broken-in jeans hugging his trim form in all the right places—underscored the evening's theme.

"And the new girlfriend?" As usual, there were a number of pretty woman loitering near the phantomist.

"Amani Falah, Class One enchanter." She followed my gaze. "She's the one in pink."

My smile faltered as I took in the gorgeous woman wearing a hot pink crop top exposing several inches of tanned and toned abs above the waistline of her snug jeans. Thick black curls tumbled down her back and framed a heart-shaped face accented with delicately arched brows. Jessie leaned in and must have said something funny because her wide mouth drew back in laughter, exposing a sparkling smile that would make a dentist swoon. She was only a few years older than me, but I suddenly felt like a gawky schoolgirl compared to her.

I cleared my throat. "She seems nice."

Layla snorted at my bland assessment. "And yet her mind is on lockdown whenever any of us come near."

My gaze returned to Layla. "What do you mean?"

"You're an empath now." She planted a hand between my shoulder blades and gently shoved me in Jessie's direction. "Go find out."

It's what I came to do, but now that the moment had arrived, it felt wrong and intrusive. Would I have thanked Jessie if he'd told me about Nicholas's longtime girlfriend when things first started heating up between us? Or would I have viewed his interference with suspicion, questioning his motives and finding them self-serving? As I trudged across the floor, the answer came to me swift and sure, and it didn't speak well to my presence there. I veered away, intent on escaping before any regrettable mistakes were made.

"Blake!" Jessie's voice called out to me. I pretended not to hear and picked up the pace.

A man stepped into my path, and I skidded to a halt just shy of a collision. He was attractive in a conventional way with a narrow face elongated by a smooth wave of brown hair rising a few inches above his scalp. His khaki pants and black polo shirt were a complete departure from the night's theme, so he was either new to town or simply didn't care.

"Where are you off to in such a hurry?" he asked with a flirty smile. The stairs were right behind him. Escape was within reach.

"Blake!" Jessie called again, making it a fine line between departing and fleeing.

Plastering a smile on my face, I turned. The Texan came trotting up, and I didn't need to be an empath to detect the joy radiating from every fiber of his being. I could only hope some of that happiness was reserved for me, but regardless, it made me feel like an even bigger jerk.

"Didn't you hear me?" he asked.

"Oh, you know, loud music, a lot on my mind…" I trailed off awkwardly. Fortunately, he didn't seem to notice.

"Come," he said. "There's someone I want you to meet."

"Maybe she wants to meet me," the stranger said from behind.

Jessie regarded the other man coolly. "Sorry, but she's with me."

Dread pooling in my stomach, I allowed him to whisk me away.

"I hope you don't mind," he said when we were out of earshot, "but he's probably just another one of your fans."

"My fans?" I couldn't have heard him right.

"They've been coming by in droves ever since you helped Thorne win the challenge for regent." He chuckled with dry amusement. "If you ever want to set up an autograph table, we could make a fortune."

I'd spent most of my life trying to attract as little attention as possible and wasn't particularly comfortable with the idea of being The Nine's current It Girl. However, since I wouldn't meekly go along with the society's tradition-bound agenda, I should probably get used to being famous—or infamous, depending on your point of view.

"Amani," he said as we neared the woman in pink, prompting her to turn with a thousand-watt smile. She was even prettier up close and smelled like the gardenias that occasionally flowered in my parents' backyard. "I want you to meet a good friend of mine. Blake Wilder, this is Amani Falah."

"Nice to meet you, Amani." I did her the courtesy of not offering my hand. Many Nines weren't eager to come in contact with a voyant, especially when it circulated after the regent's challenge that touch enhanced my ability. "Are you new to Santa Carla?"

"I'm here on business"—she sent a heated glance at Jessie—"but there's a lot to like about your city."

"Amani's a financial consultant," Jessie filled in, his hand finding its way to the small of her back. My chest tightened in response, but I did my best to ignore it. "Sutton Sinclair hired her to help restart his construction project."

The real estate mogul's multi-million dollar commercial building had been shut down mid-construction after two supposedly accidental deaths at the site. The delay must be causing him to bleed money, so it made sense he'd be taking steps to find new investors, starting with hiring a consultant who was surely both beautiful *and* smart.

"I just love a challenge," Amani gushed, "and with a visionary like Sutton at the helm, we'll have that building back on track in no time."

Visionary? He'd fought at Chancellor Hayashi's side back in the day, but since then his vision had evolved into becoming a supporter of the New Order.

"I've been expecting you for days now," Jessie said, a touch of admonishment creeping into his voice. "Harper told me you came back to town last weekend. She also said something happened with you over the holidays, but she wouldn't say what."

I flushed with annoyance. I'd agreed to let one of his spirits—in this case, the ghost of a sixteen-year-old, recently departed girl—follow me around, but nothing had been said about her reporting details of my life back to Jessie. He didn't need to know my dad was a Nine, let alone the former Prime, and I was in no mood at that moment to share.

"I didn't mean to interrupt your, ah, date, but I'm meeting Nicholas in Los Angeles this weekend. Could you let Harper know a little privacy would be appreciated?" It was gratifying to sense a downturn in Jessie's mood, but I tried not to read too much into it. Pinpointing Amani's emotions was much more difficult, which wasn't surprising given the number of people in the vicinity. It seemed the better I knew someone, the easier it was to wade through the static and home in on their frequency, so to speak. I picked up nothing from her.

"You're going to the Palmarium games with Nicholas Thorne?" Amani inquired brightly. "From what I heard he did to that poor telekinetic—" She abruptly pressed her lips together before tacking on, "Well, it doesn't matter what I heard. I'm sure you'll both have a great time." She probably didn't mean to be rude, but alluding to the false rumors circulating that we had deliberately caused the death of Balthazar Montoya—the challenger who'd inadvertently died by his own hand in the recent battle for the regent's seat—chipped away at my good intentions.

I smiled tightly. "It's amazing how fast gossip travels in The Nine, but I try not to pay too much attention to it." Since it was Marina's hunch that brought me there, the irony of my own words was not lost on me. I turned to Jessie. "Are you going, too?"

"Yes," Amani jumped in, smiling at her new boyfriend. "I was going to surprise you later tonight, but I managed to get tickets and a room at To The Nines. Please say you'll come with me."

He beamed with pleasure. "I'd be honored."

I bared my teeth, but I couldn't tell whether my mouth turned up or down. Maybe the venue would be a giant convention center, and we could go the whole weekend without running into each other. One could only hope.

"Do you plan to stay in town long?" If not, I could leave well enough alone and let Jessie enjoy his fling while it lasted.

"I'm here until my job with Sutton is finished." Her gaze once again slid to Jessie. "But it's not like I have to rush back to my empty condo in Palm Beach. There's not even a cat to miss me."

"I've been telling her Santa Carla is a great place for Nines. Don't you agree, Blake?" He rarely called me by name, preferring to address me as darlin', but suddenly we were being all formal.

"Oh, yeah," I halfheartedly agreed, biting my tongue not to mention how many Nines had turned up dead since I'd moved there six months ago.

"Maybe we could all get dinner sometime soon," Amani suggested. "If Regent Thorne isn't available, maybe there's someone else you'd like to bring to make it a foursome?"

That sounded like as much fun as bobbing for piranhas, but I went through the motions of acting delighted. "I'm sure my roommate Scarlett would be thrilled."

She snuggled up to Jessie in an unmistakable gesture of ownership. "It's a date then."

"Blake, no worries about Harper," he said, ignoring me in favor of beaming down at her as if she were the only woman in the room. "I'll make sure she gives you some space."

Two weeks ago I'd helped clear his name when he was being framed for murder, and now I was being dismissed like one of those people who handed out religious pamphlets at the airport.

"Thank you, Jessie," I said as evenly as I could manage. "It was so nice meeting you, Amani."

Other than Amani's emotions being a complete mystery, she seemed like a perfectly nice person. Maybe that would have been enough if every Nine I knew hadn't all but ordered me to check her out in my own unique way. Not giving myself time to dwell any further, I smiled sweetly and gave her bare arm a friendly squeeze.

A door crashed open. Framed in the portal was the tangled silhouette of two people engaged in a blistering kiss. Without breaking apart, they lurched into a bedroom fashioned from shadow and light. Monochromatic bedding, stark black-and-white photographs of singular subjects—a scrub desert, an arched bridge, a disinterested steer—hung on walls painted battleship gray, and accent pieces in the deepest shade of black.

My chest tightened when I realized it was Jessie's loft, and Amani was the woman in his arms. I fervently hoped it was a future vision, but that wish was quickly dispelled by the scent of her floral perfume. Damn, damn, damn.

I mentally shook myself like a dog shedding rainwater. I'd endured countless visions of sex, love, and most everything in between. What was one more? It wasn't like Jessie and I were anything more than friends.

The couple separated long enough for Amani to tug Jessie's shirt over his head, and my breath lodged in my throat. Golden skin clung to muscles honed by years of lugging cases of beer or whatever else was required from the owner of a nightclub. She raked her red nails down his chest to chase the happy trail of blonde hair sprouting at his belly button that disappeared into the waistband of his jeans. My own fingers unconsciously flexed, and I huffed at letting a glimpse of Jessie's bare skin get to me.

He grinned like a pirate about to ravage a princess as he stripped Amani of her own clothing. I really wanted to shut my eyes right then, but visions were only in my mind, and there was no blocking them out. Instead, I searched for a single detail to narrow my focus, a trick that had helped me survive a thousand episodes of violence and heartbreak without losing myself in the abyss.

The intricate tattoo on Jessie's shoulder blade caught my eye. I'd seen it in another erotic vision—the premonition of the two of us wrapped around each other still had the power to make my entire body blush with heat—but this time, I recognized the design of intersecting curves as the symbol of a phantomist.

I desperately clung to those inked lines as Jessie moved in a primal dance, one that called to the deepest reaches of my soul. Not even the sight of those wicked red fingernails biting into his flesh could break the spell. It was Nicholas my heart wanted, so how could I yearn to feel Jessie's hands on me, to take the weight of his body on mine?

Guttural moans became cries of pleasure, and I longed to cover my ears, not that it would change anything. I burned with desire, pure and simple, because there was no way I could ever fall in love with the opportunistic Texan. I clung to that thought until at last, we were each released from our own various forms of exquisite torture.

A Disturbing Message

Scarlett and I slumped at the kitchen table as we each worked through our second cup of coffee. She wore the silky pinstriped pajamas Warren had given her for Christmas with her red curls piled on top of her head in a way that came off as artful rather than messy. My sleepwear of choice was an oversized tee-shirt and stretched out sweats, and my long blonde hair had yet to see a brush that morning.

Conversation so far had been limited to "Is there more cream?" and "Look behind the milk," because we were both preoccupied—Scarlett with her new temp job as the assistant to a mercurial businessman visiting Santa Carla for unspecified reasons, and me with the leftover guilt and confusion from last night's vision. I deserved whatever consequences came from purposely invading other people's privacy without their consent, but how could I be so easily distracted by the sight of Jessie's naked skin? What did it mean for my future with Nicholas? What did it say about me?

Marina's reminder that Jessie was, first and foremost, my friend also tugged at the corner of my thoughts. Regardless of the mess I'd made of my own peace of mind, shouldn't he know what his friends and employees were saying about Amani before things between them went too far?

Scarlett's phone chimed with a text, and she sighed heavily after reading it.

"Mr. Wonderful calling?" I asked, referring to her employer.

"He doesn't like the hotel *he* chose after I presented every single option in town, and now he wants me to find the ten best short-term house rentals available immediately so he can move into one of them this weekend." She shoved back her chair. "I'd rather book the starring role in a hemorrhoid commercial than to keep working for this guy, but the agency will never send me on another temp job if I quit." The soda advertisement she'd landed last summer had paid her rent for months, but that was a dozen auditions ago.

"Will he be here long?" I asked.

She shrugged. "I don't even know what his business is. We haven't spoken on the phone yet, but I'm betting he's Scandinavian. Maybe he's scouting Santa Carla for a new IKEA store. We could use one."

Glancing over at our garage-sale-sourced living room furniture, I mock shuddered. "And compromise our taste in fine furnishings?"

"We wouldn't have to if you'd hurry up and add materialist to your repertoire," she said, rising from the table. "Chop, chop, Nine girl. Baby needs a new pair of recliners."

"Before you go," I said, halting her departure before losing my nerve. There was never a good time for us to talk about my boyfriend, but like it or not, the moment had arrived. "I'm meeting Nicholas in LA this weekend."

She dropped back into her chair with another sigh. "Pray tell. Why does Pretty Boy need you to risk your neck this time?"

The question wasn't completely unreasonable, but I refused to take the bait. "We're going to some big sporting event for Nines. I'll sit in the stands and eat popcorn. No one will even know I'm there."

She let out a snort of laughter at my wishful thinking. "I can only imagine what kind of games these people play. Juggling with chainsaws? Competitive guillotining? Fire-breathing dragons at fifty paces?"

"I don't think so, but I'll ask Nicholas to suggest those at the next regents' meeting," I said sweetly.

She groaned in mock frustration. "Can't you date somebody less hazardous to your health like, I don't know, Voldemort?"

"We can't all have the perfect boyfriend," I said in an attempt to sidetrack another lecture about my dating choices. It helped that Warren really was a great guy. As expected, she lit up from the inside out, but her dreamy expression evaporated as soon as she caught onto my game.

"Nice try." She rose once again and took the few short steps to the kitchen to put her mug in the dishwasher. "Will you at least promise not to be the one who dies this weekend?"

I gaped at her in surprise. "What makes you think anyone's going to die?"

"When that many Nines come together, someone always dies. To be or not to be," she loftily quoted as she retreated to her room. "That's *always* the question when you're with Nines."

I checked the time and downed the rest of my coffee. My shift at Jitters started in less than an hour.

As predicted, Cindy jumped at the chance to pick up my weekend shifts, though I'd miss catching up with Olive, the high school senior who'd lately only been available to work Saturday nights and Sundays. The perky cheerleader was overscheduled with fundraisers for the class trip to Disneyland, away games for her school's basketball team, and a new boyfriend.

"Gosh, the extra hours will be swell," Cindy said, her retro phrasing matching the vintage scarf she wore like a hairband.

"Todd wouldn't let me take any of our furniture, so my new roommates are letting me sleep on their couch until I can afford a mattress. This will really help."

"Didn't you buy a new sofa like two months ago?" I stood at the nearest cappuccino machine foaming organic almond milk for a triple shot latte, a drink we privately called the hipster heart attack. It was late morning, and the customers were an easy flow of twenty-somethings fueling up while pecking away at their laptops or stay-at-home parents craving a fix before picking up their preschoolers from daycare.

Cindy nodded, the shame and embarrassment of her predicament radiating from her as brightly as rays from the sun. "I really screwed things up, didn't I?"

"No, you didn't." I handed the coffee off to a yawning man with a toddler propped on his hip. "Todd did that all by himself." As much as I wanted to launch into a lecture about people only taking advantage if you let them, she was too preoccupied with beating herself up to hear it.

A warm and familiar energy drew my attention to the front door, and my throat tightened at seeing Jessie walk in. It wasn't that he never dropped in for coffee, but there was always a point to his visit. Could Harper have blurted out my true purpose in coming to the club last night? Had a telepath relayed how I'd intruded on a deeply intimate moment between him and Amani? Whatever the reason, I didn't want to discuss it in front of an audience.

"One of your hot guys is here," Cindy sang out.

"He's not *my* hot guy," I whispered fiercely.

She snickered. "Bet you want to take your break now, don't you?"

"He's just a friend, okay?" I pulled off my apron. Today it read, *Coffee, because adulting is hard.*

She chortled as I came around the bar and met Jessie.

"I'm just about to go on break," I said. "Can I get you something first?"

"Black coffee would be great." He ran a hand through the tangles in his blonde hair. "The hotter the better."

Dipping back behind the bar, I filled his order and fixed a vanilla latte for myself before meeting him at a corner table.

He took a big swallow and sighed with satisfaction. "You're a lifesaver. Nothing like discovering you're out of coffee before you've had your coffee."

"My mom will be thrilled to know I'm saving just as many lives as she is," I said, faking a relaxed air.

He raised his cup in a toast. "And without all the trouble of going to med school."

I waited for him to launch into his grievance, but his calm state of mind suggested he might truly have stopped by simply for a caffeine fix. The reprieve allowed room for Marina's words of concern to float to the surface.

"You and Amani seem happy," I ventured. The mention of his girlfriend colored his emotions with pride and pleasure.

"Yeah," he agreed. "I can't wait for you to get to know her. She's so much more than a pretty face. She's easy to talk to, laughs at my dumb jokes, and is smart as all get out. Did you know she was already chosen to be a patron?"

He tossed out the mention of the high honor quite casually, despite it being a bit of a sore subject between us. Nines traditionally designated a patron to vouch for them as they took an oath of allegiance at the Declaration, a formal ceremony I was expected to attend this coming summer. Jessie wanted to be the one to act as my sponsor, but I wasn't convinced of the need to have someone speak for me when I was perfectly capable of doing it myself.

"I'm really happy for you." I took a sip of coffee to hide the lie in my eyes. "Are she and Layla besties yet?"

His mouth turned down a fraction. "I hadn't realized how much of a bossy work wife Layla had become until now."

"She only wants what's best for you," I pointed out.

"What's best for me is for her to accept my choices, like you do." He fiddled with the lid of his cup, not meeting my gaze. "It's been a while since I've felt a connection with someone who feels the same. Lately I've been thinking how nice it would be to cook for someone and already know she hates onions, or accidentally pick up her body wash in the shower and smell like jasmine for the rest of the day, or order only one dessert because she pretends she doesn't want any, but then she asks for an extra spoon."

His musings were oddly specific, no doubt a glimpse of what he shared with Amani. I tried to be happy for him, though I couldn't help but wonder if Nicholas thought of me that way. Our time together always seemed filled with purpose, and our weekend in Los Angeles would likely be the same. Were the little romantic gestures really that important to building a relationship? As my break came to an end, it felt as if my insides were jumbled together like last year's Christmas lights, the colors blending into an indistinguishable blur that were impossible to pick apart.

Shortly after Jessie departed, a vaguely familiar guy approached the counter. He was about my age with the rangy build of the naturally thin. His unkempt hair was a brassy shade of yellow, and an uneven smattering of stubble on his chin suggested he was enjoying a lazy winter break.

His face brightened. "Blake?"

"Hi," I said weakly, unable to place him. He took pity on me.

"Aaron. We were in art history together. I'd heard Dr. Hamilton was supposed to be a jerk, but I didn't think he was so bad."

I stifled a smirk. Out of desperation, I'd once accepted a ride home from the college professor who treated female students like fresh meat served up for his dining pleasure. A vision from his past had armed me with the ammunition to shut him down when he'd made his inevitable move. A subdued version of the man had shown up to class for the rest of term.

"I ended up liking that class too." I eyed the customers lined up behind him. "What can I get you?"

He glanced up at the menu posted above my head. "How about—" He froze, only his chest rising as he breathed.

After a few moments, I ventured, "Aaron?"

His eyes, which had been trained on the menu, rolled in my direction, but the rest of him didn't move an inch. If he was having some sort of seizure, it was the creepiest thing ever. I opened my mouth to ask if I should call an ambulance when he spoke.

"You should have stayed away." The raspy monotone made the words even more chilling. "But now it's too late. People are going to get hurt, and it will be all your fault."

His eyes lost focus and he keeled over, taking down the unfortunate guy standing in line behind him. Several onlookers rushed to their aid, but I was too shaken to move. A quick search of the coffeehouse for anyone delighting in how their trick completely unnerved me revealed nothing.

First a materialist conjuring a snake, and now an enchanter delivering a disturbing message through a hapless classmate. The timing of these two things so close on the heels of my dad unburdening his conscience was certainly suspect, but why come at me? What was I supposed to have stayed away from, and who was going to get hurt?

Maybe this had nothing to do with Henry Thorne's duplicity, and the harassment came from a completely unrelated quarter. If so, who hated me so much they were driven to such tactics?

With a flash of guilt I thought of Luna D'Onofrio, the enchanter who'd tried to force my sister to kill me. I'd been totally justified in fighting back, saving my own life and probably Jordan's, but Luna had died that night. In the weeks since, memories of her last moments—her gleeful expression as she loomed over us, her scream as she flew through the air, the crash of breaking glass as she was hurled through a window—haunted my sleep and often my waking hours too. Had a member of her family learned how she'd died and come seeking revenge?

Then there was Matthias Montoya, a materialist who blamed me for the death of his twin. He would probably celebrate the day I breathed my last, but surely he had better things to do than hang out in Santa Carla playing head games. He and his brother had been in league with the voyant regent to seize control of The Nine, so petty revenge seemed out of character when their ambition had been nothing short of revolutionary. Could that have been Matthias who'd lurked outside Jitters' windows when the cobra reared its head?

What about those within The Nine who were threatened by my relationship with Nicholas? Rumors of my growing abilities had swirled among the sentinels at Alder House when I was there last month. Maybe someone beyond their sect had gotten wind I was a multi and decided my alliance with the son of the chancellor was too much political capital being consolidated in young and inexperienced hands. No one liked a power couple who wielded too much power.

As Aaron rose shakily to his feet, it suddenly occurred to me my multi status no longer had to be viewed as a burden. At first I had been afraid how Scarlett might react to my additional powers, and then I'd feared being targeted or exploited by other Nines, but it wouldn't be long before everyone knew. The time had come to own my power.

My empathic skills were growing in strength and purpose, perhaps because I practiced on almost everyone I met. In fact, it was mildly troubling how much I'd already come to rely on the additional insight when reading between conversational lines, but I liked the subtext it added to every word and gesture. Would my telekinesis develop along the same lines if I no longer regarded it as an inconvenient truth?

Whatever the answer, I was done pretending to be less than I was.

Welcome to Wonderland

The driver Nicholas sent was right on time. The woman waiting on the front steps of my apartment was in her mid-thirties and wore the obligatory black uniform of a car service driver, the jacket nipped at the waist to showcase a generous hourglass figure. Shoulder-length black ringlets framed a round, dark-skinned face highlighted by a wide mouth and deep-set eyes.

"I'm Marie Landry," she said, her gaze assessing. "Class Two phantomist."

"Blake Wilder. Voyant."

"I know who you are." Obviously, since she'd been sent to pick me up. She moved past me to grab the carryon bag parked just inside the front door.

I tottered on three-inch heels to the car. Trainers and Uggs were my winter footwear of choice, but neither went very well with the burgundy velvet dress I wore. It laced from navel to breastbone with a black silk ribbon, so depending on how close-ly the neckline came together, it was either a pretty dinner dress or a revealingly sexy garment that made the most of my limited cleavage. I'd decided to err on the side of reminding Nicholas what waited for him in California. With the front of my hair pulled back in a jeweled clip, I felt not only pretty but resolved to seek insights into my latest troubles among the people at To The Nines.

As I made for the front passenger seat, Marie slipped in front of me and opened the rear door. Her unyielding expression made it clear she would brook no refusal, so I climbed into the backseat.

"Is that so?" Marie mused as the car pulled away from the curb.

I caught her eye in the rearview mirror. "Excuse me?"

"There's a young ghost here who says you're upset about something. There's no jealous boyfriend coming after us, is there?"

"Thanks, Harper," I muttered under my breath.

The teen spirit must have overheard my phone call with Dad last night. He'd been equally mystified by my troublemaking visitors.

"Henry Thorne isn't the kind of man who plays games," he'd said, "but I guess it's possible one of his enforcers picked up the slack. They might think any threat to you would be more effective than if they came after me, and they'd be right."

"What if the warnings aren't coming from Alder House?" I recounted my depressingly long list of potential enemies.

"Let me do some poking around and see what I can find. There are still a few friends who are willing to help me out from time to time."

Shaking off the recollection, I told the driver, "Someone seems to think I've butted in where I don't belong."

She let out a peal of laughter. "Hell, sugar, that's a typical Tuesday for me."

"Well, hopefully they didn't send an enchanter to possess one of your customers." I spilled the rest of the story, and then described the cobra who'd appeared a day earlier.

Indignation filtered across the small space. "I swear, some people think being a Nine gives them license to rule the world, but you're safe with us. Madame Boudreaux says no one followed us onto the freeway, and she'll keep a watchful eye the whole way to LA."

Jessie was the only phantomist I knew well enough to ask about the spirits who dwelled in his shadow. He'd told me there were several, but Cedric, a dandified English aristocrat who'd died centuries ago, seemed to occupy a place of honor in Jessie's life. It made me wonder if all phantomists had one ghost they relied on more than others.

"Please let Madame Boudreaux know I appreciate her kindness. Have you been, uh, friends long?"

"Madame Sally started honoring me with her presence about five years ago," Marie explained with no small amount of pride. "Two hundred years ago, she was the most famous medium in the French Quarter, and a free Black woman at that. Being a phantomist herself, she was accustomed to talking to spirits, but she had the gift to summon almost anyone back from the dead."

A woman of color who'd successfully made her own way in pre-Civil War New Orleans must have been a force of nature. Nicholas had once told me phantomists attracted spirits who shared similar traits as their hosts, so Marie had a right to be proud in pulling a ghost such as that.

"She must have some stories to tell," I said.

The drive to Los Angeles sped by as Marie related tales of dark family secrets spilled by spirits out for revenge, and the frequent duels of honor fought by the city's elite as a result.

"Modern DNA testing companies do most of the dirty work these days," the driver said with a laugh. "Madame Sally says it's done wonders for helping vengeful spirits find peace."

By the time we pulled up in front of a five-story building squatting on an entire city block of downtown Los Angeles, the strain of the last twenty-four hours had melted away.

Marie insisted on retrieving my bag from the trunk, so I got out of the car and peered up at the imposing façade that bore more than a passing resemblance to a medieval castle. Sly gargoyles leered down from gray stone outcroppings, a rooftop parapet connected turrets where I half expected to glimpse archers repelling invaders, and a polished slab of wood that could probably withstand a battering ram served as the front door. Nestled amid the skyline's sleek towers of glass and steel, it was as out of place as a mustache on a chicken. I loved it.

A discreet bronze plaque affixed to the wall outside the entrance read:

To The Nines
Established 1893
Members Only

The portal swung inward on well-oiled hinges. A young woman in a dark suit, her wide shoulders straining the seams of her jacket, regarded me with a polite smile. Her pale hair was buzzed on the sides with a longer section at the crown angled across her brow. It wasn't a particularly flattering style, but it would save a ton of time on blow drying.

"To The Nines welcomes you," she said, admitting me to an inner sanctum smaller than my bedroom at home. It was bare of furniture, but intricately tiled floors gleamed in the warm glow of a handful of brass sconces lining the walls. Another set of burnished doors at the other end made it clear the room served the same purpose as Suki's antechamber at The Lower 8. There'd be no admittance without first being assessed by a sentinel.

"Stand down, Jane." Marie pulled my bag in her wake. "This is the voyant Blake Wilder."

The sentinel's demeanor instantly went from formal to deferential. Jane dashed to open the interior door for us, and Marie led the way into a spacious reception area. New arrivals were being helped at two of the tall desks, but the third was open and staffed by a familiar face.

"Hello, Blake Wilder," said the younger half-brother of my occasional bodyguard, Khalia Clarke, though there was little affection between the pair. "I didn't expect to see you again so soon."

"Marcel Pryce." I was pleased to remember his full name in return. We'd met recently at The Lower 8 when he'd been filling in as door sentinel on one of Suki's nights off. "What are you doing here?"

Amusement danced in the depths of his caramel-colored eyes. "I go where I am needed—and where I am paid." He had more in common with his practical-minded sister than he'd probably like to think, including smooth black skin, an accent that betrayed his Caribbean roots, and a great sense of style as evidenced by a three-piece suit in brown herringbone that was anything but stuffy.

"Did I suddenly become invisible?" Marie inquired of Marcel with a touch of pique.

"Of course not, Marie," he smoothly replied. "It's good to see you."

"That's a relief. For a minute there, I was afraid I'd become one of those invisible evanescents." She leaned closer to me and said in a loud whisper, "The good looking ones have a habit of forgetting their manners."

He leveled his gaze at her. "I will assist Miss Wilder from here. Thank you, Marie."

"Hmph," the woman muttered before turning to me. "I'm on duty all night. You need anything, you just pick up any house phone and ask for me." I reached for my wallet to dig out a generous tip, but she waved me off. "Regent Thorne has taken care of everything."

"Thanks, Marie. I hope to see you and Madame Boudreaux on the ride back."

She grinned. "It will be our pleasure."

Marcel pulled my information up on an electronic tablet. "You must be here to show solidarity with the Thornes."

I made a noise that neither confirmed nor denied his assumption. My presence there was in no way a political statement—on my part, at least—but the willingness to share anything personal had been beaten out of me at a young age by peers who'd treated me like the prom queen of a leper colony.

He smiled as if he could read my thoughts. "No one carries tales from this club, if that's what worries you. Not only are sentinels stationed in every room to maintain privacy, but indiscreetly sharing what you see comes with consequences most are unwilling to pay."

"That's not nearly as catchy as what happens in Vegas stays in Vegas," I pointed out.

"Perhaps not," he said, his lips still quirked, "but you have nothing to fear. We keep each other's secrets here. You will understand when you join us in one of the main rooms."

"That's good to know." I had the impression there was some deeper meaning at play, but it eluded me. "Is my room ready? I'd like to drop off my bag."

"Yes. I have you in the Alder House suite, which is always ready to welcome the chancellor or a visiting regent. It is most fortunate the stipulation was written into the club's charter since the rest of the rooms were booked within minutes of the game day announcement."

One of the double doors opened, and a young man dressed in a black suit identical to the door sentinel's entered the foyer. He gripped the handle of my suitcase as Marcel slid an old-fashioned brass key across the countertop to me. I slipped it into the black velvet clutch Scarlett had recently thrifted.

"Vincent will take care of your bag," he said with a knowing gleam in his eyes. "I suggest you go explore Wonderland, Alice."

To the Nines

I tried not to gawk like a tourist, but the club's unique exterior was tame compared to the jewel of design and style within. At the heart of the rectangular building was a five-story atrium capped by a peaked skylight inviting in the last vestige of the day. Open walkways and swooping staircases of polished oak and ornate wrought iron trailed down each floor, with bird-cage elevators nudging the spectacular into the realm of steampunk. People spilled out of ground floor bars to lounge at café tables set about the courtyard, and at least one restaurant was already open for business.

"First time at To The Nines?" Vincent beamed as if he were personally responsible for creating the architectural marvel. He wasn't much older than me and spoke in the stateless accent of a local.

"I've never seen anything quite like it." Not that I visited many places more than a century old. Central and Southern California came of age in the post-war boom, so it was largely a landscape of ranch homes, bungalows, and office buildings shaped like giant cubes.

He pointed to a closed door at the far end of the courtyard. "If you really want the full experience, you should check out the Marco Polo room."

I glanced at him in query. "Marco Polo? Don't tell me he was a Nine too?"

"An empath. Knowing what people were thinking helped him keep his head on his shoulders more than once, especially after meeting up with the Mongols." His voice was filled with longing, as if he was disappointed to have missed out on all the barbaric fun. "His private journals are in the vault at Alder House, but you can read the translations online if you have the password."

As he excused himself to deliver my bag, I wondered once again if I would ever become accustomed to such startling pronouncements.

My heels clicked across a mosaic tile floor of cobalt, terracotta, and buttercream as I took Vincent's advice and entered the Marco Polo room. My eyes widened at the chaotic scene. In a layout similar to The Lower 8, a stage and dance floor took up one end of the cavernous space while the other was outfitted with sofas, tables, and a bar. What made it unique were the scores of people behaving in strangely disjointed ways, as if each were lost in some personal fantasy.

On stage, a woman wearing a tutu, toe shoes, and a sublime expression danced as if freed from the bonds of gravity, accompanied by music only she could hear. Against a wall, a young man supported by a walker stared into a decoratively framed mirror, one hand reverently touching his hair and face as if in disbelief. On a nearby sofa, a couple happily flipped through a photo album, stopping often to chat and laugh, though the pages of the book were blank. A man on the dance floor, dressed in a suit of armor and wielding a broadsword, battled a small translucent dragon lashing its tail with hostility.

"What's your fantasy, Blake Wilder?" A voice rich and smooth as the aged whiskey Nicholas favored murmured in my ear.

Startled, I turned to meet the gaze of a most singular individual. Taut, golden skin clung to a sculpted face bearing an aquiline nose and sharp slashes of dark brows. Eyes shadowed with a rainbow of hues and heavy lashes were offset by a crown of short, platinum hair teased into a halo. A thin, boyish body clothed in a black spandex bodysuit featured a deep vee neckline revealing a swath of flat, hairless chest.

"Excuse me?" I responded.

Lips painted a vivid red curved into a wicked smile. "Isn't that why you've come to the Marco Polo? To fulfill a wish you can't experience in the outside world?"

My companion turned to look out over the crowd. "An enchanter to let you live your dream of being a prima ballerina or take away the grief of a lost child? An evanescent to turn a medieval game into reality? A materialist to restore the illusion of youth and beauty? Not that you need it, of course." They had unerringly picked out some of the people who'd caught my eye, as only a telepath could.

"Is that what they're doing?" I suddenly understood one of the unique offerings of the club. "How long will their fantasies last?"

"Only while they're here." A sly look entered their eyes. "We also have private rooms for those looking to indulge in more intimate adventures. Is that what you crave, my sweet?"

I took a step back, needing to put some distance between me and the direction this conversation was headed. "I'm good, thanks. You know my name, but you have yet to tell me yours."

"I'm Honey, here to make all your sweet dreams come true, for a small fee, of course." Stroking their naked sternum with black lacquered nails, they looked me over with interest. "Voyants are such a rare commodity that we don't have one on staff. Perhaps you'd be interested in joining us?"

I scoffed. "I see traumatic events in people's lives. Who would pay to hear about their own death and destruction?"

Their laugh was shadowed and knowing. "You'd be surprised what people will pay you to do to them."

My lips pulled back in a grimace. I'd spent my life observing people do and say terrible things to each other. Delving into their private darkness for kicks was a bridge too far.

"I think I'll wait for my boyfriend at the bar. Excuse me." Without giving the host an opportunity to respond, I ducked to avoid a woman wearing a matching red bodysuit and cape dip and soar through the air.

I'd taken only a few sips of mineral water with lime when a pair of strong arms slipped around my waist from behind. Nicholas's familiar energy engulfed me and made my skin tingle. I swiveled on my stool to meet his hungry gaze, and my body instantly responded. Wordlessly, we reached for each other, the weeks apart forgotten as our lips met.

After a searing minute that finally helped dispel the lingering vision of Jessie that tormented my dreams, he pulled away and whispered against my mouth, "If you moved to Alder House, we'd never have to be apart for so long."

It had only been a few weeks since he'd first asked me to come live at The Nine's magnificent English estate, but he pressed his case at every opportunity. Likewise, I glossed over it each time, not quite ready to pull up stakes in Santa Carla when I'd only just arrived.

My lips curled into a pleased smile. "You have to admit, though, it definitely makes our reunion more fun."

"More fun for some than others," joked a familiar voice.

"Dev!" I exclaimed, pleased to find Nicholas's personal sentinel at my elbow, and not only because I liked the man. His father Ashwin had served as Henry's bodyguard at the chancellors' challenge, and I hoped to find a private moment to ask Dev if he knew about the shady circumstances surrounding the Thorne's rise to power.

Dev had ditched the staid Alder House sentinel's uniform for an ivory turtleneck and black blazer with jeans. The subtle rebellion continued with dark stubble gracing his lantern jaw. A single gold hoop in one ear gave him the air of a pirate, a look reinforced by deep brown eyes sparkling with mischief.

Nicholas released me and pretended to scowl at his bodyguard. "Aren't you supposed to stay in the shadows and be silent and mysterious?"

"You're thinking of Batman," Dev quipped, leaning his back against the bar and observing a group of older women beautifully lit by floating orbs of warm light as they gossiped and drank champagne. "I'm more best friend, let's-do-shots material."

Nicholas slid onto the stool on my other side. He was thinner than the last time we'd been together, the angles of his handsome face more defined. He wore his dark brown hair in the Ivy League style, a cut an actor might sport in the role of a young billionaire. It worked well with his love of fine fabrics in classic cuts, and tonight he was a study in navy and gray.

"Since the murder of Bailey," he said, a note of regret in his voice for the telekinetic regent before him, a man he'd considered a friend and mentor, "all regents are now saddled with babysitters."

"I prefer the term uncanny nanny," Dev cheekily volunteered.

"I prefer the term two's company, three's a crowd," Nicholas retorted before ordering a whiskey and soda. The bartender reached for the bottle of spirits without hesitation, despite my boyfriend being only nineteen. As was often the case, The Nine was a law unto itself.

Dev turned toward us, his face alight. "There'll be no escaping a crowd tonight. The exhibition game's starting soon."

Nicholas perked up. "Did you get good seats?"

The sentinel pulled three tickets out of his breast pocket and grinned. "The uncanny nanny strikes again."

Nicholas regarded the politely interested expression I'd adopted and dialed back his eagerness. "We don't have to go. I don't have any official duties tonight."

"But it's going to be an awesome match," Dev interjected with a wheedling note before turning his powers of persuasion on me. "The two teams are made up of retired players. That means old rivals call an uneasy truce if they're on the same team, but if not, they can finally let loose without having to worry about getting ejected from the game. There's sure to be at least one player who'll need an evanescent to put them back together by the end."

Telling Dev to go enjoy himself while Nicholas and I went elsewhere for a romantic dinner was not an option. As the personal sentinel to a regent, he was both honor and duty bound to accompany his charge at all times, at the expense of his own interests and relationships. It was a lot to ask of anyone, but especially a sentinel, whose entire class was somehow regarded as less valuable to The Nine than the other disciplines. The least I could do was go along for a night that seemed to mean so much to him.

"How can I say no when you make it sound so, uh, tempting?" I asked wryly.

"Yes!" Dev exclaimed, and even Nicholas lit up with anticipation. "You'll love it. Blood, sweat, electrocutions—what more could you want in a team sport?"

I shot a dubious glance at Nicholas. "Why am I not surprised that even your fun and games are bloodthirsty?"

He took my hand as I hopped off the barstool. "Because you are as smart as you are beautiful." His admiring gaze dipped to the glimpse of skin revealed by my dress's satin ribbon, but a ringing phone put an end to the moment. Releasing my hand, he frowned at the name on the screen before answering.

"Mr. Silver." The conversation was short. "I'm staying at To The Nines… Yes, she's with me… Of course, we'll see you soon."

I raised an inquiring brow as he slipped the phone back into his pocket.

"The Prime's just landed in Los Angeles. He's on his way here and wants to see us both."

Palmarium

News of the Prime Sentinel's imminent arrival provoked a frisson of nerves. My father had told Mr. Silver I'd witnessed Henry's betrayal in a vision, so part of his agenda must be to interview me. My fury had known no bounds when I'd discovered Nicholas had known my dad was a Nine and concealed it from me. Would he believe me if I told him I'd only waited for a private moment to reveal what I knew about his father?

"Did Mr. Silver say what he wants?" Dev asked.

We'd finished our drinks and queued up with dozens of others for one of several elevators. Spirits were running high, and the courtyard echoed with conversation and laughter, but more than one person edged back when they spied the newest voyant among them. As a result, we had the next open elevator all to ourselves.

"He's been gathering evidence on Bailey's killer and accomplices ever since Blake's vision," Nicholas said as we entered the car, referring to my insight into Matthias Montoya, the materialist who'd murdered the former telekinetic regent. "Whatever he's found, we'll find out soon enough."

Dev made a sour face. "Heaven forbid we have a night to ourselves," he said, missing the irony of his words.

He hit the button for a lower level. As the car smoothly dropped, I latched onto Nicholas's arm in an irrational moment of apprehension. The last time I'd descended into the bowels of a building populated by Nines, I'd ended up fighting for my life.

Nicholas put his hand over mine and gave it a reassuring squeeze. "No challenges tonight," he said, perhaps experiencing the same eerie sense of déjà vu.

The cage door opened, and we followed the well-dressed crowd into a space resembling a much more upscale version of my high school gym. Padded bleachers lined either side of a large plank floor, the painted markings as much a mystery to me as those mapped out for a basketball game. Silk banners celebrating past winners adorned the walls—some so aged and faded they were almost illegible—but I was able to pick out a few dating back over a hundred years. Dev presented our tickets to an usher with a flourish, and we were led to three floor seats right in the center of the action.

Nicholas looked at Dev with amazement. "How did you get such prime tickets at the last minute?"

The sentinel raised a hand to get the attention of a food server before answering. "I may have, uh, mentioned they were for you."

"Dev..." Nicholas ground out, obviously not pleased at pulling rank.

"Ever since you became regent, all we do is work, work, work," he retorted. "If you want to keep your sentinel happy, you have to toss him an occasional bone." The food server, a pretty woman in shorts and a sports jersey, arrived. "Or in this case, two hot dogs with everything and a draft beer."

"That sounds good," I told the server, "but make mine a Sprite." Nicholas shook off his displeasure and ordered the same as Dev.

I didn't know if I'd ever get used to the attention that came with being a voyant and being flanked between two attractive men—one a regent—only cranked up the heat. Most of the people in the quickly filling stands across the floor stared and whispered, with many raising their phones to snap pics. It would have been easier to pretend we weren't on display if the emotions surging around us—lust, envy, jealousy—didn't make me want to take a shower. The handful of people glancing about in either amusement or distaste were most likely telepaths overhearing the thoughts that went along with the feelings.

Sutton Sinclair, the elementalist regent, had an equally prime seat directly across from us. In his sixties, his buzzcut had completed its journey from gray to white in the months since his son's death. He was accompanied by a handsome older woman who had the same long, dark hair and tan skin as his late girlfriend, Selena Flores. Sutton definitely had a type.

It would be asking a lot, but would he be able to recall anything unusual about the day Henry Thorne challenged Mitsuko Hayashi? Not that witnessing the sitting chancellor fry to a crisp happened every day, but maybe something else odd had stuck out that had remained with him all these years later. Did he blame my father for the chancellor's death? I resolved to track him down after the game.

My gaze next snagged on a familiar profile in the third row. Jessie's face tilted toward Amani as she likely told some amusing anecdote. For once he'd ditched the jeans that were the staple of his off-duty wardrobe in favor of an unconstructed herringbone jacket over a white shirt and black pants. Amani wore her mass of dark curls in a high ponytail, all the better to admire the miles of smooth skin revealed by a strapless silver top embellished with crystals. She oozed style and sophistication, giving me a sudden urge to yank a bag over my head.

She unexpectedly looked over and caught me staring. My mouth curved in an awkward smile, but she didn't immediately respond in kind. The distance between us made me wonder if her dark eyes narrowed, or if I read too much into her scrutiny. She finally gave a friendly nod before turning back to Jessie.

"So what is Palmarium?" I asked, determined not to let petty observations ruin my night.

"Only the greatest sport in existence," Dev enthusiastically volunteered before catching Nicholas's quelling side eye. "Silent and mysterious. Got it."

"Nines have been playing Palmarium almost since our history began," Nicholas explained. "In fact, certain aspects of the game will look familiar to you because they've filtered into the outside world and inspired such sports as cricket, baseball, and jai alai." He was cut off by his ringing phone. Without even looking at the screen, he silenced it before powering it off. Dev's jaw went slack.

"Are you sure that wasn't important?" I asked with an impish grin, delighted at the gesture.

He snorted. "They're all important, but apparently all I do is work, work, work. Tonight is for us." Our lips met in a brief kiss that produced titters and camera flashes from the spectators.

"I hope I'm not interrupting." We broke apart to find a woman in her mid-twenties beaming at us both. Riotous waves of long, auburn hair framed an open and appealing face while layers of gauzy fabrics in a multitude of colors and patterns floated about her reedy figure. Multiple necklaces of various lengths draped her bodice, and chunky rings sparkling with semi-precious stones adorned most of her fingers. She looked like the coolest chick at an outdoor music festival.

Nicholas shot to his feet with delight. "Francesca! I didn't know you were going to be here."

"I don't know why—this is my town, after all," she mock scolded after they'd shared a quick hug.

Nicholas glanced my way, so I stood as well. "Blake, I'd like you to meet Francesca Ricci, a Class One elementalist, and a good friend from Alder House."

"I'm so happy to meet you, Blake," she said with an infectious smile I couldn't help but return. "I met Nicholas when we were both teacher's assistants one summer for first years. I'm amazed Alder House was still standing after that."

"I barely recognized you without a mop and fire extinguisher," he said with a laugh.

"We elementalists might make a bit of a mess, but at least I didn't get blamed for destroying an entire classroom," she teased. Despite her outward show of ease, she was on edge, but too many people surrounded us to be able to pick up anything more.

He turned to me with a sheepish grin. "It was a miscommunication with one of my students, but nobody died."

The words were barely out of his mouth when he stiffened, and Francesca's smile froze.

"Well," she said after a few moments, her eyes casting about as if seeking a new topic of conversation before landing on Dev. "I see you two are still a matched set."

The sentinel had remained uncharacteristically silent. He was often the first to leap into a conversation, particularly with anyone female, but he'd slouched behind me as if hoping to go unnoticed.

"Hello, Fran." Dev smiled thinly. "A pleasure, as always."

She made a noise in the back of her throat that made clear she wasn't any happier at their meeting than he was, and I hid a smile. There was history there, and a fiery one at that.

She turned the full force of her attention back on Nicholas. "I hope you don't mind if I join you. One of our clients had to leave town unexpectedly, but she insisted such a prime seat shouldn't go to waste."

"Clients?" Nicholas inquired as we all sat back down.

"I work in crisis management PR, mostly for celebrity Nines," she explained. "We do things like keeping a certain popstar's drunken display of her materialist powers off the gossip sites last week."

A flurry of excitement at the main entrance turned every head as one of the most recognizable faces in Hollywood sauntered into the room. The handsome actor pretended not to notice the stir he created as he and a couple of buddies claimed the last remaining floor seats right across from us.

"Being an empath has helped make him a great actor, but rumor has it his latest film isn't testing well," Francesca mused before pasting on a bright smile. "Excuse me, but duty calls." She crossed the floor and beelined straight to the celebrity.

"And that, ladies and gentlemen," Dev said as he observed her pushing past the star's reluctance to engage in shop talk, "is why we broke up. Fran's ambition has no off switch."

Personally, I admired her willingness to go after what she wanted, but I wasn't there to do a deep dive on the qualities he valued most in a partner.

The arrival of our hot dogs came at the same time music started to pump throughout the room. People clapped and stomped their feet until cheers broke out at the sight of a man striding onto the floor. He wore a jacket in an edgy shade of pumpkin and had so much product in his hair, he should probably avoid an open flame.

"Ladies and gentlemen," he said into a wireless microphone, his gentle accent placing his origins as south of the border. "To The Nines welcomes you to the opening of the American league playoff! I am your host, Miguel de Palma. Tomorrow's winner-take-all game will decide which team competes in the upcoming Palmarium world championships, but tonight, we have an exciting exhibition match between two teams made up of some of our most celebrated players. Without further ado, let's bring out our champions!"

A set of doors opposite the entrance were thrown open. Excitement swelled as a grizzled set of men and women wearing padded jerseys in either white or black prowled the short distance to two long benches set at the edge of the court. There were nine per team plus a coach, and each player carried an equipment bag they tossed down at their feet as if they'd done it a thousand times before.

"Look!" Dev exclaimed, his eyes trained on a glowering woman in black whose spandex shorts showcased muscular thighs the size of both of mine put together. "That's Elaina Sackhoff. She's had more career knockouts than any other player."

Francesca made her way back over, a triumphant tilt to her lips as she took her seat.

"In the white jerseys," the announcer said, "we have the Lords of the Game, and in black, the Atomic Bombers." As he introduced the members of each team, the crowd cheered for their favorites while the players unzipped their bags and drew on shin guards and helmets complete with face masks. Gloves similar to catcher's mitts came out along with bats that flared into flat paddles at the end.

Swallowing down a bite of a hotdog, I leaned closer to Nicholas. "Why do they look like they're going into battle?"

His mouth quirked up. "No one usually dies, if that's what you're asking."

I shook my head. "Where have I heard that before?"

Once all the participants had been introduced, three players from each side took to the floor. A handful of staff dressed in red or blue T-shirts bearing the To The Nines logo skirted the sides.

"Materialists, ball and shields, if you please," Miguel commanded of the people in red. Instantly, two disks the size of dinner plates, one on each side of the field of play that corresponded with the teams' colors, hovered several feet above the heads of the players. Near the ceiling, a brown ball the size of a softball materialized dead center. All aligned with the markings on the floor.

Miguel stepped outside the red line running along the floor's perimeter that formed a rectangle. "Evanescents," he called out to the blue-clad staff stationed at each corner of the floor. "Erect the barrier." An electrified shield rose from all four corners of the court, the glowing edges visible until they knit together at the ceiling.

I took a sip of soda. "What is the object of the game?"

"It's simple," Dev said, his excitement overriding his intention not to make our date a threesome. "Each team must protect their shield from being hit by the ball while also trying to land a shot on the other team's shield. The first team to connect ten times wins."

"Unless one team loses all their players," Nicholas chimed in, his own anticipation making him shift excitedly in his seat. "Then they forfeit."

"Loses their players?" I echoed in alarm. "Where do they go?" Scarlett had been right to question the weekend's body count, and not in the fun way.

A hush fell over the place as the players on the court assumed their ready positions. Miguel commanded the crowd's attention one last time.

"The power of the one…" he called out.

"Is the power of the many!" the audience roared.

A whistle blew, and the ball dropped to the floor. A player on the white team who wore an eyepatch made a swooping motion with her arm, and the ball telekinetically rocketed toward the other team's shield. A gust of wind summoned by an elementalist in black diverted the projectile and sent it slamming into the invisible barricade. The resulting crackle of electricity made the hair on the back of my neck stand at attention.

A member of the white team scooped up the ball and lobbed it toward the black team's goal. Surprisingly, one of his own teammates flew through the air and blocked the ball with his chest, the momentum carrying him right into the electrical barrier. His body arced as power shot through it with the sound of a mosquito hitting a bug zapper. He fell to the floor as Elaina Sackhoff raised a fist in triumph. When the man didn't move, the whistle blew and play halted.

I gripped Nicholas's hand. "Is he alright?" Coming into contact with an evanescent's creation had killed his uncle, whether he was aware of it or not.

Club staff hustled onto the floor and collected the fallen man. The coach pointed to another player on the white team. He leapt from the bench and took his place.

"Elaina Sackhoff used her telekinesis on a rival player to stop the ball," Nicholas said matter-of-factly. "It happens all the time. An evanescent will shock his heart if it's stopped, and if there's no other damage, he'll probably survive." I should have known The Nine would put their own brutal spin on what they considered a knockout.

The whistle blew, and the game resumed. A player on the black team smashed the ball with her bat, and the sphere ricocheted hard off the back of a man in a white before shooting to the center of the white team's disk. The crowd leapt to their feet and roared their approval as the player who'd served as a backboard was carried away gasping for breath.

Francesca leaned in and whispered something in Nicholas's ear that made him chuckle. A burst of cheers at another brutal move drowned his response, but whatever he said made her laugh in return. Dev caught my eye and silently pantomimed a simpering laugh of his own before shaking his head in annoyance. There was definitely a story there.

Turning back to the game, my attention caught on the nearest of the club's blue T-shirted evanescents, a woman in her seventies with white, cotton candy hair and oversized tortoiseshell eyeglasses. She suddenly halted mid-stride in a move so similar to what happened to my classmate at Jitters that my skin prickled with apprehension.

On the court, a member of the white team smacked the ball at the opposing team's goal. Before it even came close, Sackhoff telekinetically propelled her paddle skyward to bat it away with a defensive swing. The ball rocketed straight at us, and without thinking, I ducked.

The hum of the orb flying over my head was cut horribly short by a meaty thud. Screams erupted as the man directly behind me flew backwards and collided with spectators in the third and fourth rows. The ref's whistle cut through the air, and chaos reigned.

Nicholas yanked me away from the surge, his grip on my shoulders fierce as he searched my face. I stared back at him mutely, shocked by the close call with major injury or possibly even death. My mind rebelled at the idea this could have been more than a terrible accident, but after the harassment of the past week, I couldn't be sure.

"Are you okay?" he asked.

I nodded shakily. "Are you?"

We clung to each other as evanescents tended to the unconscious man and a number of others who'd gone down with him. Two of the healers laid their hands on the victim's chest, and after a minute, his eyes fluttered open.

"How did you know the barrier was down?" Dev asked, making me jump. I hadn't realized he loomed protectively at my back.

"I didn't," I said, which was true. Tossing about suspicions and accusations would only hamper the inquiry that would surely follow. "I acted on instinct."

Dev's dark eyes searched the crowd, a scowl etched across his face. "You should both return to the suite while the evanescents responsible for the barrier are questioned."

It was Nicholas's turn to be startled. "Are you saying this wasn't an accident?"

"It's too early to know," the sentinel said, "but let's not forget what happened to the last telekinetic regent."

"You think *I* was the target?" Nicholas asked.

"Excuse me, Regent," Honey cut in, a folded note in hand. "The chancellor is trying to reach you, but you're not answering your phone." They thrust the paper at Nicholas with a trembling hand.

Honey withdrew as Nicholas read the contents, his face going slack before meeting my eyes. His own roiled with shock and sorrow.

"What is it?" I asked, barely able to breathe as dread constricted my throat. Dev leaned in as well.

"Akim Silver, the Prime Sentinel, is dead."

13

Work to Be Done

My heart plummeted to my feet. Death had been a frequent visitor since The Nine entered my life, but repeated exposure didn't soften the blow of Mr. Silver's fate. What could have happened during his short drive from the airport? It had to have been an accident, right?

"What can I do to help?" Francesca asked. She'd followed us out to the elevators after overhearing the news. Separated from the crowd, I didn't have to guess at her emotional state. Her earlier anxiety, presumably from encountering an ex, had been replaced by anticipation, setting my teeth on edge. What could she possibly hope to gain from this terrible loss?

"You need to move swiftly before curiosity turns to unrest," she said.

Nicholas raked a hand through his hair, the air around him roiling with grief and frustration. "You're in the business of putting out fires. What do you suggest I do?"

"Advise the chancellor to put out a statement announcing Silver's death and appointing you to lead the investigation," she urged. "Then use tomorrow night's speech as a demonstration of your ability to take charge."

While I grappled with shock, Francesca had already moved on to the political fallout—and opportunities—created by the Prime's demise. I was coming to understand Dev's disdain.

The sentinel checked his watch and made a disparaging noise. "Fifty-three seconds. That's how long it took to make this all about you, Fran. What next? A job as Nicholas's personal advisor?"

"Don't be an ass," she snapped before returning her focus to Nicholas. "This is what I do, and I can tell you the moment that will define you is here. It's your opportunity to cement your position as the most obvious candidate to carry the time-honored traditions of The Nine into the future."

His face went blank, but I sensed his anger and resentment. "You sound like my father. What makes you think I share that dream? What if I want something different?"

"Forgive me, Nicholas," she said without missing a beat. "I assumed someone willing to risk their life to become regent had no intention of stopping there."

As we rode the elevator back up, Nicholas wordlessly passed me the note. The last line of Henry's terse message ordered Nicholas to personally assess the crime scene.

My gaze shot to his. "He's going to put you in charge like Francesca said, isn't he?"

"They both must own the same playbook," he said with bitter sarcasm.

"But you'll do what he wants," Dev inserted wryly. "You always do."

The door opened before Nicholas could frame a response. The sentinel got out at the ground floor to secure a car, Nicholas excused himself to call his father, and I continued upstairs to change. I owed it to Mr. Silver to offer whatever help I could. He had been my friend, and one of the few in my new world who hadn't regarded me as an asset to be used or acquired.

I made it to the suite, but once the door closed behind me, the dam of sorrow broke. The velvet dress pooled around my feet as I wept. The jeweled clip in my hair felt frivolous now, so with an angry jerk I yanked it out before it flew unbidden from my hand and smashed against the wall. Stupid, inconvenient telekinesis.

I appreciate the sentiment, Miss Wilder, but there is work to be done. Do you not agree?

The Silver of my imagination spoke the truth. Weeping in my room would have to wait. He deserved answers, whether he'd met with a tragic accident or something worse. I was terrifyingly aware how closely his death followed the phone call with my father, but going down that road before we knew more would only send me into a tailspin.

Making my way to the bathroom, I washed my face and brushed my hair. Vincent had set my suitcase on a wooden luggage stand inside a walk-in closet, so I retrieved a navy sweater, black jeans, and boots. As I finished changing, my phone chimed with a text.

You ok darlin? Jessie had written. For a moment, all the weirdness of the last few days faded away, and he was once again the champion in my corner.

I'm fine, I texted back. *Thanks for asking,* I added, hoping he understood it to mean, *Don't stop caring just because you have a hot girlfriend.*

Nicholas and Dev were in tense but quiet conversation when I stepped out of the elevator on the ground floor.

"I'm not going to hide because an evanescent lost focus," Nicholas said in a low voice.

The sentinel's mouth flattened into a mutinous line. "Have it your way, but they will all be questioned first thing tomorrow morning."

Honey came gliding up. "We have a car waiting for you out back, Regent. Please come with me."

Our escort led us away from the atrium and through a pair of large, swinging doors that delivered us to an industrial kitchen. A chef and a half dozen cooks were too focused on their own chaotic ballet to notice the intrusion. Our journey ended outside in a stretch of alley gated at either end. True to her word, Marie was still on duty and stood attentively next to the town car.

Nicholas stopped and turned to face Honey. "A statement will be issued later tonight." Henry had apparently decided to heed all of Francesca's professional advice. "I would appreciate if you would keep the news of Mr. Silver's death to yourself until then."

A trace of melancholy traveled across Honey's face. "There's no keeping secrets for long among our kind, as you well know, but no one will hear it from my lips." They gazed wistfully up at the cloudless night sky, the stars valiantly fighting to be seen above the glare of city lights. "The Prime came here whenever he was in town. Not to indulge some fantasy, but to make sure no customer ever crossed the line with any of us." Their eyes hardened, refocusing again on Nicholas. "Please find out what happened to him, no matter where the truth takes you."

He nodded solemnly as if making a vow. "I will."

Pulsing red lights splashed across high-rise apartment buildings and ground floor shops before we'd driven more than a mile. Several police cars and a coroner's van surrounded the scene as well as a number of looky-loos.

"This is as far as I can go," Marie said when we were still a block away, "but I can pull over and wait."

Nicholas swung open the door. "Thank you, Marie. That is most kind." As distressed as he was, political instincts ingrained by a lifetime as the chancellor's son rose to the surface. An answering flash of respect came from the driver's seat.

The three of us stepped out of the car, Dev and I following as Nicholas wove his way through the loose ring of onlookers.

"Mr. Silver has a younger brother named Rafe," I said to the sentinel, folding my arms against the chill. "Did you know that?"

His head swiveled like an owl as he scanned the crowd. It was the first time I'd been in public with Dev, and he was in full guard duty mode.

"Rafe Silver is a Shadow Nine," he informed me. "I've always wondered why one brother devoted himself to The Nine while the other ran as fast as he could in the opposite direction."

My heart sank even further. The Prime blamed himself for not being there that terrible night to protect Rafe and those who had died from his power. Had penance been at the root of his devotion to duty? Would there be anyone to tell Rafe of his brother's death?

Reining in my grief, I joined Nicholas at the mouth of a narrow alley where a yellow line of police tape fluttered across the entrance. Industrial-strength metal doors and dumpsters scarred with graffiti lined the corridor's brick walls. A black sedan, haphazardly parked with the driver's side door flung open, jammed the road, and I cynically wondered if the car would have attracted such quick notice if it hadn't impeded the flow of traffic. A couple of officials from the coroner's office, a few uniformed officers, and a lone plain clothes detective all worked with calm efficiency.

"Are there any others here?" Nicholas quietly asked Dev.

The sentinel nodded toward the alley. "One of the cops is a low level enchanter, and the detective is a solid telekinetic."

Within a few minutes, a uniformed cop sidled up to our patch of cement. The silver nameplate identifying him as Officer Irving mirrored the red and yellow flashing lights from a nearby squad car. With one large hand propped on his gun belt, he made a show of inspecting the bystanders, looking at everyone but us.

"Regent Thorne?" he murmured, finally glancing our way. He was young and fair except for his nose, which was the rosy color of the perpetually sunburned. It was the mark of a tourist or a recent transplant.

"Yes, Officer," Nicholas said softly. "Can you tell us what happened?"

"He was taken by surprise, that's for sure." The man rubbed the back of his shaved neck. "It's hard to believe anyone could get the drop on the Prime."

Nicholas and Dev exchanged glances. It would be near impossible for a Nine to do so, but an outsider was another story. Sentinels were as vulnerable as anyone else when out in the world of ordinary humans.

"The car was reported stolen from a parking lot at the airport just a few minutes before the shooting," Irving added.

"Mr. Silver was shot?" I blurted.

Irving nodded. "All his valuables are gone. Detective Phillips over there, who knows who she's dealing with, says that on the surface it looks like a robbery gone wrong." Despite the sense of unreality that we could so calmly be discussing the death of the Prime, the cop's words ignited a thin shred of hope.

"Wait." I latched onto the officer's arm. "If all his things are missing, how do you know the man in the car is Akim Silver?"

Between our physical connection and my need for the victim to be anyone other than Silver, the tight rein I kept on my clairvoyance shattered.

The smell of iron, be it from the freshly pooled blood on the ground or the gunpowder still lingering in the air, confirmed I'd stepped into the past. No police photographer yet lit up the black sedan or surrounding alley with bright flashes, no crowd observed from a few dozen feet away.

Officer Irving was alone, the beam of his flashlight scanning the abandoned car's license plate, the empty leather wallet discarded on the ground, and the driver's side door standing open. He angled the light to sweep across the backseat, and we both gasped at the sight of the car's lone occupant.

"Oh man," he murmured. "I shoulda stayed in Iowa."

Mr. Silver stared back, eyes dull and unfocused, his habitual expression of calm acceptance settled permanently on his features. Snapping on a pair of blue latex gloves, the officer opened the back door and carefully leaned in. He rested two fingers on the other man's carotid for a few moments before straightening again.

He depressed a button on his shoulder mic. "Send a bus. No need to hurry."

Forget the World

Nicholas was once again on the phone with his father before the car even pulled away from the curb. Passing streetlights threw his features into high relief as he relayed the facts of Silver's death with the same self-possession that had carried him through the regent's challenge. It was what the chancellor wanted and expected, but I wondered what part of his son's soul had been forfeited to achieve that level of detachment. It was a stark reminder there was much I still didn't know about the man at my side.

His eyes momentarily darted to Dev as he listened to Henry's response. A whisper of opposition rose within him before resignation once again dropped into place.

"I understand," he murmured, ringing off as the car returned to the club, the alley gate humming shut behind us.

Dev's brows came together. He'd observed the byplay as well. "What is it?"

Avoiding the question, Nicholas directed his attention to our driver. "Thank you, Marie. I hope I can count on your discretion regarding anything you may have seen or heard tonight."

The dark eyes reflected in the rearview mirror were troubled. Surely Madame Boudreaux had filled her in on why we'd visited the scene of a murder—and who had been the unfortunate victim.

As word spread of Mr. Silver's death, so too would suspicions over whether the Prime had been the victim of random street violence, or if the target of one of his investigations had perhaps turned the tables on their pursuer. Through his son, Henry Thorne would attempt to control the narrative, probably until he figured out which scenario best suited his purposes. Of course, if Silver had been murdered to prevent my father's tale from spreading any further, Henry's game plan was already in play.

Such thoughts never would have occurred to me if my dad hadn't shared the vision of the day Mitsuko Hayashi lost her life and the chancellorship, and I wondered what else had sailed over my head due to his misguided attempt to protect me.

"Of course, Regent Thorne," Marie responded.

Nicholas took my hand as we exited the car, and the energy between us pulsed. His eyes flew to mine, and the world stopped. It didn't matter that he was in full battle mode in his position as regent, or that his father might have orchestrated tonight's tragedy, or that I was still in a state of disbelief that such a vital man as Mr. Silver had been so suddenly erased. Nor were the invisible threads drawing us together merely physical. My empathic senses responded to his yearning to be close, to know he wasn't alone, and my heart reached out to him.

"We good here?" Dev asked as he climbed from the car.

Nicholas blinked, the spell broken. "Yes. Let's go inside."

The kitchen was as busy as when we left, but now the steady beat of dance music bleeding though the walls signaled the party had begun—Nines were not the type to let the near death of a spectator put a damper on things. On any other night, I'd be intrigued to see what indulgences To The Nines had to offer a celebratory crowd, but all I wanted right then was to escape to our room.

"I really wish we could go upstairs without running the gauntlet," Nicholas said, echoing my sentiments.

"This way." Dev took the lead. Circling the kitchen, we entered a quiet hallway where a freight elevator opened at the touch of a button.

"How did you know this was here?" Nicholas asked as we stepped inside a car with padded walls.

The sentinel shot a sheepish glance at me before his eyes slid away. "The Isenberg sisters have a, uh, thing for elevators."

Nicholas pressed his lips together, the first hint of a smile since Honey had delivered that terrible note, but he refrained from comment.

The sentinel who'd admitted me earlier that day waited in a chair outside our door, her head bowed over a book. She snapped the thick paperback shut and stood at attention as we approached.

"Regent Thorne," she said deferentially. "I'm sentinel Jane Cassidy. I've been sent to relieve sentinel Trivedi."

"That's not necessary—" Dev began before she cut across him.

"Section 42, paragraph 6 of the Sentinel's Code specifically states if a regent's primary sentinel has been on duty for more than sixteen hours, he or she must be relieved for a rest period of no less than eight hours." She rattled off the passage as if she read directly from the source.

Dev's lips thinned in a patently insincere smile. "You must be new here."

"Thank you, Cassidy," Nicholas said smoothly, no hint of the past hour's ordeal reflected in his voice. "I need to speak with sentinel Trivedi for a few minutes before he departs for the evening."

There was pride and satisfaction in the look she sent Dev, but a snort of annoyance was his only response as he tromped into the suite and closed the door behind us.

I'd been too caught up in shock and grief to notice my surroundings when I'd come up earlier to change, but a closer inspection revealed no expense had been spared in making the Alder House suite an elegant retreat. Honoring the club's roots in the Gilded Age, the furnishings were opulent, yet the color pallet restrained. A fire burned low in the sitting room's white marble hearth, splashing a soft glow across walls of butterscotch, sofas and chairs in various shades of tan and cream, and hardwood floors stained a warm walnut hue.

"Silver is dead, a Palmarium ball damn near took off your head, and now you want to trust your life to a baby sentinel," Dev grumbled as he flopped down on one of a pair of camelhair sofas flanking the fireplace.

I cut the sentinel major side eye. "I don't recall Nicholas needing to duck."

"You know what I mean," he said, waving off my objection. "And did you see the book she was reading? *Lord of The Rings*? She probably imagines being your sentinel as some noble quest."

At any other time, Nicholas would have laughed, but instead he crossed the room to a sideboard where a crystal decanter mingled with a host of matching glasses. He splashed amber liquid into a tumbler, and the tangy aroma of whiskey perfumed the air.

Dev straightened, diverted from his complaints. "That bad, is it?"

Without answering, Nicholas poured a generous amount into a second glass and sent it sailing across the room to his friend before joining me on the opposite sofa. He offered the glass to me, but I shook my head, not having a stomach for alcohol. We sat close enough to touch, but perhaps after what transpired between us a few minutes ago, he kept his hands to himself. That didn't stop his eyes from straying in my direction as I tugged off my boots and tucked my feet underneath me.

He tossed back his drink before meeting Dev's wary gaze. "Henry has named you as the acting Prime. A statement will be posted on the website within the hour."

The sentinel stared at Nicholas in confusion, perhaps waiting for further explanation, but none was forthcoming. "This is Fran's doing, isn't it?"

He shook his head. "She only said what Henry was already thinking."

"But I can't be the acting Prime," Dev sputtered. "I don't know anything about tracking down criminals or coordinating the sentinel force or the million other things you need to know for the job."

"One of Silver's deputies will be here by morning," Nicholas said. "She'll assist you in carrying out your duties until a new Prime is chosen. In the meantime, I'll be assigned an interim sentinel."

"Why me?" he asked, the drink forgotten in his hand. "My father would kill to be acting Prime. So would at least a dozen other sentinels who are older and more experienced."

"There are few, if any, Henry trusts as much as your father to watch his back. Ashwin should take your selection as the highest form of compliment—for both of you."

Dev rose and stared blindly into the murmuring blaze. Mr. Silver seemed to have relished his role as Prime, and my father had expressed regret at leaving the post, yet Dev didn't act as if being the top sentinel was an honor to be coveted.

When he finally tore his gaze from the dying fire, it didn't take an empath to read the rebellion brewing in his eyes. When we were at Alder House last month, Dev had told me the new generation of sentinels didn't see being in service to other Nines as the honor their parents and grandparents did. Maybe he viewed the job of Prime, elevated though it might be, as just another act of obedience rendered to an ungrateful master.

"What if I don't want to be The Nine's good little soldier?" he spit out. "What if I refuse?"

"The Sentinel's Code—" Nicholas began.

"Fuck the Sentinel's Code," he growled. "We didn't write it. You did."

Nicholas's determination to treat his friend fairly and with respect was suddenly colored with impatience. "The Sentinel's Code—written almost three hundred years ago, I might add—states that to refuse the chancellor's orders is to be expelled from The Nine. Are you prepared for that?"

The resolve on Dev's face drained away. My father often lectured that history's victors were usually those who were clear-eyed about the challenges they faced and smart about how they engaged and deployed their resources. It would take more than one sentinel acting on impulse to wipe away centuries of tradition, and Dev knew it.

He threw back the rest of his drink, grimacing as the liquor burned his throat. "At least say my replacement isn't going to be G.I. Jane out there. I don't want to have to break you of all the good habits she'd likely drill into you."

Nicholas cracked a smile. "One of the perks of being acting Prime is you get to designate the regents' guardians."

"Fine. No Alder House-trained drone is taking my place." Setting his glass on the sideboard, Dev stood, loose-limbed with exhaustion. "I'm heading to bed, but Nicholas…" He eyed his best friend as if to underscore what he was about to say. "When the sentinels finally take a stand, I hope you'll be standing on the right side of that line."

They held each other's gaze a moment before Dev turned away. The door clicked shut, and we were alone. Sentinel Cassidy would see to that.

My head lolled back against the cushions, fatigue and sorrow leaving me drained. Nicholas should know about Henry's duplicity and what chain of events my dad might have set in motion by reaching out to Mr. Silver. My father needed to be told of the Prime's death, but I hesitated to disturb the last decent night's sleep he might have for a while. Then there were the Nines who'd been hassling me at work, and how they might factor into all this. But it was Dev's comment in the elevator, that Nicholas would always bend to his father's will, that was uppermost in my mind.

"Your father is grooming you to be chancellor one day, isn't he?" I said.

Nicholas rose from the sofa and poured another small measure into his glass. "It's hard to deny him when it's in the best interests of our people."

Or Henry's, but I didn't voice that thought out loud. "What about you? What do you want?"

His eyes were on the fire dying in the grate as he took a contemplative sip. "I used to dream of living in Portugal, of owning my own boat, and taking tourists out to fish those sweet spots only I would know about."

I smiled at the pretty picture he painted. "I didn't know you liked to fish."

He let out a self-deprecating chuckle. "I have no idea. I've never tried."

For a moment I indulged in my own version of the future if he broke free of the Nine. He could move to Santa Carla and pick me up in the mornings and drive us both to school. On Friday nights we'd get tickets to the game—football, basketball, it didn't really matter—or just Netflix and chill with Scarlett and Warren. On Sundays we'd laze in bed until we got hungry enough to go to the farmers market and—

"You've helped me see it's time for The Nine to evolve," he said, interrupting my unlikely fantasy. "I'm not saying we completely abandon the covenant, but the next leader needs to balance our traditions while also reflecting the demands of the modern world."

"Are you that next leader?" I quietly asked, already mourning the loss of what would never be.

Setting down the glass, he reclaimed his seat on the sofa. "It's time to admit abandoning my birthright is a childish dream that can never be real. The Nine is real. The people who count on us to protect and guide them into the future are real." He reached for my hand, and I bit back a gasp at how quickly every nerve in my body responded to the energy surging beneath my skin. Every worry that had been a weight on my soul slipped away like a storm blown out to sea.

"This," he said, squeezing my hand. "This is real."

Nicholas and I had spent only a single night together, and that had been weeks ago. He'd taken the lead then, and I'd eagerly followed. Now it was my turn. The many erotic visions I'd had throughout the years had fired my imagination, leaving me both bold and curious.

Despite a powerful impulse to unleash the heat sparking between us, I leisurely turned to face him. Taking the glass from his hand, I set it on the coffee table before reaching for the top button of his shirt. The pearl disk slipped easily through the opening. I let my fingers trace the hollow at the base of his throat before starting on the next.

He moved to touch me, but I captured his hand. Glancing up at him through my lashes, I kissed his palm before daring to follow with a playful nip. His breath caught, the sound adding fuel to the fire building between us.

I pushed him back against the sofa and straddled his hips, intent on returning to the task of removing his shirt. He let his arms fall to his sides, but his eyes followed every flick of my fingers. With the last button undone, I parted the fabric to reveal smooth skin running from the curve of his chest to the flat planes of his abs. I bent to kiss every tempting spot, working my way up until we were cheek to cheek. When I gave into the urge to gently tug his earlobe with my teeth, the muscles of his stomach tightened in pleasure.

I moved my mouth to hover over his, but I wasn't quite ready to give into the almost irresistible need to seize and plunder. He gazed up at me through eyes half-closed, the savage expression on his face a far departure from the political animal he was by day. My lips curled in satisfaction that I had done this to him, and I looked forward to much, much more. But first, the lights.

"Dim," I said, centering all my focus on the room's row of switches. The lights quickly obeyed. Too quickly, considering my unreliable skills. I looked at Nicholas in playful suspicion. "Do I do that or did you?"

Suddenly, his hands were on me, and the world turned upside down. He flipped me on my back, and now it was he who had the upper hand. His smile was pure devilry as he hovered over me, his hips pressing against mine.

"Does it matter?" he said in a near growl as our lips met, and the world was forgotten.

15

An Open Wound

I stretched like a cat in the sun before coming fully awake in a nest of downy pillows and silken sheets. Memories of the night just passed made my toes curl in pleasure, and I reached for Nicholas. Not only did my fingertips fail to brush warm skin, but the sheets were cold. Propping myself up on my elbows, I discovered him gone, and the bedroom door closed.

Without warning, the horrible vision from the alley came roaring back. Mr. Silver was dead. It wasn't a nightmare, but cold, stark reality. How could I have forgotten, even for a minute, what had happened?

Flopping back down, I regarded the decorative plaster ceiling and wondered if I was a terrible person. Nicholas was surely off doing everything he could to learn the truth of Mr. Silver's death, as duty demanded, while I'd indulged my disappointment at waking up alone in a strange albeit luxurious hotel room. Even now, proud though I was to be with a man who had his priorities straight, a voice echoed from the darkest part of my heart asking if that would always be enough.

Exasperated with the direction of my thoughts, I grabbed my phone off the nightstand. Waiting on the screen was a text my sister had sent in the early morning hours that wiped everything else from my mind.

Dad got a phone call that woke us all up, Jordan had written, *but he got all weird when I asked who it was. Are you ok? I wish telepathy worked on sentinels.*

Could someone have alerted him to Mr. Silver's death? And if so, who would contact a man designated as a Shadow Nine to deliver news of a robbery gone wrong?

I have some terrible news, I texted back, though being Saturday morning, Jordan probably wouldn't see it for a few more hours. *Mr. Silver, the Prime Sentinel, was killed last night. Cops say it was a robbery gone wrong but idk.* Next I called my dad. It went straight to voice mail, but I didn't leave a message. The news I needed to deliver wasn't the kind you left for someone to stumble across.

I put aside my phone. Coffee and a shower would help organize my thoughts.

Padding barefoot from the bedroom thirty minutes later in jeans and a white Henley cropped at the waist, I discovered Nicholas had set up camp at the suite's round dining table. With laptop open, phone in hand, a cold cup of tea and a half-eaten slice of toast at his elbow, he looked the picture of industry despite his loose black tee-shirt and gray sweats. He rose when he saw me.

"There was an angel in my bed this morning," he said with an intimate smile, wrapping his arms around my waist and dropping a kiss on my lips, "but I didn't want to wake her."

I returned his kiss. "Have you been up long? Is there news?"

The light in his eyes dimmed. "It looks like Mr. Silver was set up. It was no accident he was in that car in that alley last night."

"What?" I searched his face for answers. "How?"

"Coffee first." How well he already knew me.

I pulled out the chair next to his as he poured me a cup, and we both sat down.

I added cream and took a large gulp. "Explain."

"Silver always used the same car service when he was in LA, run by a materialist named Carmina Raquel. When I reached her this morning, she said he'd been scheduled for an airport pick up last night until they got a call a few hours beforehand letting them know he'd taken a later flight."

"Though he obviously hadn't." I helped myself to an almond croissant from a basket next to the coffee service. "Did she say who called?"

"A woman claiming to be one of his deputies, a sentinel named Lauren Meserve." The computer dinged with an email, but he ignored it. "When I called her this morning, she was in Rome and had no idea Silver had flown to Los Angeles. Her phone records confirm her story."

"Which means whoever called knew the name of at least one of Silver's people." I nibbled at the pastry while mulling over the development. The use of a conventional weapon had all but pointed to an outsider as the killer, but what if it had been a false flag? "And what about the stolen car? Any more news on that?"

A trace of a smile shaped Nicholas's lips, most likely at my inquisitiveness, but he readily answered. "It belongs to another airport car service that got an automatic notification when it was driven out of the parking structure. That's why the theft was reported so quickly." He tapped a few keys on his laptop before turning it in my direction. "The lead detective on the case sent this."

On screen was a still photo of the black sedan's dashboard and steering wheel captured the moment it exited the parking lot. A chauffer's cap concealed the top half of the driver's face, but a dark mustache betrayed the man's gender. Black gloves covered his hands.

I sat back in my chair. "A woman cancelled Silver's car while a man picked him up posing as the expected driver. We're looking for more than one killer."

The suite became a command post as people came and went to confer with both Nicholas and Dev, officially the new acting Prime. Francesca breezed in mid-morning still garnished with assorted necklaces and rings, but more somberly dressed in a black tunic and dark jeans. Dev abandoned the dining table at that point and set up camp in front of the fireplace, where a fresh blaze snapped and sparked. The Palmarium playoff would still proceed as scheduled, death and accidents notwithstanding, but people were understandably jittery.

One of the main topics of conversation in phone calls going to and from the board of regents and Henry himself was Nicholas's speech before the game that night. It was originally intended to be a rousing address about Nines finding common ground beyond the Palmarium court, but now everyone had an opinion about how much should be said about the Prime.

Francesca urged restraint. "I'm sorry Silver's dead, but if you announce his cause of death as anything other than a robbery gone wrong, you'll completely lose your audience to speculation."

There was little I could do to help on that front, so from the comfort of a highbacked wing chair, I observed the evanescents who'd manned the barrier around last night's game come in one by one to be questioned. The first two—a gawky man barely out of his teens whose knobby Adam's apple bobbed every time he swallowed, and a middle aged woman who'd discovered a shag hair style she liked twenty years ago and stuck with it—were genuinely mystified over the lapse in the shield.

The third evanescent in the hotseat was the older woman with the cloud of white hair who'd momentarily frozen at courtside. Her eyes were pale and watery behind her glasses, and she wore stretch jeans, orthopedic shoes, and a USC crewneck sweatshirt. The university was located right across town, but their swag was popular even in Santa Carla.

Dev opened his computer and called up her photograph. Comparing the image with the living and breathing woman right in front of him, he asked, "Lindy Lou Menard?"

"Why, yes," she confirmed, "but I had nothing to do with that unfortunate accident last night." Her emotions confirmed she believed she spoke the truth, but I perked up at the confusion and worry threatening her peace of mind.

I got up from my chair and strolled behind the sofa where Lindy Lou perched. Pretending to stumble, I briefly touched her shoulder. "Oops, sorry," I murmured before meeting Dev's gaze over the top of her head. He quickly excused the woman and almost pounced in his eagerness to know what I'd gleaned.

"She wasn't lying," I told him. "She really does think her new heart medication is giving her problems, but I saw what happened last night and then again through her memory just now. I couldn't swear to it, but I think an enchanter interfered just long enough for her to lose focus."

He expelled a harsh breath in frustration. "Our records show there were thirty-seven enchanters at the game last night. Any idea who it could be?"

I shook my head with regret before retreating back to my chair to watch Francesca and Dev continue ignoring one another. He did a better job of feigning indifference, but perhaps it was because he was immune to my ability to pick up the feelings of loss and regret that oozed from his ex like blood from an open wound.

The pace picked up with the arrival of the sentinel deputy, Greta Svedberg, a woman with a whipcord physique and a steel-gray braid trailing down her back. She wore the sentinel's traditional all-black color, but her sleek leather jacket paired with tight jeans tucked into knee boots called to mind what Khalia might look like in thirty years.

Together, she and Dev fielded a constant flow of emails, texts, and phone calls, so there was little reason either of them should notice a brief energy spike if I should dip into Francesca's head. Her confused emotion state when she was around Dev was practically an open invitation to take a peek. Ignoring the inner voice scolding me that an idle mind was the devil's playground, I lowered my mental defenses and reached out to the elementalist just a few feet away.

I'd made a daytime visit to the DaVinci solarium during my recent stay at Alder House, but the room was a different creature at night. Missing was the visual impact of the ceiling's stained glass dome depicting a flock of birds forever frozen in flight, or the myriad prisms thrown across the floor by sunlight streaming through beveled windows. Instead, it offered a quiet beauty illuminated by dozens of candles placed about the room casting a warm glow across a velvet-covered settee where Francesca and Dev lay entwined, their naked bodies glistening in the afterglow of what must have been a passionate coupling. An open window carried the scent of lavender on a warm summer breeze, a sign this was, not surprisingly, a vision from the past.

"I hear a new elementalist has been found in the Kiermayr family," Francesca said, her fingers idly stroking the sparse hair on his chest.

"Hmmm," he responded, his eyelids at half-mast.

"She's only thirteen and already Class Two, so she'll definitely need a patron soon. Don't you think I'd make a great patron for such an important family?"

Dev roused himself enough to respond. "Someday, but you haven't earned it yet."

"Who's to say whether I have or haven't?" She propped herself on one elbow to peer into his face. "It's the chancellor who makes the final decision."

He yawned. "Good luck with that."

"Maybe I don't need luck." She gazed at him with a seductive smile. "Maybe you can help him make the right decision."

Opening his eyes, he peered into hers. "How am I supposed to do that?"

She responded with a husky laugh. "You could ask Nicholas to speak to his father about me."

"And tell Nicholas what?" he asked, his languor dissipating. "The time has come for me to trade on our friendship?"

"Stop acting like you don't do it all the time," she said, impatience edging into her voice. "Aren't you the youngest sentinel to lead a summer session for first years? Gosh, I wonder how that came about."

Dev sat upright, forcing Francesca to do the same. "I didn't ask for the job. It was offered to me."

"Oh, and that makes all the difference?" she asked caustically. "It's okay to want it but not to ask for it?"

He reached for the pile of clothes discarded on the floor. "You know I don't care about advancement as a sentinel. I have other plans."

"I see. So you'll only use Nicholas for things that are important to *you*."

He pulled on his pants and angrily yanked up the zipper. "And what about us, Fran? Are we just a transaction too?"

"If you cared about me, you wouldn't be asking that question," she sniffed.

Finding his shirt among the pile, he jerked it on. "Let's be honest here. Are you only with me because you want to be part of the Thorne's inner circle?"

"Oh please," she scoffed. "If I was social climbing it wouldn't be with a *sentinel*."

Dev's fingers stilled in the midst of buttoning his shirt. After a few moments, he finished the task and retrieved his shoes. With those in hand, he turned to face her.

"It must have been a great sacrifice to lower yourself to my level." His voice was even but boiling with fury. "Don't worry, I won't ask you to do so again."

"Don't you dare walk out on me, Devraj Trivedi," she hissed as he turned to go. "You are a fool if you think you can do better than me. You will never be anything more than a sentinel, but one day I will be regent! Do you hear me?"

Her last words came out as a shriek, but Dev's strides didn't slow as he walked away.

An Army of Shadows

The vision of Dev and Francesca proved yet again I should never make assumptions about people or their relationships. I felt renewed empathy for the sentinel class, and wondered how much longer their simmering resentment could be restrained before the kettle boiled over.

It was time to make a break for it, so I laced up my Converse and slipped out the door. Our guard, Jane Cassidy, had been replaced by Marcel Pryce, whose smart suit from the night before had been exchanged in favor of a black fitted sweater and pants. He'd even found time for a haircut, his tight curls razed almost to the scalp. It looked good on him, and I told him so.

"Thanks. I'm taking over for Trivedi until a new Prime is named," he said with pride.

I raised a brow, hoping Jane wasn't too disappointed. "Congratulations."

"Thanks." A gleam of self-satisfaction entered his eyes. "I can't wait to see my sister's face when I walk through the doors of Alder House as a regent's personal sentinel."

Unless there was a stack of cash stapled to his forehead, I didn't think Khalia would care, but I left him with his dreams intact. On my way to the elevator, Scarlett called to lodge another complaint against her employer.

"I thought twenty-five bucks an hour was really good money to help some guy during a business trip, but this man is what happens when you put Regina George and Miranda Priestly in a blender, add a pair of balls, and hit puree."

When her comment didn't solicit the expected laughter, she pressed. "Blake? What's wrong?"

"You were right."

"I usually am," she said with a hint of smugness. "What am I right about this time?"

"We couldn't get through a weekend gathering of Nines without someone dying." I told her what we knew so far about the death of Mr. Silver.

"I'm so sorry." Her regret was genuine. She'd met him briefly when he'd shown up at our apartment after another Nine had broken in with murderous intent. "He seemed like a nice man."

"He was," I agreed, "unlike your new bestie."

"Oh please, don't remind me. I have to leave soon to pick up the keys to his new rental place, which he will probably hate, because his lordship is in meetings all day. Then I have to go back tonight to let him in."

"Have you met him yet?"

"No, but I'm imagining a humpbacked troll with the most misplaced sense of BDE ever."

I couldn't help but laugh, which had been her goal. I ended the call feeling better than when it started, one of many things I loved about Scarlett.

Heading to the ground floor, I wandered through the court-yard. It wasn't quite noon, but already the restaurant was full, and the various salons saw a number of people catching up with friends, presumably in town for the big game. Heads came to-gether as I passed, and hushed voices followed me all the way across the atrium. For a brief moment, the old demons surfaced, the ones who whispered I was a freak, a mutant, but I lifted my chin and refused to listen. This wasn't high school, I reminded myself, and that frightened little girl was gone.

Inside the Marco Polo room, only mundane powers were on display. A tray of food floated behind a waiter as he delivered lunch to a table, and an older man with a fringe of white hair conjured a small ball of light to better illuminate his menu, but no fulfillment of fantasies was on offer at that time of day.

A handful of seats at the same bar where we'd sat last night were open, so I hopped onto a stool. Without even asking, a menu materialized in front of me. As soon as I'd placed an order with the bartender for a chicken Caesar salad and iced tea, someone took the open seat beside me.

There was something almost boneless in the way Honey languidly draped themselves across the stool. Flowing lounge pajamas reinforced the impression, the glossy black silk falling in graceful folds from their delicate frame. Head tilted away, light glinting off a crown of platinum hair, they struck a pose that invited my perusal before turning to meet my gaze.

"Ah, if it isn't the lovely Blake Wilder, and all by herself too. Is that delectable boyfriend of yours too busy to come out and play?" They feigned a pout on my behalf. "I'm sure *I* could find something to entertain you."

"I have no doubt, but I have a feeling your version of enter-tainment and mine are about as far apart as the earth and stars."

"Oh, I don't know," Honey drawled. "All cats are gray in the dark."

This was one cat who planned to stay firmly in the light, at least for now, but perhaps there was something they could help me with. "How does one go about tracking down a Shadow Nine?"

Their lips pursed in disappointment. "You're right. Your idea of fun doesn't even *exist* in the same universe as mine."

The bartender placed a tall glass of iced tea in front of me, and I idly poked at the cubes with a straw. "Mr. Silver had a brother who's a Shadow Nine. Someone needs to tell him what's happened."

Honey straightened in their seat, liquid brown eyes suddenly devoid of cockiness, and my senses registered their anguish. Maybe I wasn't the only one who loved a Nine who had turned their back, willingly or not, on their people.

They signaled the bartender for a drink before quietly asking, "Is it true his death wasn't an accident?"

There was no other conclusion to be reached from what we knew about his driver being switched out. Henry and the regents could attempt to manage the flow of information all they liked, but I'd already heard Silver's name murmured half a dozen times in the ten minutes I'd been downstairs. How did Francesca think Nicholas could get away with ignoring the details of his death?

"The Prime was murdered." The words tasted foreign on my tongue, his loss not yet assuming the mantle of permanence. "Whether it was intentional or the fallout from a robbery, I couldn't say."

"Thank you for your honesty." A glass of club soda arrived, and Honey drank half of it down in one long gulp. "It is refreshing to have someone speak the truth, even if everyone here already knows it."

"I don't know if the chancellor would agree," I hedged.

A smile flitted across my companion's mouth. "When your grip on power is loosening, you hold on even tighter to what remains."

"Does that apply to Shadow Nines?" The question of why my family had been tracked throughout the years bobbed to the surface of my thoughts, and it made me wonder if we were the exception or the rule.

"Most people wouldn't dare attempt this conversation in such a public place." Honey's eyes searched out the dark corners of the room. "For the life of me, I can't decide if you're naïve, brave, or simply reckless."

I shrugged. "Maybe all three?"

A cynical bark of laughter escaped their lips. "I can't remember the last time I was any of those things." Their gaze turned speculative. "But your question is an interesting one."

My salad arrived and I ate in silence, hoping Honey would be compelled to fill the void. My patience was soon rewarded as they leaned closer to whisper in my ear.

"Rumors have been circulating for quite some time that Shadow Nines don't fly quite as low under the radar as we've been led to believe. I hear the regents have an entire task force devoted to tracking them."

I lowered my fork and gave Honey my full attention. "Whatever for?"

The knowing gleam was back in their eyes. "Imagine a small army of Nines who answer to no one, who could do anything you wished—for a price, of course—because no one was there to police them. How valuable would they be if you wanted to get things done that might be considered questionable? Or even traitorous?"

My appetite evaporated as I considered the implications. Had Henry employed a Shadow Nine on the fateful day of the challenge? Is that how a voyant escaped my father's notice? Could a Shadow have been hired to silence Mr. Silver as well?

A dreadful sort of anticipation stole over me. "Do you think it's possible someone has been tracking the Shadows for more than twenty years?"

A burst of laughter from across the bar was a stark reminder this wasn't the time or place to dive further into the subject. Honey's body flexed as if redonning their mental armor, and I pretended renewed interest in my lunch. Draining their glass, they slid from the stool with a grace and attitude that assured the world their devil-may-care air was firmly back in place.

"The one who could answer that question may be as close as your own bed," they archly tossed over their shoulder before leaving me to my thoughts.

A Door Opens

My phone rang as I left the Marco Polo room. It was Dad. "Hold on," I said by way of greeting. "I'm going out-side."

Veering out the same door I'd come through yesterday, now with a different sentinel on duty, I stepped out into a typical winter's day in Southern California. Pale gray clouds hung low in the sky, and a cool breeze cut through the loose weave of my cotton pullover.

"We're good," I said, choosing a direction to wander at random. The handful of people sharing the sidewalk had been smart enough to throw a sweatshirt over their gym clothes, as most were dressed in yoga pants or sweats as if running to or from an appointment with their personal trainer.

He heaved a sigh before saying a word, which told me he'd heard the news about Mr. Silver. "Are you still in LA?"

"Yeah. Nicholas is giving a speech before tonight's game, which is a story all by itself."

"I can imagine." Having once been the Prime, he probably could.

"Dad, Mr. Silver was on his way to meet with Nicholas and me when he was killed."

His swift intake of breath echoed in my ear. "I didn't realize. The man didn't say."

"What man?" My mind flashed on his middle-of-the-night phone call.

There was a pause before he said in a rush, "I'm responsible for the Prime's death."

"What?" I'd heard him fine, but the certainty in his voice left me unsettled.

"I got a call early this morning. The man sounded robotic, like he was using a device to disguise his voice. He said the Prime Sentinel had been murdered because of what I'd done, and if I kept talking about what happened twenty years ago, I could be next."

"He threatened you?" Despite my aimless path, fright lengthened my strides.

"Not exactly," he conceded. "He sounded almost apologetic, if you can believe it, like he was sorry to be the bearer of bad news."

"Dad, we're not even sure if Mr. Silver's death was intentional or not because it looked like a botched robbery." I'd vaguely taken note of a passing diner done in the Art Deco style popular a century ago when the realization hit. "Unless your caller was in on it."

"I don't know, but I feel like I'm reliving the hellish day Henry Thorne murdered Mitsuko, and I'm faced with the same untenable choice."

"There is no choice, Dad. Do what he says." Fear for my family banished any lingering doubts I might harbor surrounding his actions two decades ago. "We'll find another way to expose the chancellor's crimes."

"There is no other way," he said bleakly, probably remembering what it had been to lose his home, his job, and his people all in a single day. "If I don't take a stand, Henry Thorne will continue to get away with murder."

"Not for much longer." Justice was coming for the chancellor, but it would have to be delivered by a hand other than my father's.

"Dad, how much do you know about Shadow Nines?" It was an abrupt change of topic, but I couldn't shake Honey's claim that the group of outliers—which included my father—were in fact closely tracked and possibly more.

"You know what I know." He lapsed into the assured tones of a seasoned professor. "Those unwilling to pledge to The Nine and obey our laws and covenants are to be shunned. No aid or succor is to be offered or given to a Shadow at any time. Why do you ask?"

I reflected on the vision he'd shared, wondering if an unknown voyant could have blended in among the crowd. "Do you think it's possible the person who distracted you the day of the challenge could have been a Shadow voyant?"

He sat with that for a moment. "It's theoretically possible but highly unlikely. There was only one Shadow voyant at the time, a kid out of Germany, but he disappeared after refusing to pledge a few years earlier. How would he have known when the challenge was or what to do about it? Remember, this was in the days before texting, and cell phones were not in everyone's pocket."

It may have been before the era of instant communication, but tracking Shadow Nines could have been going on for decades, possibly centuries. If Henry had cultivated an ally among the regents, he could have known how to find a rogue voyant.

"Do you think he'd be in The Nine's database?" I asked.

"Perhaps, but you'd need Prime sentinel clearance or above to access anything about Shadows."

Regents would have that kind of access, but if Nicholas knew the purpose of my search—to find the person who could potentially reveal Henry as the murderous schemer I believed him to be—would he allow it? My odds of getting access would increase if I came up with a believable cover story, but adding a lie on top of everything else I'd yet to share with him felt wrong on so many levels.

I reached a corner and made a right turn with the intent of walking in a large square so as not to end up miles from the club. Somewhere on the street, tires squealed. I idly glanced over to see the horrified visage of a man behind the wheel of a white Range Rover as it bore down on me.

All rational thought was obliterated as the vehicle jumped the curb. I blindly ran a few steps before launching myself into the air, completely unaware someone was in my path until we collided. They bore the brunt of our landing, letting out a yelp of pain as their body cushioned the blow. The SUV swerved across the sidewalk, hot wind blasting my face as it passed within inches before veering back onto the street and speeding away.

As my senses returned, I looked into the face of my unwitting savior. Gray eyes returned my shocked gaze. Jessie lay beneath me, his hands gripping my waist almost painfully as we lay face to face, but discomfort was suddenly the last thing on my mind. Spurred on by adrenalin, the paranormal energy pulsing within us both flared to life at the full body contact. I reeled as it overpowered my senses. His body tensed beneath mine, telling me he too experienced the unique connection we shared.

"Are... are you alright?" I stammered.

The thud of running feet halted next to us. "Hey, you guys okay?"

I gingerly rolled off Jessie, and we both struggled to sit upright. A young guy in a Hawaiian shirt and scuffed Vans hunkered down next to us.

"I saw it all from inside my store." Under a thatch of bleached blonde hair, he regarded Jessie with admiration.

"Dude, the way you caught the hot girl was awesome, like Marvel movie awesome. It would totally go viral if I'd gotten it on video, but at least I got a pic of the license plate. Here, I'll airdrop it to you."

Jessie dazedly reached for his phone, and my attention wandered to the souvenir shop at our backs. The chaotic window display of colorful hats strung on a clothesline between two cardboard palm trees barely registered as I tried to unpack what just happened. Los Angeles was infamous for its terrible drivers, so maybe the guy had simply lost control of his car. The other option, the one that cast a far more sinister light on the supposed accident, was that the enchanter who'd been stalking me had just upped the stakes.

Jessie's jacket was torn, and we'd probably both have bruises, but otherwise we'd escaped unharmed. I found my phone where it landed under a rack of souvenir T-shirts and discovered five freaked out texts and three missed calls from my dad. I typed a quick message to let him know I was okay and would call him later. My phone buzzed immediately with another text from him, but I was too scattered to read it.

We thanked the guy from the tourist shop before staggering off without a particular destination in mind. Neither of us spoke or acknowledged the energy that had spiked between us, and I wondered if he too still felt the fire singing in his veins.

"Thank you for being there," I said belatedly.

"You looked upset," he said. "I was about to ask if everything was okay."

We walked another minute while I mentally replayed all the strange occurrences of the past week. Finally I said, "Do you think it's weird the Palmarium ball went out of bounds right when it got hit in my direction, and then that car almost nailed me today?"

His jolt of surprise rippled through me. "You don't think that driver losing control was an accident?"

"I don't know," I admitted. "They're not the only freaky things that have happened lately."

He drew me over to a slatted wood bench in front of a used bookstore. The window at our back held an array of books, posters, and photographs in homage to Los Angeles, from compilations of classic Hollywood movie stills to the famous Black Dahlia murder.

"What's going on, Blake?" I felt as well as heard his agitation.

"I was targeted by a materialist and an enchanter at work last week," I confessed. "I believe an enchanter interfered in the game last night. Dev thinks the ball was meant for Nicholas, but I'm the one who almost got my head taken off."

"Hold on—what do you mean, targeted?" After I related the two events at Jitters, he asked, "What does Thorne think about it?"

I didn't answer right away. Nicholas had enough to deal with without me adding to it. Telling him would mean I'd likely be assigned a sentinel to watch my every move, and that kind of special treatment would raise questions about our future I wasn't prepared to answer.

"You haven't told him," Jessie concluded.

"It would just make him worry." Even as the words left my mouth, I knew how weak they sounded.

He let out a humorless chuckle. "You don't need to explain your boyfriend's pig-headedness to me. He'd probably try to hide you away in Alder House if he knew."

"He's not like that," I said, though his campaign to get me to move there showed no sign of flagging. "What happened between you and Nicholas anyway?" I asked, suddenly curious.

He blinked at the rapid change in subject. "What does Thorne say went down?"

He'd once mentioned some small interference in the phantomist's one-time quest to become regent, but there had to be something more.

"Not a whole lot," I admitted.

"I wouldn't want my words to color your opinion of either of us," he said. "It might be best if I just showed you."

It wasn't the answer I expected, but it wasn't the first time he'd invited me into his memories. The last time had been to share his recollection of meeting Cedric for the first time.

He held out his hand as a bus lumbered by, an advertisement on the vehicle's side displaying the local morning news anchors in action hero stances. Before the reporters' blindingly white teeth passed from view, I had tumbled into the past.

From the refuge of a leather club chair, one of two arranged in front of a massive stone hearth, Jessie stared moodily into the flames of a crackling fire while sipping golden liquid from a crystal tumbler. His hair was cut short, further contributing to him looking a few years younger than he did now, and his shirt sleeves were rolled back to reveal a glimpse of his Casper the Friendly Ghost tattoo.

Only one other source of light, a table lamp with a stained glass shade, repelled the darkness seeping through a bank of tall windows. A suit jacket and tie lay abandoned on a nearby sofa in a room richly appointed with thick carpets, bookshelves stuffed with leather-bound volumes, and sprays of exotic blooms.

"Don't be so glum, dear boy," came a disembodied voice. Cedric, in all his lace cuffs and waxed mustache glory, materialized in the companion chair. His velvet doublet of royal blue accented by the crisp, white ruff at his throat must have been all the rage five hundred years ago. "There will be other opportunities to win the regent's seat."

"No, there won't." Jessie's flinty expression didn't change. "I should have known better than to go up against people who buy their way through life."

The aristocrat had the grace to look slightly chagrined. "One must do one's best with the gifts God has given them. Yes, I had the great fortune to be born the first son of a landed duke, but you, dear boy, were graced with the drive of a randy ox."

The phantomist's lips twitched with the first stirrings of amusement. "It's called a work ethic, Cedric. You make it sound like I'm good breeding stock."

"Well, there was that lovely empath we sampled last night," the ghost said with a leer.

"I'm glad to keep you entertained," Jessie responded dryly, "but since I'm not a regent, there's no way I can afford to stay here after tonight."

Cedric glanced longingly at the luxurious surroundings. "Not that I don't enjoy rubbing elbows with the proletariat from time to time, but Alder House is much more to my taste than the public houses where you insist upon working."

The click of a door opening arrested further conversation. Sutton Sinclair entered and surveyed the room as if he stood on the bridge of his own personal yacht. He'd retained the muscular form and broad shoulders of his younger days, which probably required the services of a tailor to make his expensive suit fit so well. He took care to shut the door firmly behind him.

"The elementalist regent has joined us," Cedric observed, flicking an imaginary speck of dust from his sleeve. "What do you suppose he requires? And why does he desire privacy to discuss it?"

Sutton Sinclair helped himself to a hearty splash of spirits from a well-stocked sideboard before coming to join Jessie by the fire. Cedric's double chin quivered with indignation as he was forced to vacate his seat to make way for the man who had no idea the chair was already taken.

"I'm sorry how that went down back there, son," the real estate developer said as he settled his bulk. "I'm sure you'll make a very fine regent someday, but today isn't it."

Jessie didn't comment or even acknowledge the other's presence. Instead, he contemplated the blaze and took another sip of his drink.

"You don't strike me as the kind of man who takes defeat lying down," Sutton observed though silver-rimmed glasses.

That got Jessie's attention. "What do you suggest? That I go back in there swinging?"

"Of course not." Sutton's gravelly voice tightened with irritation at the other man's flippant response. "But I would certainly hope you plan to come back better prepared next time."

Jessie's eyes narrowed. "How do you suggest I do that? I have no money, no connections, and I maxed out both my credit cards just getting here. Tomorrow I'll go back to the roadhouse I manage in a town that's barely a wide spot in the road. I'll remind myself to be grateful to even have a job after being fired from my last place for fingering a thief who framed me for it. But sure, I'll keep saving my pennies because hope springs eternal, right?" He threw back the last of his drink as if it could wash away the bitterness of his situation, but the resulting cough spoiled the effect.

"What if you didn't have to go back to that podunk town?" Sutton asked. "What if you didn't have to go back to Texas at all?"

Jessie cleared his throat. "I happen to like Texas, but I'm listening."

"I've just closed a deal to open a club in Santa Carla, California. It's not that far from Los Angeles, but I want it to be a world away from To The Nines. It'll be something fresh and new and completely different, and I want you to create it with my son, Marcus."

"Not to look a gift horse in the mouth, dear boy," Cedric volunteered, having perched atop the fireplace's wide oak mantel, "but nothing comes without strings attached. Why, I remember the time the king promised Lord Burnley he'd keep his wife and lands in trust if the earl would lead an army against—"

"Why me?" Jessie said, ignoring his spirit's harrumph at being interrupted.

Sutton took another swallow before answering. "I've done my research. You're hungry, hardworking, and you have vision. I also don't believe you had anything to do with that missing money—it's not your style. Running a sanctuary club would bring you visibility and the connections you need the next time you make a run at the regent's seat." He paused, and both Jessie and Cedric leaned in slightly, knowing the true reason was about to be served up. "You're also known to keep company with some canny ghosts."

"Ah," Cedric murmured, stroking his goatee. "He knows it was our skullduggery that exposed the blasted embezzler, and he's looking to buy a network of invisible spies. Clever man."

"What part would my ghosts play in this venture?" Jessie didn't mince words.

"You know as well as I what's happening to our people. Negotiation and compromise are no longer a common language. Divisions are growing wider by the day, and I'm deeply concerned where this path will lead." The elementalist discarded his empty glass on an occasional table set between the two chairs, his gaze sharpening as he got down to business. "I plan to fill that club with Nines, and I want your ghosts to report back what is being said. Who's content with the way things are, and who might be ready to fight for change. And if there are people interested in fomenting rebellion against Henry Thorne, I'd be especially pleased to know about it."

A log in the fireplace cracked apart. A shower of sparks rained down upon the hearth as Jessie weighed Sutton's sales pitch.

"Half," Jessie said after a long minute.

Sutton raised his brows in query. "Excuse me?"

"For what you're asking, I won't be an employee. I want an equal partnership in the club. I don't give a damn who leads The Nine because they've done nothing for me, but I want to build something that is mine. In return, my ghosts will be your spies on the west coast, and I'll tell you whatever I learn."

Sutton sat back in his chair with the whisper of a smile, probably pretending he didn't anticipate the Texan's demand all along. Jessie relaxed as well, letting the moment play out. Both men started when the door blew open, although there were no open windows in the room. Neither moved to close it again.

"I think that's my cue to leave before you ask me for a house on the beach or an unlimited expense account," Sutton said with a chuckle as he got to his feet. He stood in front of Jessie and stuck out his hand. "Young man, you've got yourself a deal. I'll draw up a contract and expect to see you in Santa Carla in one week's time. Contact my office for any assistance you might need with moving expenses."

Jessie stood as if in a daze and shook his benefactor's hand. With a final nod, Sutton left him to absorb how his life had changed in a few short minutes.

"Bravo, dear boy," Cedric crowed from the mantle where he now reclined on one side, his elbow propping up his head. "California will be a delightful adventure. I hear that part of the New World is famous for their beautiful lasses. I for one am always delighted to eavesdrop on your behalf, but are you quite sure the other ghosts will dance to your tune?"

Jessie smirked. "Everyone should do as their conscious dictates. I only promised to pass along what y'all tell me."

The ghost sniggered as his host departed through the open door. Out in the hall, Jessie was brought up short by someone sharply calling his name. "McCabe!"

It was Nicholas, his mouth clamped in a narrow line as he marched up to Jessie. Behind him lurked his former girlfriend, Julia Martin, this vision having gone down a few years prior to their breakup. When Jessie's gaze landed on her, she raised her chin with righteous indignation, as if she might have something to do with her boyfriend's agitation.

It suddenly occurred to me that she probably did. Julia's talents as an evanescent included the gift of invisibility. I would have bet my meager bank account that the door opening had been Julia slipping out to report what she'd overheard to Nicholas.

"Something I can do for you, Thorne?" Jessie asked, though he looked to be in too good a mood to care what might be on the teenager's mind.

"I want you to know I was one of the people who lobbied against you being regent," Nicholas said with a certain amount of satisfaction. "I heard how you framed that accountant for your thievery."

"Why, the blackguard," Cedric exclaimed, his hand reaching for a sword that hadn't hung from his belt in centuries. "How dare he make such a spurious charge?"

Jessie's bright expression dimmed, but he only stared at his accuser.

"But now that I know how wholly your integrity is for sale," Nicholas continued, confirming my suspicion of the role Julia played, "I will make it my life's mission to insure you never rise above the gutter where you belong."

Death by Nine

The breeze picked up and I shivered, though the wind wasn't solely to blame. Jessie pulled off his ruined jacket and wrapped it around my shoulders. Traces of his musky cologne lingered on the collar.

"We should get back," I murmured, rising from the bench.

Nicholas had done as he thought duty demanded, but that didn't give him the right to condemn Jessie on Julia's say so. Not that Jessie would have set the record straight even if given the opportunity because the truth was he *had* agreed to be Sutton's eyes and ears, albeit to a limited degree. He'd been in no position to refuse.

"It doesn't bother you to be judged without being given the chance to explain yourself?" I asked after we'd gone half a block.

Jessie shrugged. "Look at all the bullshit that's heaped on the rich and famous. It doesn't seem to stop any of them, and it won't stop me."

"That's what you want, isn't it? To be so successful it doesn't matter what people say."

"What I want," he said, stepping aside to allow a professional dogwalker escorting a string of well-behaved canines to pass, "is to be successful enough to be free. Money is freedom, so don't let anyone tell you wanting it is shallow or greedy."

Having never gone hungry or worried about a safe place to sleep, I hadn't really given serious thought about what it would be like to do without. However, it made sense that privilege could change a person as much as poverty.

"Do you hate Nicholas?" I was unsure how I'd feel if he said he did.

He adopted a lazy smile. "I don't hate anyone. Who has the time?"

We both made a concerted effort to relax into idle chatter and put as much distance between us and the speeding Range Rover as possible. He was effortlessly charming and self-deprecating, with no talk of politics or ringing phones diverting his attention. I soaked in the moment, knowing reality would hit as soon I returned to the suite. Julia Martin had warned me there would be no separating Nicholas from his position, but at the time I hadn't really grasped what she meant.

"Do you mind if I make an observation?" he asked, breaking into my reverie as we reached the club's front door.

I braced myself. People never asked that question if you were about to hear something nice about yourself.

"Whether or not the people you've pissed off have escalated their harassment," he said, nodding a greeting to the door sentinel, "you need to start taking this seriously. No more walks alone."

I nodded, relieved at the simple request.

"And secondly," he added, pinning me with a look that was sympathetic but troubled, "you need to ask yourself why you're keeping what could be threats on your life from the one person you should be sharing them with."

Marcel looked up from his phone as the elevator came to a stop on the fifth floor. He relaxed his guard in front of the Alder House suite when the cage door opened, and he recognized me as the car's sole occupant.

"I have a text for you from my sister," he said as I neared.

My relationship with Khalia had made the monumental leap from total disdain on her part to grudging respect, but I would still never expect her to remember my existence outside of her official duty as my occasional babysitter. This should be interesting.

"Tell her," he read off his phone screen, "to remember what I said about the nine chairs, and to ask herself who stands to gain the most from the change." He squinted up at me as if to decipher my take on the cryptic message before he read the rest. "She also says, watch your back, princess."

I suddenly wished the prickly sentinel was there to do exactly that. Her reference to the nine chairs pointed to the growing unrest of the sentinel class, and how Silver's death might be tied to that, but what rumors had she heard about me that had prompted a warning? Thoroughly unsettled, I extracted the room key from my back pocket.

"Thank Khalia for me, and please tell her if she ever gets tired of Alder House, I really hope she comes back to Santa Carla."

He crooked a brow, probably surprised anyone would purposely seek out his sister's company. "Careful what you wish for."

Nicholas was much as I left him, stationed in front of his laptop with a pile of notes beside it, but he was out of his chair before I'd even closed the door. The only other occupants of the room, Dev and his deputy Greta, were deep in conversation and barely looked up as Nicholas greeted me with an embrace.

"This is not the way I expected our weekend to go," he murmured against my temple. Regret dominated his emotions with determination running a close second. Did his resolve apply to his upcoming speech, or was it reserved for uncovering the truth about the death of the Prime?

"Me either." With Jessie's parting shot still ringing in my ears, I said, "I need to tell you what—"

His phone rang, and he dropped his arms. "I'm sorry. There's a lot going on."

Including his girlfriend almost being flattened on a downtown sidewalk, but that would have to wait.

A knock came at the door, and Marcel popped his head in. "Regent, Detective Cory Phillips of the LAPD is here."

The woman who led the charge at last night's crime scene stepped into the suite as Nicholas ended his call. She wore the shapeless crewneck tee, sturdy pantsuit, and sensible shoes that seemed to be the default uniform of female detectives on TV and in real life. Her sagging ponytail may have once been tight and smooth, but wisps of light brown hair had escaped to curl around her angular face. Sharp eyes crowned by dark brows surveyed the room, quickly summing up the rest of us before zeroing in on Nicholas.

"Regent Thorne." She offered a shallow nod of deference.

"Come in, Detective." Nicholas gestured to a seat at the table. "What can I get you—coffee? Tea? Something to eat?" He too must have noticed the detective's mouth pinched with weariness.

"Nothing, thanks, I can't stay." She didn't budge from her spot just inside the door. "Is the acting Prime here?"

Dev rose to his feet. "I'm Devraj Trivedi."

"It looks like we got him," she reported. "The perp who did the Prime."

"Did he confess?" I blurted.

At her hesitation, Nicholas made the introductions. A subtle shift in her expression when she heard my name let me know she knew exactly who I was.

"The man who we believe killed Akim Silver won't be talking, now or ever," she said. "He was discovered dead in a short-term rental late this morning along with several items belonging to the Prime. The gun found at the scene is the same caliber as the one used in the crime. I'm on my way there now."

A man murdered Mr. Silver last night and then was dead himself by morning, conveniently in possession of evidence tying him to the Prime's death as well as the gun most likely used to kill him. How very tidy.

"How did he die?" Nicholas asked.

"Inconclusive," reported the detective. "No marks on the body, but there are signs of asphyxiation."

In other words, death by Nine.

Those Things Will Kill You

"You look beautiful," Nicholas said as I emerged from the bedroom in a black cocktail dress permanently borrowed from my mom's closet. A sleeveless jersey bodice clung to my modest curves, and the taffeta skirt, tied with a matching sash, belled out at the waist. It seemed fitting for the tribute he would pay Mr. Silver during tonight's speech.

"Does this look okay?" He stood in front of the sitting room's mirror putting the finishing touches on his tie.

"Perfect." The hint of vulnerability I picked up from him made me lean in for a kiss. "Nervous?"

"Not about the speech." His eyes warmed with expectation. "Have you made a decision about moving to Alder House?"

I stiffened at the unexpected question. His willingness to take such a meaningful step in our relationship made me yearn to do the same, but the myriad visions I'd had through the years of promises made and broken, of good intentions paved over with shards of glass had left their mark. I also couldn't shake

Jessie's remark about Nicholas's need to lock me away for his own peace of mind.

My gaze dropped to his lapel, and I reached up to smooth the already perfect fabric. "When are you leaving this time?"

"Tomorrow night." A stab of disappointment at my evasive answer soured the air between us.

"It's a big decision," I said.

"What's there to decide?" He stepped back. "You can't quit your minimum wage job to live at Alder House on a generous stipend? Or bail on a state school for online university classes and tutoring from some of the most talented Nines in existence? Or is there *someone* you don't want to leave?"

Words of protest sprang to mind, that I was supposed to drop everything while he risked nothing, but so too did thoughts of Jessie. All Nicholas asked was we give our relationship a chance to grow, while Jessie offered nothing but a political alliance with benefits, if that, now that Amani was in the picture.

"Don't be angry," I said defensively. "I need time to figure out what's best for me, when you aren't being asked to do the same."

His features immediately softened, and both of his hands found mine, but before he could respond a perfunctory knock came at the door. Marcel stepped inside.

"It's time," the sentinel announced.

"What did you think of the speech Francesca wrote?" I asked as the three of us waited for the elevator. The woman was an opportunist, but that didn't mean she couldn't also be useful.

His mouth twisted in a mocking smile. "If I hadn't seen her write it, I would have thought it came straight from Henry. She hit every talking point my father clings to."

"Will you be using any of it?" I'd noticed how he'd glossed over my question.

"Let's just say," he said, seeming to enjoy the suspense he'd created, "that my speech might not be exactly what either of you are expecting."

The elevator arrived, and we climbed aboard.

"Did something happen when you and Francesca were teaching assistants at Alder House?" I hadn't forgotten the way they'd both abruptly broken off reminiscing about old times when Nicholas joked about death.

His smile faded. "A girl died. Anya, a sentinel around my age. She was found early one morning outside Alder House, and it was presumed she'd fallen out of a window sometime during the night. Dev took her death especially hard because she was one of his first years."

"Was it an accident?" I asked.

He shrugged. "No witnesses, no suicide note, and a window in the Da Vinci solarium was found open. Telepaths were allowed to listen in freely in the days afterward, but no one came forward to report any additional information. At the same time, Dev and Francesca had a thing that didn't end well, but Dev has a lot of things that don't end well."

Maybe the solarium was a popular hookup spot at Alder House, or simply a place known to promise solitude. Whatever the case, there was no reason to think Dev or Francesca had crossed paths with the troubled girl, or that their breakup and her death had even occurred on the same night.

The low rumble of voices reverberating from below grew into a cacophony as the open-air car descended to the ground floor, ending further questions. Nines crowded the atrium, anticipating an exciting playoff game, and their infectious spirits were intoxicating.

Nicholas was immediately engulfed in the chaos. Marcel shouldered his way into a more protective position as dozens sought to shake the newest regent's hand or have a quick word.

People nodded to me in recognition but generally maintained a more respectful distance, and I soon found myself relegated to the perimeter of his admirers. We weren't the only ones to cause a stir, however. A major popstar who'd had a meteoric rise in the last few years held court a short distance away. A popular network news anchor known for his ability to get his interview subjects to spill their guts rubbed shoulders with an actress who was as famous for her love affairs as she was for racking up Academy Award nominations.

Jessie sidled up to me. "Small minds only recognize power when it's put on a pedestal."

He'd once again upped his style game, and tonight he wore a jacket, pants, and button down all in the same shade of rust. With his collar open to reveal several inches of golden skin and his blonde hair left loose to curl around his shoulders, mine weren't the only eyes straying in his direction.

"To be honest, I'm pretty happy to be on the sidelines tonight," I said truthfully. "How are you feeling?"

He rolled his shoulders and grimaced. "I once took a chair to the back while trying to break up a bar fight in some dive near Waco. It's kinda like that, but I consider today's adventure a much better return on the investment."

"I'm glad I'm a better cause than a couple of drunks," I said with a laugh, turning to regard the glittering crowd once again. "Do you suppose people get rich and famous because they're Nines, or do you think they'd be successful no matter what?"

He perused the celebrities speckled throughout the room. "I think it depends on the person and the ability. The news guy over there who always gets world leaders to practically confess state secrets is a telepath. You can't tell me that hasn't played a huge role in his success. Meanwhile, the famous actress at the bar is a sentinel, but I have no clue how you'd use that to get ahead." He turned to me, his gaze thoughtful. "Are you reconsidering using your voyancy for more than helping the Thornes?"

"Blake is too noble for such a thing," said a feminine voice. "Isn't that so?"

The scent of gardenias registered at the same moment Amani cozied up to Jessie and placed a possessive hand on his arm. She wore a column of pink silk held up by straps so thin, one deep breath and the dreams of her many admirers would come true. Considering the woman barely knew me, it was a weird thing to say, but her guileless expression was absent even a hint of malice.

"I don't know about that," I said, giving her the benefit of the doubt.

"Really?" She feigned surprise. "The word is you're willing to do almost anything to protect the Thornes. Perhaps even kill for them."

It was the second time she'd let a self-serving rumor slip into conversation. My empathic senses were overwhelmed by the excitement of so many people, but even if I had the training to zero in on one individual within a crowd, I bet she still had her emotions on lockdown.

"Amani—" Jessie said before I cut him off. Even beautiful women could be insecure, but it didn't mean I had to pander to her jealousy.

"You know how people love to talk," I said, smiling sweetly, "even when they've got nothing to say."

Her little trill of laughter grated on my ears. "But don't you find it amusing to look for the kernel of truth behind the wildest stories? That rumor had to start somewhere."

"Are you sure about that? I would hate to think everything I've heard about *you* is true." I knew next to nothing about her, but I couldn't resist.

Her hand fluttered to her mouth, seemingly taken aback by my barb, and it made me wonder if I'd read the situation all wrong. I'd give up my tips for a week to know if Amani was devious or just socially awkward. Fortunately, I was rescued from further discomfort by Nicholas, who swooped in with some urgency.

"Dev has something for us," he said, grasping my hand.

With an apologetic glance at Jessie for letting my irritation get the upper hand, I allowed Nicholas to whisk me to the far corner of the courtyard, where Dev held open the door of a private dining room, unoccupied that early in evening. He instructed Marcel to guard the door.

"The man police believe killed the Prime has been identified as Andrew James Holstead," Dev said when the three of us were alone. "He's known to law enforcement for his ties to organized crime, but there's nothing on him in our database."

I shrugged. The name meant nothing to me. "If he wasn't a Nine, what possible motive could he have to hunt down Mr. Silver?"

"Detective Phillips thinks it was murder for hire." He got out his phone and started searching for something. "Police were responding to an anonymous call when they found his body with items tying him to the crime."

"The call was probably made by the person who hired him," Nicholas said. "They've practically giftwrapped everything the police needs to close the case."

"Not everything." The sentinel tilted his phone screen so both Nicholas and I could view it. "Look what the detective found on the killer's cell."

The video was shot from the vantage point of a man relaxing in a green upholstered armchair. An amber bottle of beer sweated on a side table, and the smoke from a lit cigarette between his fingers trailed lazily toward the ceiling. Disjointed jazz played at a low volume in the background of a bland living room furnished straight from a catalogue.

"Hey, Caroline," a deep, masculine voice drawled. "You'll be happy to know the job's been done to the client's specs. I have the items the client requested, and I'll drop them in the mail tomorrow. By the way, thanks for renting a place with a decent restaurant across the street. I had a great…"

His voice trailed off as the camera zeroed in on the cigarette. The smoke no longer curled upwards. Instead, it arched slightly sideways before dissipating.

"What the hell?" He was puzzled but far from panicked until the angle of the smoke stream became more pronounced, and a newspaper discarded on the nearby coffee table fluttered.

A cough tore from the man's throat. Then another. His breaths suddenly came in shallow gasps as he lurched to his feet. The phone dropped from his hand, giving us a stationary view of a short hall leading to the front door. The glowing cigarette landed on clean beige carpeting before the man crawled into frame, his face reddening and his mouth gaping like a landed fish as he tried to draw breath. Collapsing, he rolled onto his back and clawed at his throat. The cigarette in the foreground extinguished itself. I looked away, having seen enough, but the sounds of his struggle went on until finally, it was silent.

I shuddered. "What did we just see?"

The two men locked gazes before Nicholas turned to me. "The work of an elementalist."

Open Your Eyes

Dev and I stepped out of the manager's office while Nicholas called Henry to inform him Silver's killer had been executed by an elementalist who'd drawn the air from the room, most likely from under the front door. I had never even considered such an application of the gift, but it didn't surprise me to discover yet another way a Nine could cause pain and death.

Marcel stood guard a few feet away with his back to Dev and me, so I had a minute alone with the man who, before last night, had seemed more interested in finding ways to combine business with pleasure than serving as sheriff to The Nine.

"You're really good at this," I told him, impressed with how much progress had been made in less than twenty-four hours.

Since the day we'd met at Alder House, his eyes had always reflected a perpetual sparkle, but he regarded me now with a new sharpness to his gaze. Even his smile had lost some of its brightness.

"I'm doing it for Mr. Silver." He turned to survey the nearby groups of chattering people while we spoke. "When the job's done, so am I."

"What if the chancellor decides otherwise?" Normally I wouldn't poke a sleeping bear, but both he and Khalia had made me aware of the inequities suffered by the entire class of sentinels. It would be harder to lead a call for change if he was no longer part of The Nine.

"He will do what he must," he said, his tone bleak, "and so will I."

"But if you're going to reform the—"

"Reform?" He barked out a laugh. "You make it sound as if we plan to *ask* for parity."

An arrow of sadness pierced my soul as I realized where this was headed. He and Nicholas had been best friends most of their lives, but if Dev chose to be the flashpoint in a stand against The Nine's leadership, their relationship might not survive. Nicholas allowed very few to penetrate the steep walls he'd erected around his heart. Losing Dev would isolate him even further.

I had further questions about the future the sentinel envisioned, but I had a more pressing issue for our limited time alone.

"Dev…" I hesitated, then pushed ahead. "Has your father ever told you about the day Henry Thorne became chancellor?"

Surprise and curiosity warred for dominance in his expression. Whatever he'd thought I'd say wasn't in the same zip code as the topic now on the table. He quickly schooled his features into the standard mask of watchfulness most sentinels wore.

"No, but is there something in particular you wish to know?" he asked.

"Only this," I said, leaning close to whisper into his ear. "If you knew Henry cheated to win the challenge, could that information be helpful to your future plans?"

Dev let out a breath as if he'd been sucker punched at the same moment Nicholas emerged from the manager's office, straightening his cuffs as if he'd done some heavy lifting.

"Ready for battle?" Nicholas asked, offering me his arm.

It was my turn to be startled by a question. "Yours, mine, or the one on the court?"

"I've got an elementalist to find," Dev brusquely cut in. "Good luck with the speech." He stopped to say a few words to Marcel before disappearing into the crush.

His abrupt departure left Nicholas nonplussed. "Did Dev just pass up a courtside seat for the big game?"

"He's the acting Prime now." My eyes lingered on the place where he'd melted into the crowd, feeling like I'd ignited a spark without any idea who might get burned. "I'm sure he has much to do."

Our three courtside tickets had been delivered to the room a few hours ago, and with Dev's departure, there was a definite bounce in Marcel's step as we joined the cue for the elevators.

I elected to take my seat while Nicholas moved about the Palmarium court with Marcel hovering over him. He was in his element, warmly greeting friends and shaking hands with new acquaintances. The talk would invariably turn to politics and other Nine gossip, something I definitely had my fill of for the moment.

"He's a natural, isn't he?" Francesca said with a touch of pride as she slipped into the seat beside me. A velvet dress in an electric shade of blue served as a vibrant backdrop for her signature layers of necklaces and assortment of rings. "No matter what he says about not wanting to follow in his father's footsteps, he was born for this."

"You think so?" I kept my gaze on Nicholas. It had been so much simpler when we'd first met. I'd been a girl longing for love and acceptance, and he'd been a boy yearning for connection. Now he was the regent and scion of a man who'd stepped over bodies to seize power, and I'd been cast in the very public role of his supporter and defender. If I had known where that first kiss would lead, would I still have courted it?

She let out a small laugh. "That's supposed to be a good thing."

I mentally shook myself. Too many eyes were upon me to indulge in private reflections.

"Maybe it is." I pasted on a pleasant smile. "If that's what he wants."

A dozen trumpets magically appeared overhead and blasted a short but regal melody. The floor cleared of spectators, and every seat filled except the two reserved for Nicholas and Marcel, who lingered near the locker room door. The same master of ceremonies as the previous night bounded onto the court with hair slicked into a pompadour towering several inches above his scalp. Dressed in a suit of cornflower blue, all he needed was a ruffled shirt to look like the world's oldest prom date.

"Welcome, ladies and gentlemen, to the American Palmarium league playoff game!" The cavernous room thundered with cheers and applause, and the onslaught of so much positive energy felt like adrenaline being pumped directly into my veins.

"I'm your host, Miguel de Palma, and as you know, the winner of tonight's match will compete in the international games taking place next month in Sydney, Australia! While the teams take a few minutes to finalize their strategies, we have a very special guest to kick off the night. My fellow Nines, please put your hands together to welcome our new telekinetic regent, Nicholas Thorne!"

The applause was welcoming if not exactly booming. Nicholas strode confidently to the center of the floor with his now ever-present shadow Marcel in tow. He shook hands with the MC, who handed off the wireless microphone.

"Thank you, my friends. It is an honor and a pleasure to be with you tonight, despite the tragic loss of our Prime, Akim Silver." If he hadn't completely held everyone's attention before, the mention of the late Prime brought absolute silence to the room. "We do not yet know the motive behind his death, but I can tell you it was no accident, and that at least one Nine was involved."

Beside me, Francesca expelled her breath in a hiss before it was buried by the rumble of heads coming together to murmur in surprise or confirmation of what they already suspected. Nicholas waited for the shock of his announcement to fade before continuing.

"Mr. Silver was that rarity among us, one who didn't judge a fellow Nine by their politics or personal beliefs. It makes his death even more troubling, for if a man such as that can be targeted, what about those of us who hold strong opinions on how we should shape the future of our people? Are any of us safe?" He let them ponder that question a few moments.

"No matter what your politics may be, I plan to follow in the footsteps of Regent Bailey Foster-Simms, a man who recognized The Nine has survived these many centuries because of our diverse talents, not in spite of it. He believed a path could be forged that includes all of us, and so do I. He once told me, 'Politics is war without bloodshed, while war is politics with bloodshed.' So, I ask you, my friends, my fellow Nines, let us find a common ground where there is no room for bloodshed of any kind."

As his eyes scanned the crowd, they seemed to settle on me. "A newcomer in our midst recently questioned our need to cling so tightly to our traditions. I defended them by saying our history is what binds us and holds us together as a people, but now I wonder." His voice turned thoughtful. "I wonder if they also prevent us from growing and adapting."

He tore his gaze from mine to address the room at large. "I believe we can come together again as one people united by our desire to live free from the limitations outsiders would place on us. I, for one, plan to listen more and speak less, seek solutions to our problems instead of turning a blind eye, and to be a positive force for change. I hope you will join me."

As he stepped away from the podium to polite applause, Francesca muttered, "Nicholas always did know how to walk a fine line, but Henry's not going to like it. His son all but announced the New Order is right to demand change."

Pointing out there might be valid points of view other than one's own was hardly revolutionary, but she must have taken my silence for agreement because she added, "Anyone who's lived at Alder House knows about the strain in the Thornes' relationship. I'd hoped Nicholas would choose the path of least resistance, for his sake if not for ours."

"I haven't known Nicholas very long," I said, my gaze remaining on my boyfriend as he made his way around the room, shaking hands and inclining his head as people engaged him in conversation, "but I do know he will always do what he believes is his duty, no matter what the chancellor or anyone else demands."

She scoffed. "You're too wrapped up in your little romance to understand what's at stake here. Grow up, voyant, and open your eyes." With an angry toss of her head, she left her seat and marched to the exit.

She and Henry might not be happy, but Sutton Sinclair, once again seated across the floor, caught my eye and raised a brow to convey his surprise at the door Nicholas had just opened. I tipped my head in acknowledgment, hopefully paving the way for a future frank conversation, one I'd been unable to have last night. I may be among Nines, but a second murder in a single weekend was over the top, even for them. Scarlett's jaded snicker echoed in my ear.

Nicholas's arrival cut short my brooding. Marcel was right behind him, taking the spot occupied by Dev the previous night.

"Well done," I murmured in Nicholas's ear.

He forced a smile, likely anticipating the expected blowback from his father, but the thump of a drum echoing through the venue cut short further chatter. People picked up the beat, clapping along as the tempo escalated. Just when it reached its zenith, the locker room doors flew open.

Modern day gladiators strutted through the portal. They were all markedly younger and, for the most part, less battle-scarred than yesterday's players. A few had various joints taped or braces on limbs marked with bruises, but they lacked the permanent damage the retired veterans had sported, both visible and unseen. The older crew had squinted doggedly at the world, doing their job with little fanfare, while the people now taking the court bounced with the enthusiasm of puppies.

The teams were introduced—it was a matchup between the Kansas City Wolves and the hometown Los Angeles Outlaws—and after a bit more fanfare, a shrill whistle cut through the air. The game began.

21

Ring of Truth

Ever since word of Silver's death had gotten out, the club's atmosphere had been thick with every manner of emotion. Suspicion, sadness, anticipation, avarice, and more all braided together into an electrical current pulsing just under my skin. I overheard one Class One empath, her face drawn with exhaustion, tell another it was like living in a haunted house—she didn't know what would jump out at her from one breath to the next. It made me grateful my empathic abilities were still in their infancy.

For her sake and mine, I was thrilled when the Outlaws, the local favorites, won the playoff with only two players requiring life-saving measures. Excitement and joy washed over me as I rode the high of other people's happiness. The atrium and sur-rounding rooms quickly filled, music blasted everywhere, and people swayed to the rhythm as the celebration began in earnest.

I scoped my surroundings for Sutton, but Nicholas pulled me into his arms, and our bodies began to sway in time with the beat. We tried various moves, some more graceful than others, and soon we were laughing with abandon. The weight of the past twenty-four hours lifted, and I could just be a girl twirling and dipping in the arms of a boy.

Until Marcel tapped Nicholas on the shoulder.

He stopped dancing. The sentinel spoke into his ear, and the joy drained from his face. Nicholas's eyes met mine, and my mind dredged up a dozen terrifying scenarios.

Nicholas must have sensed my fear because he didn't wait until we'd escaped the mass of gyrating bodies to put his mouth next to my ear. "Dev needs us upstairs. I don't know what's happened, but he told Marcel it was urgent."

At the elevator, he lifted our joined hands and brought my knuckles—bleached of color— to his lips. "Whatever it is, we'll face it together."

"Sorry," I said, trying to relax my fingers before the circulation in his own was cut off.

My heart thudded in time with our steps as we walked from the elevator to the suite. The sentinel deputy, Greta, pulled open the door before we could unlock it ourselves. Dev waited in front of the room's big screen with the remote in hand.

"What have you got?" Nicholas asked.

"The man who killed Silver was in a short-term rental across the street from a restaurant called Bistro Annabelle," he said. I sagged in relief to hear our summons had nothing to do with me nor had somebody else dropped dead.

"They've had a few break-ins lately," Dev continued, "so the owner of the place invested in a security system that includes wide angle cameras covering an entire section of the street directly in front of the restaurant. Their range includes the townhouses across the way." He clicked a button on the remote. "See what they picked up early this morning."

The video, timestamped 1:47 a.m., showed a handful of parked cars lining the curb in front of a connecting row of identical townhomes. The lack of light leeched most of the color from the scene and rendered the residences even more indistinguishable from one another. Only random personal touches, such as potted geraniums on the front porch of one and a leftover Christmas wreath on the door of another, differentiated the units.

A late-night visitor strolled into frame and stopped on the street in front of a door lacking any such individuality. The figure's shapeless jacket and loose pants gave nothing away, nor did the hood drawn up over their head. With their back to the camera, the person stood unmoving as the timestamp ticked away one, two, and finally three minutes. I mentally replayed the images of a dying man's last moments behind the door of one particular unit during those same three minutes. At last the killer turned to leave, dodging an oncoming car as they crossed the street.

Nicholas glanced over at Dev, who stood pinching his lip in thought. "Any leads on who that might be?"

The sentinel heaved a tired sigh. "Detective Phillips is running—"

"Stop!" I commanded, trying to make sense of what may have been revealed in the brief moment headlights passed over the unknown elementalist. "Back it up thirty seconds."

"What is it?" Nicholas asked, but Dev didn't have to be told twice. He pressed a button on the remote and rewound the video as requested. Everyone gathered closer to see if something had been missed.

"Slow it down," I ordered as lights from the car partially illuminated the scene. Frame by frame the video advanced until I said, "There."

The others examined the image for several long seconds before Dev drew in a swift breath. He too had found what had caught my eye.

"What am I looking at?" Greta asked in an accent that placed her homeland as somewhere in the Netherlands.

Nearing the screen, I pointed to the killer's hand. For a fraction of a second, it had caught the light… as did the distinctive collection of rings topped with colored stones decorating most of Francesca's fingers.

Fire and Water

The party had ramped up even higher in the few minutes we'd been away, the lights dimmed to spotlight the evanescent creations sparkling in the air overhead. A flock of fantastical birds winged about the room, dolphins appeared and disappeared as they leapt through waves of light, and a shower of shooting stars created a strobe effect across the faces of hundreds of dancers.

"How are we supposed to find anyone in this?" I raised my voice to be heard over the music.

"Shield the regent and Blake," Dev tersely ordered Marcel before he plunged into the crowd. Greta followed suit, going in a different direction.

Nicholas reached for my hand. "Let's work our way around the side."

It was slow going as we circled the courtyard, and we stopped completely when Honey stepped into our path. They were hard to miss in white pants and a matching double-breasted jacket plunging low over their naked chest.

"Francesca Ricci just went out the front door," Honey said.

My brows shot up. "How did—"

"Another telepath warned her you were coming, and it wasn't for a dance." Honey glared at Marcel with pursed lips. "Do better, sentinel."

Nicholas already had his phone out and pressed to his ear. We pushed our way to the main entrance where we were met by Dev and Greta. The sidewalk outside the club was well lit and sparsely populated at that time of night, making it easy to spot a flash of electric blue nearing the end of the block.

"There!" I pointed to the elementalist about to disappear around the corner.

Francesca happened to look back, her step faltering as she realized we weren't far behind. Dev, Greta, and Nicholas—followed closely by a chastened Marcel—were instantly in motion, but I chose a different tack. Whipping out my cell, I called Marie, who picked up on the first ring.

"Marie, it's Blake Wilder," I said before she could even say hello. "How fast can you have the car out in front of the club?" Wading through the crowd to reach the back entrance would take forever.

"I'm pulling out of the alley right now," she said before calling out to someone, "Hang on! We have an emergency!" The squeal of tires echoed through our connection. "I'll be right there, Blake!"

My next call was to Nicholas, who along with the sentinels, had disappeared from view.

He answered breathlessly, the slap of his running footfalls keeping time with my racing pulse. Sentinels may be immune to paranormal abilities such as voyancy or telepathy, but Francesca was an elementalist. Could they shield themselves from a wall of flames or a deluge of water at the same time they protected another? I didn't want to find out.

"Where are you?" I asked.

"Uh… Temple and Broadway," he panted before abruptly yelling, "Greta! Watch—"

The line went dead. I willed myself not to hyperventilate.

True to her word, Marie screeched to a halt directly in front of me in less than a minute. Heedless of protocol, I threw myself into the front passenger seat.

"Drive! Make the first right and keep going." I'd learned enough of the local geography on my walk with Jessie to have a general idea of where to go.

Marie slammed her foot on the gas.

"Blake Wilder?" A feminine voice came from the backseat.

Twisting around, my eyes met those of an elegantly dressed, middle-aged couple. She jangled with diamonds along with the makings of a second chin, and he a stocky silver fox with deep laugh lines around his mouth.

The woman offered a sunny smile. "What a thrill it is to meet you in such exciting circumstances. We're the Loudon's. Janet and George."

"We have reservations for a late supper at Park 42," said her husband. "Took us months to get. The short ribs in a red wine reduction are supposed to be divine."

We took the corner with tires squealing, and I gripped the door handle to stay upright.

"Are we chasing somebody?" Janet politely inquired.

"An elementalist who may be responsible for the death of Mr. Silver," I threw over my shoulder. "And now she's turned on Nicholas and the acting Prime."

"My stars!" Janet exclaimed. "You heard the young lady, Marie. Hit it!"

Marie swore under her breath. Traffic was light, but we were in imminent danger of getting boxed in at the upcoming intersection.

"Hang on!" She jerked the wheel to the left, sending the car careening towards oncoming traffic. Horns blared as she ran a red light and slid between two vehicles traversing the crossing as if she were threading the fast moving needle on a sewing machine. With a flick of the wheel, the car was back on the right side of the road.

"I'm all for doing our part," George said after we'd all expelled a breath, "but I'd hate to lose that table."

"George," Janet said reproachfully. "We can't let that elementalist get away. Besides, this is the most fun we've had since Nat and Danny's wedding."

The car slowed as we approached a geyser of water flooding the street and surrounding sidewalk. A toppled fire hydrant lay nearby.

"There's Greta!" I rolled down my window as the car pulled over. The sentinel deputy lay on the sidewalk with hair and clothing drenched. Despite the deep chested coughs of someone who'd swallowed a gallon of water, she feebly waved us on.

"Shame on that elementalist," Janet scolded in much the same tone I would use to admonish Chico for trying to lick plates as they were loaded into the dishwasher. "She could conjure plenty of water on her own without adding to it from the hydrant. That's not just dangerous, it's plain rude."

Two blocks further on we caught sight of Dev, Nicholas, and Marcel pelting down the street. Francesca, in high-heeled boots and bright blue dress flying out behind her, had managed to preserve her hundred-yard lead.

"I remember when I could run in heels like that," Janet lamented with a sigh.

George smiled at his wife. "You still look as young and beautiful as the day we met."

Without slowing, Nicholas slashed his hand through the air, and a van parked at the curb tumbled into Francesca's path. She raised both palms as if warding off the obstacle, and a blast of wind sent the vehicle skittering off the sidewalk and into traffic. Tires screeched and horns blared as cars swerved to avoid it.

A public park lay directly in their path. Francesca halted at the entrance and whirled around. With a flick of her wrist, a blast of air roiled down the street, knocking her pursuers to the ground along with a few innocent bystanders.

Marie pulled to the curb as Nicholas and Dev dragged themselves to their feet. Marcel, grimacing, struggled upright while clutching one of his shoulders. The pedestrians who'd been hit were a bit slower to recover, but no one other than Marcel seemed to have sustained more than minor scuffs and bruises.

"Stay on her," Nicholas told Dev, lurching to the car.

Marcel muttered a feeble protest about Nicholas leaving without a sentinel to guard him, but he didn't rise from the pavement.

Opening the back door, Nicholas shoved a startled Janet to the center seat. Dev took off just as Francesca disappeared into the gardens.

"Go around to the other side of the park," Nicholas ordered Marie, who obeyed without hesitation. "We'll cut her off there."

"That was an inspirational speech you gave tonight, Regent," Janet said as we sped through the night.

Jacket torn, tie askew, and still breathing heavily, Nicholas gawked at the woman before finding his voice. "Er, thank you, Mrs.…?"

"Janet Loudon," she said, offering her hand before almost falling into his lap as the car veered around a corner. Righting herself with a pat to her neat updo, she added, "Class Two evanescent. This is my husband, George, a Class Two materialist."

George nodded. "Have you ever eaten at Park 42?"

Marie brought the car to a squealing stop in front of one of the entrances to the park, ending further conversation.

"The elementalist is heading right for us," Marie announced. No one questioned how the phantomist knew.

Nicholas and I both jumped out of the car. A cement footpath lit with old fashioned streetlights snaked through the rambling green space dotted here and there with stands of trees. We raced past a darkened playground outfitted with climbing towers and swings. A handful of people strolled the quiet grounds or lounged on the benches placed at random, while at the center of the park, a couple admired a grand fountain, its multiple levels illuminated by an underwater circle of colorful lights.

Dev rounded the water feature at a run. Wet clothes were plastered to his body, and his jacket had been singed in several places.

"Where did she go?" Nicholas asked, his head on a swivel.

The sentinel braced his hands on his thighs as he gasped for breath. "I lost sight of her… when she threw a fireball… but let's not stand… next to water… shall we?"

After Janet's comment about outside water sources giving elementalists additional firepower, I wholeheartedly agreed with Dev. Turning back to the car, I called Marie and explained the situation in a few words. "Would Madam Boudreaux mind helping us out again?"

"I can ask," she replied, ringing off.

The three of us emerged from the park to find Janet taking selfies with her bemused husband. Marie was alone in conversation several feet away but broke off to join us when we reached the car.

"Madame Sally says the woman you seek ducked out the park's side entrance while the sentinel was extinguishing the flames on his clothing."

"Thank heavens you're soaked to the skin," Janet pointed out to Dev. "It probably saved your life."

"Yeah," Dev agreed with a scowl. "Yippee."

"Does she know which way Francesca went?" I asked the phantomist.

"Get in." Marie hopped behind the wheel.

"We're good," George said, holding up his phone. "I just called an Uber."

The rest of us left a disappointed Janet along with her relieved husband on the sidewalk as the car peeled away.

The Point of No Return

Marie slowed the car as Dev ended a phone call ordering a team of evanescents to fry the circuits of any cameras that may have caught Francesca and Nicholas using their paranormal powers. The minor temblor that dislodged the fire hydrant could be shrugged off—this was California, after all—but not the resulting wall of water she'd sent rocketing down the street. Likewise, enchanters would be sent to the city's operations offices to delete the footage and wipe the memories of anyone who may have viewed it. Videos that might later pop up on YouTube or TikTok would be dismissed as fake by thousands of Nine-controlled bots. I had never considered the magnitude of the operation required to cover up something like this, and seeing Dev put all the pieces into place was impressive.

"Make sure Greta and Marcel see a healing evanescent," Dev added before putting away his phone.

We stopped in front of a footbridge paved with brick and topped with a Japanese-style gate on which gold lettering announced we'd arrived at the entrance to Los Angeles's Little

Tokyo. In the street beyond, red and white paper lanterns embellished with images of tigers and dragons were strung over the heads of visitors. The pedestrian district was packed with restaurants, houses of worship, and souvenir stores.

The phantomist eyed tourists posing on the bridge and mugging with their camera phones. "Madam Sally says your rogue elementalist passed through here a few minutes ago."

"Lost in the crowd and protected by them too," Dev surmised. The area on the other side of the bridge wasn't exactly teaming with shoppers, but there were enough people to obscure Francesca from casual view if she mingled among them.

Nicholas opened the car door. "Let's go."

The three of us left Marie to find parking while we merged with mostly couples and families out for a late night bite to eat or a bit of retail therapy. Our path was eased by people leaving a wide berth around Dev, whose wet, torn, and burned clothing made him look like he'd escaped the underworld by swimming through the River Styx. I'd begun to limp in my stiletto heels, and I idly wished trainers with cocktail dresses would become the hot new trend.

Peering through each doorway we passed, the scent of cooking meat, brewing tea, and a variety of tantalizing spices made my stomach growl, our room service dinner ancient history by then.

We came to a small plaza where a large round planter with a wide lip offered weary shoppers a place to rest. The towering tree at its center would offer welcome shade on a hot summer day, but the chill of winter had stripped it of its leaves, leaving a stark tangle of branches overhead. Turning in a circle with no clue as to where to continue our pursuit, I too felt a chill, this one the sting of lost causes. We were in Francesca's town after all, and she'd chosen her escape route well.

"I'm not picking up any other Nines in the area." Dev's subdued tone conveyed he too suffered from a lack of optimism. "Maybe we should split up."

As we parted from the sentinel, I sensed Nicholas's dogged determination to find the elementalist as clearly as if he'd shouted it. Maybe feelings of betrayal kept him devoted to a search growing more hopeless with each passing minute.

He was several steps ahead of me when a glimpse of electric blue from within a vintage clothing store made me pause. Stepping into a shop the size of a single-car garage, I found a young woman aggressively mopping the area behind the sales counter, the scowl on her face barely downgrading to a glower when she spotted me.

"Excuse me." I reached for the pile of blue velvet discarded on a glass-topped display case. Shaking out the material, there was no question it was Francesca's dress. "I'm looking for the woman who—"

"That makes two of us," she snapped. "This isn't a flipping lending library where you drop off one dress and check out another."

The elementalist was probably long gone, but it couldn't hurt to ask. "Do you know what she's wearing now?"

The salesgirl planted her mop as if it were a sword she could drive through the hearts of her enemies. "Do I look like Google to you?"

"Ah, no problem." Placing the velvet dress back on the counter, I let my fingertips graze her hip before returning to the street.

The clerk's most recent memory revealed Francesca had stolen a vintage shirtwaist dress in a muted shade of green. She'd swapped clothing while the shopgirl dealt with a flooded toilet in the backroom's minuscule bathroom, something that had occurred within moments of the elementalist entering the shop. She'd also traded her boots for a pair of penny loafers and covered her hair with a scarf, thefts the angry salesgirl hadn't fully realized in her brief glimpse of Francesca's departing form.

Shooting off a text to inform the guys of Francesca's change of clothes, I made to follow after Nicholas when a flash of green disappearing into a nearby alleyway caught my eye.

Ignoring the discomfort in my swollen feet, I picked my way past kitchen dumpsters and practiced using telekinesis to flick a few discarded cardboard boxes out of my path with limited success. The alley emptied out into another plaza, this one devoid of people. The businesses lining its perimeter—a cultural center, a library, a museum—were shuttered at this time of night. The area's only distinguishing feature was a wooden tower at least fifty feet high, the design of its red beams and blue tiled roof lifted straight from feudal Japan.

A glimmer of movement near the base of the tower made me call out. "Francesca!"

The click of my heels bounced off our unyielding surroundings and echoed about the square. The figure turned and, with her hair hidden under a scarf, Francesca's face was fully revealed. As I neared, she jerked her wrist in the same gesture that had summoned the punishing wind. I braced for some type of onslaught, but instead a dividing line of flames whooshed into existence, preventing me from going any further.

"Whoa," I exclaimed, flailing my arms to stay upright. Another step and I would've been charbroiled.

The dull rumble of the surrounding city seemed to recede as we faced one other. Silent tongues of flame made the shadows behind her flicker and dance. With a lack of witnesses or aid should the elementalist decide to light me up like a Roman candle, I felt the first stirrings of fear, but astonishingly, the emotions swirling about her were akin to defeat.

"Why couldn't you just let it go? I don't want to hurt you, Blake." Her emotions grew even more bleak as she considered our stark surroundings. "I never wanted to hurt anyone."

"Isn't it a little late for that?" I ventured.

A humorless chuckle escaped her lips. "I suppose it is. How did you know it was me?"

"Your rings." Even now the faceted stones on her fingers sparkled in the firelight. "You were filmed."

She briefly closed her eyes as she absorbed the blow. "Dev once said I shouldn't wear them on the street because they made me a target for thieves, and he was afraid I'd get hurt." A sad smile lifted the corners of her lips. "I should have listened."

"Why did Mr. Silver have to die?" I asked. "Did it have anything to do with my father?"

Her shoulders lifted in a shallow shrug. "I do as I'm told, but that ends tonight."

"Who told you to do it?" I pressed.

She shook her head. "It doesn't matter. I just need to disappear. It's the only way I will ever be free."

So strong was her desire to escape whatever or whoever had forced her to do their bidding that my skin prickled with her fear, relief, and hope. I leaned into it, hoping the emotions thickening the air between us would be enough to make the connection, to summon the moment she'd been ensnared in such a trap. *Show me…*

A deep sense of foreboding gripped me when I realized I was once again in the Da Vinci solarium. It looked the same as the night of her tryst with Dev, the same candles burning, the same lavender-scented breeze making their flames sway and dance.

Francesca was alone as she tugged on a summer dress, cursing and hurling a sandal when the buckle proved difficult. A small squeak came from the direction she'd thrown the shoe.

"Who's there?" she demanded. "Dev? Have you come to your senses?"

A young woman emerged from the shadows. She was in her late teens, her unblemished skin dusted with a trace of color, and a sleek fall of black hair hovering about her waist.

"I… I'm sorry, I didn't mean to intrude," the girl stammered. "I saw Dev, that is, Sentinel Trivedi come up here and I…"

"You what?" Francesca challenged, her voice thick with scorn. "You thought the strong, handsome sentinel needed help from a little nobody like you?"

"I'm not a nobody," the girl said with quiet dignity. "I'm Anya Patel. I'm in Sentinel Trivedi's class."

"Oh, let me guess. You gaze adoringly at him all day long, hoping he'll finally notice you," the elementalist taunted as she advanced.

"N-n-no." Anya's cheeks flared scarlet as she backed away. "I was concerned, that's all."

"I just bet you were." The older woman edged closer, like a tiger stalking a kitten. "Will you tell him how you dream of him at night when you're all alone in your little room?"

Anya stopped in front of the open window and stood her ground. "That's not really your business anymore, is it? From what I heard, Dev wants nothing more to do with you."

Francesca's eyes filled with unhinged rage. With fists clenched, she unleashed a primal scream. A fierce wind howled through the room, gutting the candles and plunging the space into darkness. When the wicks sprang back to life, Francesca was alone.

Hesitantly, she crept over to the window and peered down at the ground five-stories below. The dim light of the moon revealed Anya's unmoving body sprawled across the flagstones. Francesca immediately ducked back inside, frozen with shock and fright, but not for long. She soon moved with purpose, searching the shadows for her lost sandal, and when that was done, she straightened her shoulders and smoothed down her dress.

The door opening caused her to whirl about.

"Oh Francesca," said an unseen man, his voice dripping with censure. "What have you done?"

A Reasonable Explanation

I blinked, the vision at an end. "You killed that girl."

Her face turned ashen. "What did you see?"

"The night in the solarium with Anya. I saw enough to know you didn't mean to do it," I said, hoping to draw her out.

"No," she burst out, as if desperate to be believed. "I didn't. I was angry at Dev, and I should have gone straight to the Prime, I know that now, but I was too scared to think straight." A bitter laugh escaped her lips. "Maybe if I had, we wouldn't be here."

"Who found out you were in the solarium that night?" I hadn't heard enough of the man's voice to guess his identity.

Running footfalls echoed across the square, and Francesca stiffened. Nicholas and Dev came thundering across the plaza from different directions, but with another wave of her hand, the flames spread out until the fiery barrier completely walled her off. Nicholas was the first to reach me.

"Are you alright?" His eyes anxiously swept down my form.

"I'm fine," I assured him.

Dev came skidding to a stop, his lip curled as he regarded Francesca. "Fireballs? Really, Fran?" He tugged on his ruined coat. "This was my favorite jacket."

Despite her desperate circumstances, she rose to the occasion. "As I recall, you used to like a little heat."

"Turn off the flames before someone calls the authorities," Nicholas urged. "We'll go back to the club and figure this out."

She eyed him through a veil of sorrow. "It's way too late for that, Nicholas. People are dead. I've played my part, and now it's time for me to disappear."

"What part was that, Fran?" Dev's voice had lost its ire, as if her reminder of what they'd once meant to each other had hit its mark. "Who else is involved?"

Her eyes cut to Nicholas. "It doesn't matter now."

"You killed Akim Silver," Dev said in the same dejected tone. "You know I can't let that go. You can run, but there's no place where I won't find you."

Her eyes glazed with unshed tears as she studied the sentinel's handsome face. "I once would have done anything to hear you say that. You will make a wonderful Prime, Devraj Trivedi."

She took a step back but froze—as did we all—at the terrible cracking sound that reverberated off the hardscape. It was impossible to tell which direction it came from as the noise intensified.

A flash of movement behind Francesca made me gasp. "Watch out!"

The decorative tower tipped off its foundation as Francesca turned to see what held me transfixed. She shrieked as the tower fell towards her.

"Francesca!" Dev screamed. Nicholas lunged for the sentinel, latching onto his arm to hold him back.

With a deafening crash, Francesca disappeared beneath a pile of timber. The flames keeping us at bay winked out, and we were plunged into gloom. Within moments, panicked shouts raised the alarm.

"We need to go." Nicholas's eyes darted about as if he expected to be apprehended at any moment. He released Dev, who stared vacantly at the spot where a woman he'd once cared about had stood moments before.

"What happened?" I barely comprehended what we'd just witnessed.

Nicholas grabbed my hand and tugged me into motion. Dev shook off his horrified disbelief and stumbled along behind us.

"We're just going to leave her?" I asked as we hurried across the square.

"There's nothing we can do for her now," Nicholas tersely pointed out, steering us through a gap in the perimeter very much like the alley that had delivered me there. Back among the sights and smells of one of the main shopping arteries, he confidently led the way while I trailed him in a daze.

Madame Boudreaux must have informed Marie of our imminent arrival because the car pulled up to the gated exit at the same moment we did. We all piled in and were on the road as sirens screamed in the distance. Dev was already on the phone, once again taking measures to cover our tracks. Nicholas too was busy on his phone, his mouth set in a grim line as he shot off a series of texts.

I met Marie's dark eyes in the rearview mirror, wondering if Madame Sally had relayed the remarkable coincidence of the tower falling at the exact moment Francesca had let down her guard. It almost certainly had to be the work of a Nine, perhaps tying up another loose end. With the elementalist dead, we might never know her motive in bringing about Silver's death, nor the names of others who may have been involved.

As I glanced over at Nicholas, all I could think was the tower must have been toppled by a telekinetic, but that telekinetic hadn't been me.

Marcel met us outside the suite wearing a change of dry clothing, his shoulder presumably repaired by one of the healing evanescents. Not much could be done for the purplish bruise spreading across the side of his face.

"My sincerest apologies, Regent," he earnestly addressed Nicholas. "I could have sworn my shielding extended to both you and Miss Wilder. If I had known you were being observed by a disloyal telepath when you were searching the club—"

Dev, as wrung out as the rest of us, cut him off. "You *should* have known, sentinel. Francesca Ricci is dead because of your failure. We will talk about this later." Marcel's stricken expression stayed with me as we let ourselves into the suite.

Making my way to one of the sofas, I kicked off my shoes and stretched out across the plump cushions. Nicholas sat down beside me and pulled my aching feet into his lap. His fingers gently probed the abused arches, sending waves of relief through my limbs, but the thrilling connection that always accompanied his touch didn't burn quite as brightly.

Dev grabbed Nicholas's laptop and claimed the opposite sofa. "I'm too bloody knackered to go get my computer," he explained, opening the lid, "but there'll be a hundred messages on my phone in the morning if I don't send a report tonight. What's your password, Nic?"

Nicholas hesitated, self-consciously clearing his throat before answering. "Uh, Blake with a capital b, then capital m, lowercase a, y, then 2, 0."

My brows rose in surprise. It was my name and birthday.

Dev shook his head in weary amusement. "Smooth move, my friend. I'll have to remember that one."

All levity drained away as Dev took us through moment by moment everything that happened after he'd left us in the marketplace to continue the search on his own. His fingers tapped the keyboard as our responses were entered into the formal record. Mr. Silver had preferred a notebook and pen when he conducted an interview, and I felt a twinge of loss at how much I would miss the Prime's old fashioned quirks.

As I relayed the vision of Francesca's jealous encounter with the teenage sentinel, Dev stopped typing and stared at me. "She killed Anya?"

"I don't think she meant to do it, if that helps," I said.

Both men gazed at me with dumbfounded expressions, and in Nicholas's case, I could tell his sense of shock was genuine.

"We broke up that same night," Dev murmured.

"I know." His eyes flew to mine, and I let him read the truth there.

"I always wondered if things hadn't ended like they did, if I'd been in the solarium later that night…" His voice trailed off, as if in a daze.

"It wasn't your fault," I assured him. "But someone discovered her secret and used it against her."

Nicholas started. "Are you saying she was blackmailed into arranging Silver's murder?"

"I believe so, yes."

"Do you know who?" There was trepidation behind his question, but no deceit.

I shook my head. "It was a man, but I don't know who."

Dev typed for a moment. "What happened next?"

"You two showed up." My gaze flitted to Nicholas. "And then the tower fell."

Dev also focused on Nicholas. "Did you use telekinesis to bring it down?" My chest constricted as I waited to hear his response.

"No. I had nothing to do with it." My empathic senses registered only his overriding sense of vexation tempered with exhaustion, but it had been a very long twenty-four hours for us all.

I was surprised when Dev redirected the question to me.

"N-no," I stuttered. "Why would I?"

Nicholas turned the tables. "Did *you* sense the presence of any other Nines?" When Dev shook his head, he added, "That doesn't mean there wasn't someone else there. We were all so focused on Francesca, it would have been easy to overlook another Nine if they'd hidden in the shadows."

Was that possible? Could Dev have missed the presence of another telekinetic? After all, there was no proof Nicholas had anything to do with Francesca's death—or was that explanation as convenient as the timely destruction of the tower?

Dev seemed to accept our denials and Nicholas's explanation at face value, and the conversation turned to more minor details. My mind began to lose the thread of what was being said, and my last conscious thought before drifting off was that my eyelids had somehow turned to lead.

The soft light of a winter's morning filtered through the windows and illuminated the empty sitting room. I was still on the sofa wearing the now hopelessly wrinkled cocktail dress, a warm blanket covering me from chin to toes.

I'd committed the cardinal sin—at least according to Scarlett—of falling asleep without washing off my makeup. Padding to the bathroom via the bedroom, I discovered the bed slept in but vacant. The bedside clock said it was only a few minutes past eight, but Nicholas was used to living on London time. He'd probably hit the first-class gym somewhere within the club or was conducting regent business someplace where he wouldn't wake me.

After a quick shower and a change of clothes, I strolled through the suite to find it still empty. As I considered going downstairs for coffee, my eyes fell on the big central table where Nicholas's laptop slumbered. Thanks to Dev, I knew the password. Access to The Nine's database was a few keystrokes away.

The right thing to do, of course, would be to tell Nicholas what I'd witnessed the day his father seized power and ask that we comb The Nine's archives together. We'd likely be searching for different things—me for evidence a Shadow voyant had been at the chancellor's challenge, he for proof that would clear his father's name—but that bothered me far less than the very real chance he might outright refuse me. I'd be no closer to helping my dad, not to mention the cloud it would cast over our relationship.

I took a seat in front of the computer, its silver case dull and unremarkable.

The chancellor had not only put my dad in an untenable position all those years ago, he'd broken their agreement. Then there was the recent spate of attacks on me. If yesterday's near miss with an SUV wasn't an accident, someone's vendetta against me had taken a giant leap forward. If this were happening to Henry Thorne, he wouldn't be sitting here with his hands in his lap.

With one ear trained toward the door, I opened the lid of the computer. What would Nicholas say if he walked in and found me using his credentials to access privileged information? My worries faded into the background as the computer woke, and I navigated to the database's homepage. The spaces for the user and password were already populated, a virtual invitation to take a peek. One click, and the names and personal information of every Nine would be at my fingertips.

Biting my lip until pain spurred me into action, I hit return.

A Convenient Death

My leg jiggled with nerves during the few minutes it took to get past two different firewalls protecting the trove of information on Shadow Nines, but Nicholas appeared to be a big believer in saving passwords in the cloud. I might lack the grit to be a spy, but he'd practically left the key in the door.

Once the outer defenses were breached, I found an archive of Shadow Nines divided by skill. There were thousands of names, but for once it was a blessing voyants were so rare. Only a few dozen people were grouped in alphabetical order under the rogue voyant heading.

Remembering what my dad said about the gender of the singular Shadow voyant of twenty years ago, I started clicking on the obviously male names. The first three profiles were for people who'd been born well before the twentieth century, though only one listed a date of death. The other two had certainly lived up to their moniker, disappearing at some point never to be seen again.

The first living voyant I came across was Bolin Foon of Hong Kong. His bio noted he hadn't come into his power until the age of thirteen—imagining a childhood free from torment caused unexpected jealousy to rise like bile in my throat—but at the current age of twenty-seven, he'd been just a child at the time of the challenge.

My petty emotions dissipated as I read the rest of his file. It had been almost ten years since he'd refused to pledge to The Nine, but you'd never know it from the way his whereabouts were tracked. The dates Foon had moved to and from Taiwan, then New York, and finally Adelaide, Australia, were noted along with his home address and place of work. Even creepier were the candid photos of the bespectacled boy who'd grown into a thin-faced, tight-lipped man. Each shot had been captured in a public place and apparently without the subject's knowledge. They gave credence to Honey's claim the Shadows were kept under watch.

A loud knock at the door made me jump so fast, the chair crashed to the floor. I slammed down the computer lid, righted the overturned seat, and took a few steps away as if that would proclaim my innocence.

"Who is it?" I called, my voice unnaturally high.

"Housekeeping."

I was lightheaded with relief. "Can you, uh, come back later?" There was no response, but the faint sound of a cart being pushed down the hall made my breath come easier.

Foon's file was still on screen when I reopened the computer, but he was obviously not our guy. I returned to the master list and clicked on the next male name: Otto Klein. His birth year was forty-three years ago, and he hailed from the German city of Cologne. He would have been a young man at the time of the challenge.

Scanning his short bio, I read of his ascension to Class One at the age of fifteen followed later by his refusal to pledge to The Nine at eighteen. Reports noted sightings in a handful of

European cities over the next few years. Curiously, the only picture in his file depicted an angry teenage boy with a mop of brown hair threatening to overpower a face ravaged by acne. Aware he was being photographed, he faced the camera with a contemptuous snarl, showcasing rows of teeth lurching in various directions like drunken pals staggering home after a night on the town.

The final sentence in his history explained the lack of further pictures or details. *Witnesses confirm Klein threw himself in front of an oncoming train in London's Waterloo station.* The words made my blood run cold. The date of his death was July 14, a little over twenty years ago.

Wild imaginings ping ponged around my brain, but before allowing anything to take root, I snatched up my phone and texted my dad. *What was the date of the chancellor's challenge?*

A key rattled in the suite's front door just as I hit send, but this time I didn't panic. Quickly exiting the database, I closed the laptop, and jumped up from my chair. When Nicholas entered with a cardboard tray holding two tall cups and several white paper bags, I turned from the window. Despite my racing heart, I greeted him with a welcoming smile.

"Good morning," he said, setting down his burden on the table. We both took seats as he parsed out the bags. "I didn't know if you wanted a blueberry scone, a banana nut muffin, or another croissant, so I got one of everything."

He grabbed a muffin while I bit into a still-warm scone with an appreciative sigh, but it didn't slow the whirring gears of my thoughts. Would he notice the tab for the database had been closed? What if access to the Shadow Nine section was tracked? If so, wouldn't it be better to come clean rather than wait for him to be questioned about his search activity?

"I heard from Detective Phillips this morning," he said, breaking into my internal debate. "She said the official report of the collapsed tower will mention the extensive termite damage it suffered throughout the years. There's even supporting documentation filed with the city on the dangers posed by the tower because it was scheduled for renovations next year." He brushed crumbs from his fingers before reaching for his phone. "She also sent me this."

He held up the phone so I could view the picture displayed on its screen. As soon as I realized what it was, I no longer had to hide my agitation.

"It was found on Francesca's body." He turned the phone back around to consider the image of a gold coin engraved with the image of a dagger—its handle topped with a crescent moon—plunging into the heart of a blazing sun. It was linked to the New Order, but where had the coin come from? If Francesca was a clandestine member of the New Order, why had she been acting the part of Henry Thorne's good soldier by taking out Silver? Or could the coin have been given to or planted on her by someone wanting to make it appear that way?

I took a sip of vanilla latte prepared exactly the way I liked before asking, "What do you think Francesca planned to do with it?"

He appeared startled by the question. "I don't think she planned to do anything with it. I believe it was left behind by her killer."

If that was the case, it would confirm he too believed the tower falling at the precise moment it had was no accident. Since he'd never gotten close enough to Francesca to plant the coin, something both Dev and I could confirm, was he suggesting the true killer had waited for us to flee before leaving the distinctive calling card? It would effectively erase any suspicion Nicholas had executed Francesca before she could reveal anything further about who'd sent her to kill Mr. Silver.

It was a perfectly reasonable explanation, so why did I continue to harbor doubts?

My phone chimed with a text, and I glanced at the screen. My swift intake of breath sharpened Nicholas's gaze.

"What is it?" he asked.

"Just some Scarlett drama," I said, waving away his concern. "No big deal."

His phone rang then, and he rose from the table to answer. Unless the call required notetaking, he tended to pace during phone conversations. I took the opportunity to read the text my dad had sent more carefully.

The challenge was on July 12, he wrote, in the same year Otto Klein had supposedly taken his own life. To put a fine point on it, a Class One Shadow voyant had conveniently ceased to exist two days after Henry Thorne became chancellor.

When the Unthinkable Becomes the Inevitable

Vaguely aware of Nicholas wearing a path in the carpet while deep into his phone conversation, I rose from the table and made for the bedroom. My thoughts skipped down a variety of paths, churning up a mess of conflicting emotions, and I wanted time alone to sort them out.

A Shadow voyant had almost certainly been in England the same day as the challenge for chancellor. At least one member of Henry's team, the enchanter Solenn, had been poised for the moment my father lost focus and Mitsuko was left unprotected. The Shadow voyant had died, supposedly by his own hand, shortly thereafter, removing any direct link between him and the new Thorne regime. It was all circumstantial at this point, but it was too damn convenient not to contain some kernel of truth.

I'd stumbled into dangerous territory. If Otto Klein and Mr. Silver had both died to protect Henry Thorne's secret, and my father had agreed to disappear in exchange for the life of the woman he loved, what might happen if I revealed what I knew to Nicholas? Last night's speech indicated his loyalties were solidly with The Nine, but did that also include protecting his father's legacy at all costs?

I sank into a thickly upholstery chair while sorting through more pieces of the puzzle. The harassment I'd endured since my father's call with the Prime seemed to be heating up. Did Henry fear my ability to ferret out old secrets? How did the New Order and the golden coin found on Francesca's body factor into all this? Who had been blackmailing her?

On impulse, I pulled up Julia Martin's name on my phone. The clever evanescent with a gift for invisibility had the run of Alder House. Maybe she'd be willing to part with a secret or two that would impose order on all the chaos. I considered what information she might have gleaned in her covert wanderings and carefully typed out a text.

Do you know about the gold coin found with Bailey Foster-Simms? If she didn't, at least my fishing expedition wouldn't reveal too much.

My phone chimed with a response as I folded yesterday's clothes into my suitcase. I'd be returning to Santa Carla in a few hours.

Yes, she replied, equally enigmatic.

You know there is more than one? I wrote back.

Yes. A text bubble revealed she had more to say, so I stared at the screen until her next message came through. *There are 28 in the chancellor's safe.*

That raised my brows. Twenty-eight dead Nines found with mysterious coins stretching back at least seven years, when Nicholas's mother had been murdered, yet it wasn't common knowledge within the society. Why was a key piece of evidence connecting all of the deaths being kept quiet? And what the hell was being done to figure out who was doing this?

My phone chimed with another text. *Don't tell me it's about to become 29.*

I stared out the bedroom window, unable to appreciate the sight of the snow-capped San Gabriel Mountains in the far distance. If there had been no other Nines in Little Tokyo last night, it would mean that not only had Nicholas lied about knocking over the tower and causing Francesca's death, but that the coin had been in her possession before she'd died.

I typed out my next question to Julia and stared at the words on the screen for a few moments. Once I sent it, there'd be no going back. Whatever the answer, I would be laying bare my suspicions—real or imagined—about who had ordered the killing of Mr. Silver, and who had silenced Francesca.

Can you check to see if all of the coins are still in the safe?
I hit send.

I jumped when my phone rang while it was still in my hand. Seeing Warren's name on the screen, unease rippled through me. If Warren had something to say, he texted. The only time he'd ever called was to ask for Scarlett's clothes and shoe sizes while standing in a boutique right before Christmas.

I skipped the usual greeting. "Everything okay?"

"I don't know," Warren slowly replied, upgrading my apprehension. "Scarlett was supposed to call me when she got home from handing off the rental house keys to that douchebag last night, but I fell asleep. When I woke up this morning, she still hadn't called, and all I'm getting is her voicemail. I'm at your apartment now. The car is gone, and she's not answering the door. Have you heard from her?"

"No," I answered, "but let me track her phone."

"I already did," he said before I could open the app that would reveal her location. "Her phone is either off or dead."

Dread clawed at my chest. Why hadn't I warned her about the Nines toying with me from the shadows? The answer came as swiftly as the accompanying stab of guilt. I'd kept it from her because I was afraid it would drive another wedge between us.

Trying to keep panic at bay, I thought for a moment. "The car! We can track the location of the car." After the electrical circuits on the old Volvo Scarlett and I shared had been fried by a murderous evanescent, The Nine had gifted us with a Tesla. The accompanying app served not only as the car key but as a way to track mileage, charge status—and the vehicle's location.

I read off an address somewhere in Santa Carla.

"I'm going there now," he said.

"I'm coming home." I rushed to the bathroom to throw my lotions and potions into a bag.

"Okay, I'll call you when I get to the address," he promised before ringing off.

I called Marie and explained the urgency of my situation.

"I'll be there in fifteen minutes, hon," she said. "Meet me out front."

Bursting out of the bedroom, I found Nicholas, Dev, and Marcel seated at the dining table. From their sober expressions, Khalia's half-brother was in the process of being beaten down a peg or two. Nicholas half rose from his chair when he glimpsed the fear etched on my face.

"What's happened?" he asked.

"We can't find Scarlett." The words made the unfathomable real. "She went to go meet the guy she's been working for last night, and no one's heard from her since. I have to go."

He squinted at me in confusion. "I thought you were texting with her a few minutes ago."

I was thrown for a moment, but part of concealing who I was for most of my life had made me an accomplished liar. It wasn't something to boast about, but neither could I deny it had helped me survive.

"It was Warren asking for advice," I said.

He left the table. "I'm coming with you."

"What about everything else?"

"Dev can handle it."

Marcel rose from his seat. "Please allow me to accompany you, Regent." The cocky young sentinel was gone, at least for the moment, replaced by a humbler version uncertain of his welcome. "If you still feel the need to replace me when we return, I understand, but please let me prove I'm up to the job."

Nicholas looked to Dev, who weighed in with a reluctant nod. "Only because we don't have time to vet anyone else. But Pryce," he said, turning a frosty glare on the sentinel, "if anything should go sideways even a little, no one outside of a dive bar in the deepest backwater will ever hire you. I'll make sure it."

"Yes, sir," Marcel meekly agreed.

Trusting another to protect his best friend must be hard for Dev, but he had his hands full dealing with the fallout of the deaths of two Nines, the sidelining of one deputy, and the imminent arrival of her replacement. Greta had been tended by a healing evanescent, but she would need a few days of rest to ward off the pneumonia that often followed a near-drowning.

I was so anxious to get home we were downstairs in the atrium with time to spare. Nicholas and Dev had their heads together a short distance away while Marcel scowled at anyone who glanced their way. If I wasn't so keyed up about Scarlett, I would have found his new attack dog attitude entertaining.

Honey floated into the room wearing a chest-baring gold brocade smoking jacket and black cigarette pants. Gucci loafers studded with bees and stars whispered on the tile floor as they made their way over to me.

"Marie tells me there's trouble afoot in Santa Carla," they said.

"When is there not?" I wrapped my arms tightly around my body as if I were in danger of flying apart.

Honey moved closer and spoke quietly in my ear. "You may *see* what people have done or intend to do, but I *hear* the choices they make that takes them there. The one thing I know is everyone has an agenda, and they can rationalize almost any violation or sacrifice if it will get them closer to achieving their ultimate goal."

Their words unnerved me. "What are you saying?"

"I'm saying each person, even those you may love and trust, has a price where the once unthinkable becomes inevitable. Those who survive learn to recognize the signs and proceed with caution."

I pulled back slightly, jolted at the pronouncement. What had the telepath overheard to prompt such a warning? More importantly, who was the source?

The front door banged open, and I jerked around. Marie had arrived. When I turned back, Honey was gone.

All In

We were on our way to Santa Carla with Marcel riding shotgun when Warren called again. I lunged for the phone.

"Did you find her?" Fear made my question come out sharper than intended.

"No," he said, a catch in his voice. "I knocked on all the doors on the street where the car's parked, but either no one was home or the people who were said they hadn't seen her."

I put the phone on speaker. "We're on our way. Nicholas is coming with me."

"Is it time to call the police?" Warren wondered.

"I've been targeted by a materialist and an enchanter in the last week," I said, not meeting my boyfriend's startled gaze. "I'm worried they went for Scarlett when they couldn't find me, and maybe they did, but I also had at least one near miss in LA yesterday when a car almost mowed me down." We still didn't know who had been the target of the out-of-bounds Palmarium ball.

"Wouldn't somebody at least call you if they were trying to use her to get at you?" Warren asked.

"Unless keeping me off balance is part of the fun. What do you know about the guy she's been working for?"

"I don't even know his name," he said helplessly. "We've just been calling him the douchebag."

"How did she get the job?" Nicholas spoke up for the first time.

"Through a temp agency," Warren replied, "but I couldn't tell you which one."

"The cops won't take us seriously until Scarlett's been missing for at least twenty-four hours." I knew that from my steady diet of *Law & Order* shows. "But we need more help than just the three of us. I'll meet you at The Lower 8 in an hour."

I rang off and immediately hit Jessie's name on my favorites list.

"Who are you calling?" Nicholas asked at the same moment Jessie answered, the sound of his voice bringing all of my raw emotions to the surface.

"My roommate is missing," I said, swallowing back tears.

"How can I help?" he asked without hesitation.

"Can you ask Harper if she knows anything about the Nines who seem to hold a grudge against me?"

"Hang on." The one-sided conversation that followed was muted, as if he held the phone against his chest. I glanced at Nicholas to find him staring out the window as the car hopped on the northbound 101 freeway. It was midmorning on a Sunday, so traffic was light.

He came back on the line. "She wasn't there when the enchanter possessed your classmate, but she saw the materialist. She says it's a man with brown hair, and he drove away in a silver car." He cleared his throat before reluctantly adding, "She says he was a, uh, bit of a snack."

"Please tell Harper thank you for me, and that we're meeting Scarlett's boyfriend at your club in about an hour if she wants to hang out with me again." I regretted the jealousy that had caused me to sideline the teen spirit. "I hope you don't mind, but I'm hoping Suki or Layla might have seen something that could help."

"I don't mind in the least," he assured me.

We ended the call, and I took a deep breath to calm my rattled nerves. The idea of Scarlett breaking even a fingernail due to someone's vendetta against me churned up both panic and rage. Resentment also entered the fray, but it wasn't mine.

"Are you angry I didn't tell you what's been going on?" I quietly asked Nicholas, not wanting to include Marie and Marcel in our conversation.

He turned from the window. "What else does McCabe know that you haven't bothered to tell me?"

"I tried to tell you yesterday," I said evenly.

His jealousy faded into sadness. "How is this supposed to work if we're always six thousand miles apart?"

We could probably string our relationship along for a while longer until one of us finally admitted the physical distance between us was too great an obstacle to overcome, or I could do something about it. The choice would have to be mine, a situation I found both comforting and unsettling. I wanted power and control over my destiny, but that also meant taking responsibility for my decisions.

I'd spent a lifetime witnessing all the ways people screwed up their relationships—infidelity was by far the most popular, but right behind that came neglect, selfishness, jealousy, envy, the list went on. Had those painful lessons in love made me too scared to let anyone in? Would the need to examine the motives behind Nicholas's every thought and deed be so strong if I could view romance through the lens of any other eighteen-year-old girl?

Maybe moving to Alder House was the answer to everything. Scarlett would certainly be safer without me around once she came home—I refused to accept any other outcome—and I would have a fleet of sentinels protecting me from vindictive Nines. Nicholas and I would finally have time to dive beneath the surface of our long-distance relationship, and without Jessie haunting my dreams, maybe I could finally risk opening up my heart. The idea of living my life closed off to the possibility of love frightened me, perhaps even more so than the pain of a broken heart.

Then an inner voice I almost didn't dare admit was mine weighed in. *What better way to topple a king than from inside his own castle?*

Alder House was the one place Henry Thorne might relax his guard. I didn't expect to break into his office and find a folder labeled, "How I murdered Mitsuko Hayashi and screwed over Luke Wilder," but Henry hadn't acted alone. Unless he'd murdered every one of his accomplices, there were others who knew what he'd done. The key to finding them and exposing the truth might be found at Alder House.

Putting aside misgivings of how Nicholas might react if he learned of my intention to bring his father to justice in order to protect mine, I swung out onto the highwire with no net to catch me if I fell.

I caught his hand in mine and squeezed. "I'll move to Alder House."

On the Grid

The Lower 8 wouldn't open for several hours, but Gustav, the house materialist, had almost completed the task of transforming the club into the deck of a Spanish galleon. Raised platforms at the bow and aft hosted the bar and dance floor, and a starlit sky completed the illusion we were at sea on some balmy, windless night.

Layla was on the foredeck cutting fruit for drink garnishes while Ricardo loaded beers into a cooler disguised as a weapons locker. Suki lounged at a table in front of the ship's wheel scrolling on her phone. Across from her, Warren sat hunched over, his arms folded protectively against his body as if that could ward off the terror flirting around the edges of his psyche. They all looked up expectantly as the four of us entered, Marie having volunteered to help in any way she could.

"Oh my," the phantomist said, craning her neck to take in the canvas sails high overhead. "I'd heard this place was something else, but man, it's like we've gone through a time machine."

The diminutive head waitress trotted down the stairs to the main deck. She wore jeans and a tee-shirt knotted at the waist, which would soon be replaced with a costume corresponding to the night's theme before the doors opened.

"It's Adventure on the High Seas night," she politely informed our driver before her dark eyes, warm with sympathy, landed on me. "How are you doing, Blake?"

I shrugged, since tearing out my hair and shrieking until my throat burned would do nothing to help my best friend. I wasn't the one, however, who'd harbored feelings for Akim Silver. When he'd been in Santa Carla last month, Layla had confessed her hope he might return those feelings. It hadn't gone well.

I placed a comforting hand on her shoulder. "How are you?"

Her eyes glazed with tears. "I was angry at him, you know? He said he couldn't be in a relationship while he was Prime, especially when there were only two years left in his term. Why would anyone postpone happiness?"

"Oh Layla." We hugged for a moment, both of us sniffling, until she pulled back and dabbed at her face.

"We'll have tons of time to talk about the stupidity of men," she said with a shaky laugh, "but first, what's going on with your friend?"

"At least one Nine might be behind Scarlett's disappearance, maybe more. I'm hoping if we go over everything that's happened in the last week, you might be able to fill in the missing piece that can help us find her."

Ricardo closed the cooler and rubbed a hand over his bald pate. "If a Nine has taken your friend to punish you, then we have sunk deeper into the morass than I feared."

The club's bouncer was generally a man of few words, and I looked at him curiously. "What do you mean?"

"For centuries it has been understood we do not involve outsiders in our business." He picked up four chairs—two in each meaty hand—on his way to Suki and Warren's table. "That custom was violated last month by the evanescent who murdered the innocent woman outside the club. Now it's happening again."

"Scarlett is not dead," I insisted, my voice rising along with my anxiety.

"Of course not," the bouncer backtracked. "But as those in the New Order chip away at the foundation of who we are, how far will we allow them to push us before we push back?" His words made me think of Francesca, and I wondered if Ricardo would also have regarded Nicholas's pre-game speech as building castles in the air.

By silent agreement, everyone but Gustav pulled a chair into a loose arrangement around the table. The house materialist ignored us in favor of making small adjustments to his artistic design.

"Good to see you, Nicholas," Layla said, settling next to him. I wondered what she made of the contentment zinging through his veins that wasn't quite masked by his concern for Scarlett. I couldn't fault him for being delighted at my announcement about moving to Alder House because the ill-fated timing had been mine, so I did my best to shake it off.

I gestured to the phantomist. "This is Marie Landry."

"Class Two phantomist," she added. Everyone else was acquainted, so we made quick work of going around the table introducing the group to Marie.

"Warren Hartman, Scarlett's boyfriend, Class Three elementalist," he murmured when it was his turn, a reminder to everyone that whoever had taken her had trespassed against more than one Nine.

Jessie and Amani arrived just as I brought out my phone with a picture of Scarlett, but rather than drag over more chairs, they remained standing with hands entwined, their backs against the ship's wheel.

"I'm sorry to hear about your friend, Blake," Amani volunteered. She came across as sincere, but the side-eye Layla cast her way let me know I wasn't the only one who found the barrier she'd somehow erected around her emotions both mystifying and frustrating. I mumbled my thanks as we got down to business.

"This is Scarlett Sloan." I passed around my phone, the picture of the two of us dressed up for New Year's Eve. Warren and Scarlett had invited me to a party hosted by one of his friends.

"About a week ago, she took a temp job assisting a businessman who's new to the area, or at least that's how he presented himself. We don't yet know the name of the temp agency who connected them, but I don't think Scarlett communicated with him by any means other than text or email."

"She didn't," Warren confirmed.

"Then are you sure it's a man?" Layla sagely inquired.

"No," I admitted, "but since that's how Scarlett referred to him, let's go with it for now."

I went on to describe the man's changeable nature, though now I wondered if his unpredictability had been intentional. Instead of being cautious about meeting someone she didn't know, Scarlett had chalked up the task of letting him into his latest dwelling as yet another example of his capricious behavior.

"Soon after she started working for this guy, I was harassed at work first by a materialist and then an enchanter."

"What makes you think these things are connected to your friend's disappearance?" Amani asked with a frown.

"What makes you think they're not?" I challenged, probably overreacting to her perfectly reasonable question. "Was the out of bounds Palmarium ball that could have killed me Friday night an accident? What about the car that almost ran me over yesterday?"

"Your near miss with a car is news to me, but don't you think you would have heard from this kidnapper if your friend was taken to get back at you?" Her voice was shaded with skepticism.

I slammed my hands on the table at the same moment several nearby chairs toppled, my telekinesis choosing the most awkward moment to slip its leash. "How am I supposed to know what goes on in the mind of some psycho?"

Jessie eyed the overturned chairs with some speculation before straightening up from his slouch. "I know tensions are running high, but let's remember we're all on the same side here."

Amani pulled her phone out and turned away from us both, but not before I caught sight of the anger tightening her jaw.

"We do have a general description of the materialist," Nicholas said, getting the discussion back on track. "One of McCabe's spirits saw what happened, and said it was a brown-haired man who drove a silver car."

"That describes a half dozen of the materialists who've come here in the past week," Suki chimed in.

"What about any unfamiliar enchanters?" Nicholas asked.

Suki shrugged. "None that I know of."

"What about you?" Marie asked Amani. "There's a young spirit named Harper here who says you're an enchanter who just showed up a few weeks ago."

Amani was visibly startled. "Well yes, but I'm here for a job. I only just met Blake, and I don't know anything about her friend."

"Harper's still adjusting to having Amani around," Jessie said, leaping to his girlfriend's defense. His eyes narrowed on a spot a few feet from the table. "The time has come for that long overdue chat, Harper."

Marie pursed her lips, as if she harbored doubts Harper's point should be dismissed so easily. Could Amani have been the enchanter who messed with me? I'd assumed the two incidents at work were connected, but what if two people with separate agendas just happened to play dirty tricks on me within days of each other? My classmate had been assaulted the day after Jessie introduced us, so maybe Amani was petty as well as insecure.

"I assume your friend has a computer?" Suki said, cutting into the prickly moment. "Has anyone looked at her texts or emails?"

Warren shook his head. "I don't have a key to the apartment."

"We drove right here from To The Nines, but I'll check as soon as I get home." I'd borrowed her laptop a few months ago when my ancient one had finally died. I could only hope she hadn't changed the password.

"Did you try tracking her phone?" Amani asked. I wondered if her patronizing tone was all in my mind.

"It was the first thing we did." I did my best to give a measured response to her basic question, but the smirk on Layla's face said I hadn't quite succeeded.

"I'll be damned," Warren said a moment later. He held up his phone, his face alight with hope. "Scarlett is back on the grid."

Try Not to Kill Us

"Where is she?" I jabbed Scarlett's name on my favorites list. Once again, the call went straight to voicemail.

Warren chewed his lip in puzzlement as he stared at his phone. "It says she's in the car."

Nicholas pushed out his chair. "Let's go."

Everyone else stood as well, but Ricardo, Layla, and Suki made no move to follow. They, of course, had to get the club readied for the coming evening, but Jessie took a step in my direction. Amani latched onto his wrist.

"I'm sure they can handle picking up a girl who probably just woke up from a wild night out," she said.

Warren whipped around to give her a hard stare, and a stack of napkins on a nearby table burst into flame. It seemed I wasn't the only one whose talents were barely under control. Jessie shook off his girlfriend's grip and lunged for a nearby a pitcher of water, putting the fire out.

"Keep me informed," he said grimly as the rest of us hurried out to our cars.

Not for a second did I think Scarlett had willingly dropped out of sight without a word to me or Warren, and my entire body clenched at the thought of what she might have endured during those missing hours. For the entire fifteen-minute drive—which Marie accomplished in ten—I concentrated on the dot on my phone screen signaling her location. Having witnessed thousands of ways people were capable of inflicting pain on each other, it was the only way to keep my imagination from spiraling out of control.

Marie slowed as we entered a neighborhood of pleasant streets, wide sidewalks, and well-kept, single family homes. Here and there was a forgotten trike or the occasional basketball hoop, but the chilly afternoon kept most of the residents inside.

We spied the white Tesla Scarlett and I shared parked at a curb midway down the block. The moment Marie came to a stop, both Warren and I jumped out and peered through the vehicle's windows. Except for a cardboard Jitters' cup in the center divider and a hoodie abandoned on the floor, there was no sign of Scarlett or her phone. Warren and I locked frightened gazes over the roof.

Nicholas came to stand next to me as we gathered at the back of the car. The foreboding pumping through his veins drained me of hope.

I swallowed hard, unable to stop the tears. "She can't be in there, can she?"

Warren dragged a sleeve across his own welling eyes. "Her phone says she is."

"Why don't you go wait with the others while I open the trunk?" Nicholas asked. Marie and Marcel had kept a respectful distance.

Turning my back to the car, I glanced at Warren, who also turned away. He nodded. Using the app on my phone, I pressed the icon that opened every lock on the car. Nicholas moved to lift the lid of the trunk while I buried my face in my hands. The trunk opened with a whisper. Nicholas breathed out.

"She's not in there." He pulled me against his chest as I trembled with such relief my teeth chattered.

"Who would do this?" Warren asked. I turned to see Scarlett's cell discarded on the trunk's carpeted floor, the bright rainbow colors of her phone's protective case unmistakable. "They had to have turned on her phone, dumped it, and then left it for us to find. Why?"

"Somebody's playing games," Nicholas said flatly. "And my guess is they're not done."

What was happening to Scarlett in the meantime? She must be so scared, but was she also hurt, in pain? Was she being punished by proxy for whatever my perceived crimes were?

"I'm going home." I pocketed her phone and moved to the driver's side door. "Since we don't know for sure a Nine is behind this, I think it's time to call the police."

"Do you want me to drive?" Nicholas asked.

I glanced up at him in surprise. "Don't you need to get back to Alder House?"

Resting his hands on my shoulders, he gazed at me with compassion. "Do you think I'd leave you like this? I'll send Marie back to LA, and Marcel and I will take a taxi to the airport when Scarlett is back."

I appreciated his use of *when* rather than *if*.

Marie's lips flattened into a straight line when we told her she should return to Los Angeles. "I've only known you folks for a few days, but it seems to me you need all the friends you can get. To The Nines can do without me for a bit longer."

Impulsively, I hugged her, and she patted my back as if she were comforting a child.

"Keep the faith," she whispered in my ear. "Madame Boudreaux is a very powerful spirit, and she says your friend is still among the living."

I pulled back and stared at her, but she met my gaze un-flinchingly. She believed in Madame Sally, and I desperately wanted to as well. Shards of hope pushed me to the edge of shattering all over again, but I could almost hear Scarlett's voice in my ear telling me to stay in character, there'd be plenty of time to fall apart later.

"Thank you," I said, meaning it more than I ever had in my life.

I took the Tesla's front passenger seat as Nicholas slipped behind the wheel. Warren hopped in Marie's car to navigate the drive back to our apartment, while Marcel, ever mindful of Dev's directive, jumped in the Tesla with us.

The route home took us onto Adolfo Street, the main artery connecting the town's richest neighborhoods to the shabbier ones like Rosewood Gardens, where I lived. Two lanes in each direction were divided by a median bursting with greenery Scarlett predicted would bloom into a riot of pink and purple come spring. Lost in that memory, it took a few seconds to register the liquid sloshing over my feet from several inches of water on the floor of the car.

"Pull over!" Marcel yelped before I could react.

The water rose another three inches before Nicholas could escape traffic and yank the car into the narrow bike line running alongside the road. I pressed the release button on the door, but it refused to open.

"I can't open the door." I jabbed the controls with increasing alarm.

"The windows aren't working either," Marcel said, fear undercutting his words.

"Don't worry," Nicholas said, remaining calm. "There's a manual release on both front doors." He reached for the lever in front of the window controls, but it didn't budge. I tried to wedge my fingers under the lever on my door with the same results.

"Why isn't it opening?" I exclaimed.

"The release lever has been glued shut, and I'm guessing the door's mechanisms have likewise been frozen somehow." Nicholas was no longer quite so relaxed. He flicked his fingers to open the doors telekinetically, but nothing moved.

Water had risen to my knees. I tried not to panic, but in another few minutes water would completely fill the cabin. Death by drowning in the middle of a busy street was bizarre even by The Nine's standards.

Nicholas turned to Marcel. "Where is he? Where's the Nine who's doing this?"

Marcel craned his neck in all directions before his gaze locked on something behind us. "There's a Nine in a silver Mazda about two hundred feet behind us." The car in question had also pulled to the side of the road a fair distance away, the emergency flashers keeping time with the thrum of my heart. Tinted windows made it impossible to see the driver.

"Can't you block them?" Nicholas questioned tersely.

"He's too far away," the sentinel said. "From this distance I can only keep someone from using their power directly on you, Regent, but I can't stop an elementalist from filling a container that you—or us—happen to be in."

I unbuckled and turned to face the door. Lifting my sodden feet, I kicked at the passenger window several times, but the glass didn't even crack. Marcel picked up the idea and tried it on one of the back windows but with similarly dismal results. I shivered as the water level rose to my waist, but it wasn't from its cold temperature.

Nicholas released his seatbelt and glared out the rear window. "Let's break his concentration, shall we?"

Holding out his arm with his fingers splayed, he waited for a break in traffic before twisting his hand as if turning a dial. The Mazda flipped, coming to rest on its roof.

Nicholas swore as the water kept rising, reaching the level of my chest.

Cars slowed to avoid the overturned vehicle and a few pulled over, but we didn't have time for some good Samaritan to notice our bizarre predicament and fetch a tool to break a window.

"There's got to be something nearby we can use to shatter the glass," Nicholas said.

We peered out the windows at the surrounding landscape of dirt, trees, cars, and shrubs while Marcel pounded against one of the side windows, yelling to get the attention of passing cars.

My eyes landed on a construction vehicle creeping along on the other side of the median. Traffic had slowed in both directions as looky-loos gawked at the overturned sedan.

"There!" Water splashed my chin as I pointed to the truck loaded with metal pipes coming towards us in one of the opposite lanes. I turned to Nicholas. "Have you ever seen that horror movie with the logging truck?"

His mouth thinned with determination as my words clicked.

"Come to this side," he said to me before barking, "Marcel! Press yourself as hard against the window behind me as you can!" The sentinel didn't need to be told twice. He plastered himself to the side of the car while I maneuvered to sit across Nicholas's legs with my back against the driver's side door.

"Try not to kill us," I joked weakly.

He gave me a quick kiss before tucking my head against his shoulder. "I'll do my best."

Training his gaze out the window, he growled as if lifting a heavy weight. A second or two later, a silver metal pipe speared the windshield and impaled the front passenger seat where I'd sat moments before. The window spidered into a million cracks before giving way, and a deluge poured over the hood of the car.

A handful of drivers stared at us in shock, including the bearded driver of the construction truck. Who knew how much they'd seen of the pipe flying through the air and skewering our windshield, or what they thought of a car overflowing with water. All that mattered was we were alive, and there was no longer any doubt that at least one Nine wanted me dead.

30

Fish on a Hook

Maybe if we had more than five minutes to concoct a cover story explaining how the interior of our car had flooded on a perfectly dry afternoon we could come up with something convincing, but as it was, Nicholas, Marcel, and I crawled over the dashboard and slid off the hood with no idea how to talk our way out of our present predicament. Nicholas had the foresight to stash the metal pipe in the gutter to hopefully eliminate that particular line of questioning.

A couple of concerned citizens rushed over to where we stood dripping on the sidewalk.

"Everyone okay?" asked an older woman dressed in her Sunday best, from a wide brimmed hat to a skirt suit, all in a bright shade of purple.

A younger man pulled off his sweat-stained ballcap and scratched his balding pate. "How on earth did y'all get so wet?"

As Nicholas and I assured our would-be rescuers we were fine and that a little water never hurt anyone, Marcel jogged off in the direction of the silver car, his leather shoes squelching as he went. Several people had gathered around the overturned vehicle, blocking it from view.

My mind flashed on Detective Navarro in the homicide division of the local police department. She and I had recently tangled when Jessie had been hauled up on murder charges, and I could only imagine what she'd do if she came across my name in yet another police report—the first two being when a Nine had broken into my apartment followed by me being a witness to a construction "accident" where I'd been the intended target. If we continued to cross paths, I'd have to add her to my Christmas list.

Nicholas pulled out his waterlogged phone, expelling a relieved breath when the screen lit up. As he put in a call to Dev, I too checked my phone for service. It appeared unharmed—the ads claiming the latest smart phone models were water resistant appeared to be true—though nothing had come through from Scarlett, or the person who had taken her. I quickly shot off a text telling Warren and Marie of our situation.

"Dev is sending enchanters to deal with the authorities," Nicholas said, ending the call as a large firetruck arrived on the scene. "Say as little as possible. It'll make it easier to remove their memories later."

"What do we say about Scarlett?" I'd resolved to call the police as soon as we reached my apartment, but now I wasn't so sure. A Nine had just tried to kill us, and I didn't want well-intentioned detectives trying to sideline me while they pursued a kidnapper with abilities they didn't understand.

Nicholas echoed my sentiments. "The police can't help. If a Nine has her, which is all but certain, they'll just get in the way."

Marcel hustled over to rejoin us. "The driver of the Mazda took off, but a witness said it was a woman. Dark hair, jeans, a baggy sweatshirt, and a baseball hat."

There was no opportunity for further discussion because two EMTs loaded with gear trundled over. After they declared us uninjured and handed out metallic space blankets, a couple of police officers took over.

"Who's the owner of the car?" asked an apple-cheeked young cop with strawberry blonde hair razed into a buzzcut. A silver metal nametag identified him as Officer B. Novak, and he was so clean and pressed, I wondered if he ever cut himself on the sharp creases of his pants.

"It's a company car," Nicholas volunteered, and I realized no paperwork had ever arrived declaring it mine. Perhaps Detective Navarro wouldn't hear about this after all.

"I was driving it," he added.

"Would you unlock the doors, sir?" The command phrased as a question came from the other officer, an older Black woman with her lips pursed in a seen-it-all attitude, which only became more pronounced when Nicholas told her the locks had frozen. Her nametag said she was Sergeant C. Lewis.

The sergeant directed her partner to call a pair of tow trucks—a flatbed for the Tesla and a hitch for the overturned sedan. He jumped to do her bidding, making me think no one wanted to see what happened when her expression soured more than it already had.

Water pooled inside the car to the level of the shattered window, and Sergeant Lewis eyed it suspiciously. "Is this a college prank or something?" She gave Marcel, who was in his early twenties, a serious once over. "Aren't you old enough to know better?"

"Yes, ma'am," he said noncommittally while Nicholas and I remained silent. Her brows beetled as she took in the still-vivid bruise on his face, making the woman come across as even more intimidating.

"Break out the IDs," she commanded.

We remained huddled by the side of the road as night fell, occasionally stamping the feeling back into our sodden feet, while she retreated to her squad car to run our names through their database. Officer Novak took our statements, which consisted mostly of "I don't know" and "I didn't see it." Fortunately for us, he didn't press further.

The Tesla was in the process of being loaded into a trailer when the sergeant finally returned with our IDs and a ticket she presented to Nicholas, citing him for reckless driving.

"I could find more ways to jam you up, but since it looks like you've destroyed a very expensive car, I'm guessing you've got problems enough." She likely imagined an irate parent waiting for him at home. "Of course, once we take a look at how your car's locks were disabled, there may be additional charges."

Not once the enchanters arrived, I thought.

"Thank you," Nicholas said, ever the politician.

Marie texted to let us know she waited for us on a nearby side street, so we trooped off to find her. She had the heat on full blast when at last we gratefully slipped into the backseat of her car.

"You are a lifesaver, Marie," I groaned, slumping against the soft leather. I was cold, wet, and shaken to my core, but it could be a million times worse. I was alive, and no one held me against my will.

Hang on, Scarlett. We're coming.

Warren happened to have a pair of sweats in one of Scarlett's drawers, and a gym bag with clean workout gear in his trunk. Along with a couple of my oversized sleep tees—Nicholas grabbed the one that said *Reading Is Sexy* while Marcel got stuck with a giant picture of Tweedy Bird on his chest—they had enough apparel to exchange their wet clothes for dry, even if the results did leave them looking like thrift store refugees.

The chill had sunk into my bones, so after a hot shower I nestled against Nicholas on one end of our sofa while Warren sat at the other. Scarlett's laptop rested on his knees as he tried various combinations of words and numbers that were significant to her, the password having changed since I'd last logged on. It was our best hope at tracking down the name of the temp agency or finding contact information for the man who'd hired her, since her older model phone hadn't weathered the flooded Tesla as well as mine. Her fried cell now rested inside a bag of rice we kept solely for that purpose. Scarlett had a habit of losing an earbud while leaning over a sink of dishwater, or even once while washing her face and listening to an audiobook at the same time.

The wrath in Marie's eyes flared as I described how quickly the Tesla had filled with water, and that someone must have tampered with the windows and door locks to prevent our escape.

"The driver of the silver car, a woman, must have been an elementalist, so now I've got three Nines who have it in for me." I felt heavy with exhaustion and confusion. Who were these people popping up like weeds?

Marie quirked a brow. "Not necessarily. I wish we'd been there when it happened, but as soon as we got your text, Madame Sally doubled back. She said there was a Nine wearing a hoodie and mingling with the folks who'd gathered to watch. It was a man, and she thinks he was a materialist."

"A materialist?" I repeated. "Could a materialist have filled the car with water like that?"

Nicholas nodded. "They can conjure almost anything inanimate from the material world, including water."

"Kind of clever, if that's the case," Marcel weighed in. "Using a power associated with an elementalist to throw us off the scent."

"That explains why his focus wasn't interrupted when the car flipped," I mused. "He wasn't in it."

"His ruse may have saved our lives," Nicholas added. "A powerful elementalist could have filled the car within seconds."

A fresh wave of apprehension shot through me at how quickly we could have died if the materialist had chosen a more effective weapon, but maybe that hadn't been his intent. Come to think of it, he'd been playing me like a fish on a hook, enjoying the game of reeling me in. I'd been on the defensive, but what would he do if I started throwing some curve balls of my own?

"We need to find out who owns that Mazda," I said. "Maybe then we can track down the woman behind the wheel."

"I took a picture of the license plate and sent it to the acting Prime," Marcel informed us.

"It may take a few hours to get an answer," Nicholas cautioned. The Nine were far-reaching, but even they might need a minute to rouse a hacker on a Sunday night who could break into the California DMV's database without leaving a trail.

"Do you mind if we get some dinner in the meantime?" the sentinel suggested.

I didn't think I could possibly eat after what we'd just endured, but my empty stomach ignored me and rumbled at the idea of a meal. Nicholas pulled up a food delivery app on his phone and got to work.

"I'll be right back." There was a question that needed answering, but it would be better asked in private. I padded to my bedroom and closed the door. Sitting cross-legged on my bed, I called Jessie.

"Hey, darlin'." He sounded tired, but his use of the old endearment gave my spirits a boost. "I hope you're calling to tell me Scarlett is back, safe and sound."

Tears unexpectedly welled at the warmth and concern in his voice. Why did I feel the need to be strong and resilient in front of Nicholas, but one kind word from Jessie left me ready to share every fear and doubt that had ever crossed my mind?

"No," I sniffled, spilling the tale of my latest encounter with a Nine who'd made it clear his campaign of terror would end only with my eventual demise. As I spoke, the background music of the club devolved into pots and pans banging out meals, tracking his retreat from the main floor to the kitchen. Except for the squeak of his desk chair as he took a seat, all was quiet when he reached his office.

"This has gone way beyond some petty vendetta," he said when I finished my story, his voice crisp with anger. "Where is the acting Prime or one of his deputies? What is Thorne doing to keep you safe? You should be laying low while the rest of us find your friend. You're welcome to stay at my place while we track down these people."

As tempting as his offer was, I couldn't leave the search for Scarlett to others. If our positions were reversed, she'd scorch the earth to find me, and I could do no less for her. He had, however, given me the opening I needed.

"Amani would love that," I said with a healthy dose of sarcasm.

"Maybe she won't care." He exhaled a deep breath. "We had some words after you left, and we haven't spoken since."

My fingers tightened around the phone at his response. If Amani hadn't been with Jessie, could she have been the darkhaired woman behind the wheel of the silver car? I had zero evidence and even less justification to suspect her, and it wasn't like I had any right to object to her relationship with Jessie, but I couldn't help disliking her. It didn't matter why, I told myself.

"Taking relationship advice from me would be like jumping into a taxi driven by a toddler," I said, "but I have learned one thing. We all make mistakes. It's what you do afterwards that matters most."

"You think I should call her?" he asked with such hope you'd think he needed my permission.

Mustering every ounce of selflessness I possessed, I said, "Yes, Jessie. If you care about Amani, go make it right."

"Thanks. I will," he said quickly and hung up.

I stared at my phone another minute, debating the consequences of my next call but knowing there really wasn't much choice. I clicked on a name on my favorites list, and my father picked up.

"You make it home in one piece?" he said, not bothering with hello.

"More or less." News of Scarlett's disappearance would probably send him into a full-blown panic attack, but he had once been the Prime and would understand what I was up against. Now I had the added weight of potentially hurting Jessie.

"Dad, Scarlett's missing, and it's possible an enchanter named Amani Falah is involved."

Princes and Legends

Nicholas had ordered one of everything from a local Indian restaurant, or at least it looked that way from the number of containers covering much of the kitchen counter. The scent of curry and other spices made my mouth water, but how could I eat when Scarlett might be going hungry?

Marie rested her hand on my shoulder. "Your friend lives. Eat. You won't be doing her any favors by starving yourself."

"Are you also a telepath?" I asked, startled at how easily she'd read my mind.

She thrust a plate into my hands. "No, just a good judge of character."

Tucking into the various stews, rice, and naan with determination, I realized I hadn't eaten since Warren had called that morning with the news that had made me forget everything else. Even now, between bites of chicken curry, he tapped away at Scarlett's computer trying to get past the lock screen. It made me think of Dev doing the same on Nicholas's laptop the previous night.

"Have you tried your name and birthday?" I met my boyfriend's knowing gaze.

Warren nodded. "Hers and mine in various combinations."

"What's your birthday?"

"August 2nd."

"Try WarrenAugust2," I suggested.

He shrugged and typed, then his eyes widened as they met mine. "We're in."

Within a few minutes he had the name of the temp agency who'd engaged Scarlett. Putting his phone on speaker, he dialed their number. It rang three or four times before predictably going to voice mail. Warren ended the call without leaving a message.

Diving back into Scarlett's emails, he soon had the name of the man—Max Amleth—who'd employed her, but it was probably as fake as my occasional spray tan. This was seemingly confirmed when Warren plugged the name into a search engine.

"Maybe he's a real guy," he said, his statement coming across almost as a question, "but the first thing that comes up is a Scandinavian legend about a Prince Amleth who seems to have inspired Shakespeare to write the character of Hamlet."

"*That's* why she thought he was Scandinavian," I said, recalling one of our last conversations. Of course Scarlett would know the origins of Hamlet.

"Why Hamlet?" Marcel asked. "Or this prince guy?"

"Hamlet seeks revenge against his uncle, who killed his father and then married his mother," Nicholas explained. Leave it to him to have read or seen the play, or likely both.

Marie made a dismissive noise. "This talk of vengeance is absurd. It's not like Blake killed anybody." The room went silent long enough for the phantomist to turn to me with an expression of disbelief. "Have you?"

"Not on purpose," I said defensively. "Did you hear about Nicholas's challenger dying during the battle for the regent's seat?" At Marie's nod, I added, "I think his brother may blame me for that."

She frowned, taking that in. "Well, then I think we have our answer."

Again, nobody spoke, and she turned back to me. "You're kidding, right? There's more?"

"Just one," I said, as if killing off people was all in a day's work. "An enchanter named Luna D'Onofrio tried to make my sister strangle me, and in self-defense, I threw her out a window." My gut tightened with guilt, even knowing the only other option was to die myself.

She sat back in her chair, eyeing me in a new light. "Remind me never to piss you off."

Warren cleared his throat. "I'll call the temp agency again in the morning. Maybe they'll tell me more about this Amleth guy."

Conversation lulled as we ran out of new ideas to explore. If I was going to share my admittedly ill-founded suspicions, the time had come.

"There's something else you should know," I said, setting my empty plate on the coffee table. "It's possible Jessie's girlfriend, Amani Falah, may have been the woman in the car."

I relayed the highlights of my conversation with Jessie, ending with Amani's departure from The Lower 8 in plenty of time to meet up with the homicidal materialist. Beside me, Nicholas quietly simmered as he realized I'd escaped the room to have a private phone call with the Texan, but I didn't have the bandwidth right then to examine my own annoyed reaction that I was expected to keep Jessie at a distance simply because my boyfriend did.

Marcel let out a low whistle. "Imagine finding out a hot babe was using you just to get close to her target."

"We don't know anything for sure," Warren protested, having struck up an easy friendship with Jessie.

"You didn't see her in the dress she wore last night," Marcel told Warren in a low aside. "Don't feel too sorry for your friend."

"Getting back on track," I said with a pointed glance at the sentinel, "Amani said she's here to help Sutton Sinclair find new investors for his construction project. Since I don't think he would be down with some murderous agenda—assuming she's part of this, which I'm not necessarily saying she is—I'd like to know how he ended up hiring her."

Nicholas's phone chimed with a text. "It's from Dev," he said after reading the message. "The Mazda is owned by a national rental company. He'll let us know when they have the name of the person who rented it, but I'm guessing it'll be Max Amleth."

"How do we figure out his true identity?" Warren pondered, but the harsh buzz of our doorbell interrupted his musings.

Marie clutched her chest and looked around. "Is that the door or did somebody get electrocuted in the next room?"

I bolted from the sofa. Had Scarlett somehow escaped her captor and come home? Before I could rush to the door, Nicholas stayed me with his hand. "Someone is trying to kill you, Blake. Let Marcel get it."

The sentinel did as instructed, peering over at us when he reached the door.

"It's a Nine," he said warily.

Everyone in the room went on high alert. Nicholas, Warren, and Marie gathered behind Marcel, forming a human barricade between me and whoever waited on the other side of the front door.

"Madame Sally says it's a man," Marie murmured, "but she can't pin down what else he might be."

"You need to shield us all," Nicholas instructed Marcel. "Can you do that?"

The sentinel drew in a nervous breath. "I think so." He took a moment to gather himself and presumably do Nicholas's bidding before slowly opening the door.

The man on the threshold cocked his head with his own measure of unease as he regarded his unwelcoming committee. A pair of suitcases were at his feet. His eyes found Nicholas, his mouth quirking at seeing *Reading Is Sexy* written across his chest.

"Regent Thorne?" he tentatively asked. "Acting Prime Trivedi sent me. He thought you and your sentinel could use some dry clothes."

The room let out its collective breath, and Marcel moved to retrieve the bags.

My phone vibrated in my pocket with an incoming text. Without much thought, I opened the message from an unknown number and let out a strangled cry. I heard more than saw everyone whip toward me. My hands trembled as I passed Nicholas the phone. A shocked silence followed as everyone took in the image that had stolen my breath.

It was a photo of Scarlett. She sat on a carpeted floor, her back against a wall and her knees drawn to her chest. Her long red curls were mussed as if she'd dragged her fingers through them numerous times, and tears streamed from eyes closed against the misery of captivity. At least there were no outward signs of abuse.

The phone vibrated again. Nicholas's lips thinned as he looked at whatever now appeared on the screen. Meeting my eyes, he turned the phone toward me. A caption had been added to the picture.

You did this.

A Gift or a Curse

If we were in a movie, receiving the photo of Scarlett would have elevated the DEFCON level another notch. At Nicholas's request, Dev traced the number belonging to Scarlett's captor—The Nine's resources being on par with any big city police department—and pronounced it as coming from a burner phone.

We poured over the photo seeking clues to her location, but other than Warren observing the low weave brown carpeting as being similar to the floor covering in his own rental apartment, we deduced nothing from her clothing or the off-white wall behind her. All the responses I texted back went unanswered, and calling the number yielded nothing more than a robotic voice informing us a voicemail box had not been set up for incoming calls.

It was nearing midnight, but no one seemed willing to admit there was nothing more to be done until morning. Marie's phone chimed, and after checking the screen, she stood up. "I hate leaving you, but I have to work in the morning."

We met at the front door, and impulsively, I threw my arms around her. "Thank you. To you and Madame Boudreaux."

She gave me an answering squeeze. "We'll be keeping tabs on you through that young firecracker, Harper. She wants to stay with you until things are settled, and then Madame Sally and I will host her for a while."

"You mean after we get Scarlett back?" I asked, my tired brain not catching her meaning.

"That," she said with an arched brow, "and other things. She's no fan of Mr. McCabe's dead aristocrat. Some old white guy named Cedric."

Once Marie had gone, Warren crashed in Scarlett's room while I rummaged a blanket and extra pillow from the linen closet for Marcel's makeshift bed on the sofa. In my room, Nicholas and I crawled under the covers. He spooned against me, one arm draped across my hip, and his breath gently tickled the back of my neck as the rise and fall of his chest deepened into sleep.

Despite my bone-deep exhaustion, I stayed awake a few more minutes, reveling in the wonderous sensation of human touch. It was such a simple thing, something most people probably took for granted, but the warmth, comfort, strength, and the absolute rightness of it all quieted some of my angst.

Though my family loved me unconditionally, it had been agreed early on it was best if we limited physical contact. One of my earliest memories was climbing into my mom's lap and telling her the lady she would see at the hospital later that day would stop breathing soon. Much to my confusion, Mom abruptly set me on my feet and left the room. When my dad tucked me in that night, he said the lady in my premonition had a sickness in her lungs, and that my mom was sad she couldn't help her. He also said I was too young to see the things my doctor mom had to deal with, so it would be better if we tried not to touch each other. The precaution of a moment became a habit of a lifetime.

I drifted off to sleep, grateful to finally understand the intimacy of human connection, and to find it in Nicholas's arms.

Nicholas moved about a spacious bedroom beautifully furnished in the soothing colors of a California desert: the greens of cactus and sage, the beiges of sand and white fir, and the deepest brown of a Joshua tree. Tall French doors leading to a balcony dripped with rain, and beyond that was the familiar forested landscape surrounding Alder House. The rich smell of ozone and damp earth tethered me to the past.

An impatient knock at the door was almost immediately followed by Henry Thorne letting himself in, not waiting for his son to issue an invitation. Nicholas automatically straightened his already upright posture at the sight of his father.

"Are you ready to go?" the elder man inquired.

Nicholas zipped up a garment bag and nodded. "Just about. I'll only be there a few days, so I don't need much."

The chancellor crossed the room to gaze out at dark clouds hanging so low in the sky they snagged the tops of the tallest trees. "The Wilder girl meeting you there?"

With his father's back to the room, Nicholas didn't need to mask his thoughts, but his face remained inscrutable. "Yes."

Henry turned away from the windows and reached into his coat pocket. "I have something for you."

Approaching his son, he held out his hand. A gold coin, identical to the one that would be found in Francesca's keeping, lay on his open palm. Nicholas stared at the metal disk a long moment before meeting his father's calculating gaze.

"Why are you giving me this?" he warily asked.

"Interesting bit of metallurgy here." The chancellor nudged the bit of gold on his palm. "In my hand, it is nothing but dead weight, cold except for the warmth it takes from my skin. But out there," he said, glancing once again out the window, "it's worth is inestimable, for it becomes imbued with the ability to buy the most precious and elusive of all commodities: time."

Nicholas made no move to accept the offering. "How so?"

"What is life but a series of random events given meaning by their sequence?" Henry said. "Change the order and you change the outcome. Toss something unexpected into the mix, and the future splinters into a thousand different possibilities."

"Planting that on someone as a smokescreen, you mean," Nicholas said, staring at the coin as if uncertain whether he was being offered a gift or a curse. "If I take that, what makes us any better than those who are assassinating our people? From those who killed my mother?"

"We've been playing by rules our enemies ignore," Henry said. "It's time to meet them where they live. Take it, and if the opportunity arises, let our enemies hang themselves."

Henry tossed the coin into the air. It spun, catching the light, before Nicholas reflexively caught it.

He regarded the object in his palm. "I will carry this because you want me to, but I don't promise to ever use it."

"I'm not saying you must," the chancellor replied, striding toward the door, "but it's better to be a warrior in a garden than a gardener in war."

Nicholas frowned. "Meaning?"

Henry paused to answer.

"Hope for peace. Prepare for war."

My eyes opened, and I stared unseeingly at the dark silhouette of my nightstand. The scent of rain lingered in my memory, telling me what I'd witnessed was no dream. It also drew a straight line from Henry to Nicholas to Francesca.

To Be a Telepath

The crows who often perched on my building's front railings heralded the rising sun with a cacophony of gleeful squawks. The call to tumble out of bed came almost as a relief. I was still tired because with sleep had come dreams of Scarlett pacing a room without doors or windows and fractured images of Nicholas's future that only provoked more uncertainty.

Pushing aside questions I wasn't yet ready to face, I plodded to the kitchen. My boss had gifted me with an expensive bag of imported coffee beans for Christmas, so I broke them open in a small bid to lift everyone's spirits. The automatic drip machine sputtered its last gasp when Marcel trudged over to the kitchen table, yawning and bleary-eyed.

I held up a mug, and he nodded. Putting cream and sugar on the table, I poured us each a cup and set one down in front of him.

"It's good," the sentinel said with some surprise after taking a sip. "It reminds me of the coffee back home."

"Did you grow up in Jamaica?" I knew his half-sister had been raised there.

"Kingston." He wrapped both hands around his mug and stared into the depths as if it were a window into the past. "Our mother is a Class Three telepath, which explained a whole lot when she finally told us about The Nine. We'd probably never have found out we were sentinels if Khalia hadn't run into an enchanter who tried—and, of course, failed—to use his power to make her throw a fight."

"A fight?" I echoed.

"Mom's a hotel concierge. Works all hours, but my sister has no skill for hospitality." His understatement almost made me spit out a mouthful of coffee. Khalia was many things, but deferential was not one of them. "She landed in the underground fight clubs. You can make good money there if you've got the stomach for it."

The story of Khalia's youth was unexpected but not totally surprising. The woman often reminded me of a feral cat, including her almost obsessive need to protect her financial security. She'd literally shed blood, her own and others, to build a future.

"And you?" I prodded.

"I started working as a freelance sentinel when I was eighteen and never looked back." He lightly stroked the bruise on his cheek. "I just never realized this job might require more than being a glorified babysitter, you know?"

I hoped his minor epiphany would translate into a newfound respect for his older sister and what she'd accomplished. In return, while Khalia might think she was content to go through life as a lone wolf, it couldn't hurt to know her brother truly did care if she survived another day.

A knock at the door made us both stiffen. Marcel slipped out of his chair and moved on cat's feet towards the door.

"It's not a Nine," he mouthed at the same moment my bedroom door flew open. Nicholas strode out, his hair sticking up in every direction, followed a moment later by Warren emerging from Scarlett's room. He looked about as rested as I felt, and I wished Scarlett could know how much her disappearance tormented her boyfriend.

Marcel quietly repeated his observation to them.

"Who is it?" Nicholas called out in a loud voice.

"Blake Wilder?" came the muffled reply. "Delivery from a, uh, Devraj Trivedi."

At his boss's nod, the sentinel opened the door. On the threshold stood a dark-haired man with a five o'clock shadow already laying claim to his jaw at barely eight o'clock in the morning. Clean blue coveralls strained to contain his ample belly, and he carried a clipboard. On the street behind him was a flatbed trailer with a red Tesla coup glinting in the pale sunshine.

He peered at the collection of faces just inside the door. "One of you Blake Wilder?"

"Here," I said, coming forward.

"I got a message for you." He ran a thick finger down the page on his clipboard until he found what he sought. "It says, 'Don't let Nicholas ruin this one too.'"

Sutton Sinclair's assistant responded to the message I'd left the night before with an invitation to drop by their construction offices that morning. When I relayed my plans to meet Sutton to the others, Nicholas volunteered to accompany me. While I'd been anticipating a private moment to finally ask the developer about the day of Mitsuko's death, going anywhere alone while unknown assailants wished me harm would be foolish.

"What time do we leave?" Marcel asked.

"I'll stay here," Warren said. "I want to call the temp agency as soon as they open."

Nicholas and Marcel took quick showers, and in between I washed my face and tossed my hair into a ponytail. Dressed in their own clothes, they both looked like themselves again when we set out in my new car. There'd been a certain satisfaction at signing off on the vehicle's delivery and noting the car was registered in my name.

The first time I'd visited the site of the anticipated high rise that was supposed to be the crown jewel in the Sinclair family empire, it had been a hive of industry. Workers and machinery had carved a massive hole in the earth. Pillars of steel jutted up from the depths to serve as the foundation for several levels of underground parking. Scores of employees' cars and pickup trucks had nosed against the perimeter's chain link fence, but that morning when we pulled into the dirt parking lot, only a handful of cars remained.

A side entrance set well off the main boulevard had been left open, but I stopped the car well short of a parking spot as haunting memories of my last visit there flooded my brain. It had almost ended with my death. Nicholas reached for my hand, likely aware of what I must be feeling.

"I won't let anything happen to you," he promised.

"Everything okay?" Marcel asked from the backseat, unaware of the significance of our destination.

"Fine." I parked the car, vowing to be done with indulging my inner turmoil while Scarlett could be suffering any number of real torments.

A thin, slightly stooped old man dressed in the uniform of a private security company met us when we stepped inside the gate. A utility belt slung about his spindly hips looked to weigh more than he did, but he moved with alacrity to welcome us to his domain.

"Empath," Marcel murmured. "One other Nine in the vicinity, but they're inside one of those trailers over there." Three portable structures placed end to end served as the company's construction offices.

"Mr. Sinclair's assistant said we were expecting a young lady today," the guard said, a grandfatherly smile appearing beneath his gray mustache. After surveying my companions, he marveled, "You must be important if you come with your own sentinel."

"I'm Blake Wilder," I said. "This is Regent Thorne and sentinel Pryce."

"Well if Bob ain't your uncle," he exclaimed, his eyebrows shooting up so high they were shadowed by the brim of his cap "We get some important visitors here, but Beatrice—that's my wife—will never believe this." He fumbled inside a jacket pocket and extracted his phone. "Mind if we take a selfie?"

As we moved to oblige, I took a shot in the dark. "Did you get a picture with the materialist who came by here in the last week or so?"

Curiosity flared in the old man's expression. "That good looking fella? Should I have known who he was?"

Nicholas picked up the conversational thread. "That's the guy. I met him at The Lower 8, but for the life of me I can't remember his name. Not a good look for a regent," he added with a rueful laugh. "Do you know who he might be?"

The drone of passing cars filled the loaded silence as the guard gazed up at the sky as if the answer might be found in the clouds. At last, he shook his head. "You'll have to ask Mr. Sinclair. Beatrice says I have the memory of a goldfish."

Pictures taken, he showed us to the trailer where Sutton kept an office. The same middle-aged woman with unnaturally bright red hair as the last time I was there occupied the assistant's desk. After inquiring with barely concealed indifference if we wanted water or coffee, which we politely declined, she waved us through to her boss's domain.

Sutton rose from behind his large desk, but he lacked the same vitality as when we'd first met. The elementalist had lost weight in the months since his son Marcus had died—or more accurately, since the father had executed his offspring as punishment for multiple murders—and the newly sagging skin of his jowls and neck added years to his appearance. He'd maintained the build of his youth, but now his suit jacket hung on his frame as if it had been made for a larger man. He sat down heavily in one of the four modular chairs gathered into a seating arrangement and beckoned for us to do the same.

"I must confess," he said, once we were all seated, "I'm at a loss as to know what you want with me." His gaze shifted to Nicholas. "I figured you'd have your hands full dealing with the Prime's death. Good man, that."

"We know who killed Silver," Nicholas responded, "and justice has been done."

Based on the spike in Sutton's interest, he hadn't yet heard about Francesca's involvement and subsequent death, so I jumped in with my own inquiry before he could sidetrack us with his.

"We're having problems closer to home," I explained. "My roommate, Scarlett Sloan, went missing Saturday night. In the days before that, I was harassed by an anonymous materialist as well as an enchanter. Then yesterday, we think the materialist attacked again, but it was more serious this time. He tried to kill the three of us, and then, last night, I got this."

Sutton viewed the picture of Scarlett, his expression registering nothing, but I sensed from his emotions this was all news to him. That's when something else occurred to me.

"You don't have a sentinel," I blurted, stating the obvious. It was the first time I'd been in his presence without Khalia or someone of her ilk protecting his every thought and move.

His smile was dryly amused. "Should I be concerned?"

"Not at all," I insisted, wishing I'd kept the observation to myself. Even if I barged into his past without permission, there was little chance of calling up an incident from so long ago. Unless he specifically dwelled on the day of the challenge, as my father had, I'd much more likely stumble into an instant replay of the recent death of his son. My query into his memory of that day would have to wait for another time. "It's just that all regents are supposed to be guarded by a sentinel."

"Oh, I am. Sydney's out running a few errands for me, but it's a complete waste of time and money as far as I'm concerned." He let out a self-deprecating chuckle. "None of my secrets are particularly interesting these days."

"Then would you mind telling us how you met Amani Falah?" I asked.

Once again I felt his surprise, but that didn't mean he was in the dark about her possible involvement with the unknown materialist. He could simply be jolted we'd connected the dots far enough to reach his doorstep.

Sutton answered with a question of his own. "Are you suggesting she had something to do with your roommate's disappearance?"

I was in no mood to play twenty questions. "Amani is an enchanter, she's new in town, and no one can get a read on her. You tell me what to think."

Based on his quicksilver emotions, it would have been interesting to be a telepath in that moment, but I would have to settle for guessing at the cause of his concern, followed by disappointment, and finally fatigue.

"How did you come to employ her as a consultant?" Nicholas asked. "Was it your idea to bring her to Santa Carla or did it come from elsewhere?"

"I vet everyone I do business with. I wouldn't have made it this far if I didn't know who I'm working with, and Ms. Falah is a highly qualified consultant with a solid track record." Sutton ran a hand across the white bristles of his scalp and sighed. "The reason she's a mystery to you is because she's a multi. An enchanter and a sentinel."

It was my turn to be thrown for a loop, but then I recalled Mr. Silver had also been a multi, though he'd identified as a sentinel with telepathic tendencies.

"That explains a lot," I muttered.

"She was recommended to me when I was at Alder House last month," the developer added.

I gripped the arms of my chair and leaned in. "By whom?"

"Matthias Montoya," he said.

My body flushed with dread, but Nicholas had the presence of mind to ask, "Did Montoya come see you recently?"

Sutton's brows drew together. "How did you know?"

34

A World Gone Cold

I was scheduled for a midday shift at Jitters, and despite Nicholas's increasingly heated protests, I was determined to go, and not just because it wouldn't be fair to my coworkers to leave them shorthanded.

"Somebody has made tormenting you their entire personality," he argued. We stood in the middle of my apartment's common room, and both Marcel and Warren studiously avoided looking in our direction as if that would render them invisible. "We know Matthias Montoya was in town, and he may still be here for all we know. It's not safe."

I looked beyond him to where my housekeys sat on the dining table and willed them to jump into my hand. Instead of floating across the room as I intended, the keys took off as if they were jet propelled, whizzed past me, and flew straight at Warren. He dove from the sofa as they crashed into the wall where his head had been.

"Sorry," I murmured sheepishly while retrieving them from the floor.

"Don't mention it," he said, getting shakily to his feet.

"Dev has people looking into Scarlett's every move in the hours before she went missing," Nicholas continued. "Why put yourself at risk?"

I reeled off the reasons. "We can't call the police, whoever has Scarlett won't tell us what he wants, and until we hear from Dev, we have no other leads to go on. I can't hide anymore while my best friend suffers, and maybe this will get the guy to make a move."

"Then I'll come with you." His phone rang, as it had done several times that morning, and he glanced at the screen in indecision. Finding Scarlett may be all consuming for me, but the business of being regent didn't stop for Nicholas.

"Take it," I snapped, tired of justifying a decision that had already been made. "I'll be fine."

With one last exasperated look, he turned away and answered the call.

A twinge of guilt surfaced as I drove by Jitters without slowing. I hadn't lied about being scheduled to work that day, nor in my belief it might lure my tormentor out into the open, but there was something else that needed to be done without the added complication of my regent boyfriend.

Ten minutes later, my knuckles rapped on a weathered metal door, the tinny echo momentarily silencing the bright chatter of a dozen sparrows flitting about the branches of a curbside tree. The surrounding street of industrial buildings converted to apartments and lofts was tranquil in the late morning, the area popular with the young and childless.

The door opened on well-oiled hinges. Shirtless and wearing only a pair of gray sweats slung low on his hips, Jessie pushed his disheveled hair off his face and greeted me with a yawn. It hadn't occurred to me that he might still be in bed, but maybe there was a reason he hadn't yet risen—and it had nothing to do with keeping nightclub hours.

"I hope you're here with good news about Scarlett," he said.

"No," I said quietly. "Is this a bad time?"

"There's never a bad time for you, darlin'." He swung the door wide in invitation.

My nose twitched at the scent of freshly brewed coffee, and without a word, he poured us each a cup. I took a seat at the kitchen counter while he retrieved a carton of half and half from the fridge and stirred in exactly the right amount before sliding the mug across the stainless steel countertop. Knowing he cared enough to remember how I took my coffee brightened an otherwise bleak day.

"What's being done to find your friend?" he asked, the brew in his own cup resembling black tar.

"Nicholas has people on it, but we have no clue where she is. This is all we've got to go on." I turned my phone screen so he could see the image of Scarlett I'd received.

As he scanned the photo, compassion filled the air between us and completely shredded my composure.

"She must be so scared," I said, my voice thick with unshed tears.

"Oh darlin'," he said, coming out from behind the counter. Wrapping his arms around me, I allowed him to pull me against his naked chest, having momentarily forgotten what happened the last time I was in his arms.

My entire body suddenly pulsed with energy and fire in equal measures. It was a purely involuntary reaction, I told myself. Jessie's arms tightened around my waist, and he lowered his face to my neck as if to breathe me in. He must feel it too.

The heat of his desire assaulted my senses, and I shivered in anticipation. Never had my empathic abilities been so in tune with another, his excitement amplifying my own. He raised his face until our lips were inches apart, and I suddenly didn't want to overthink it or deny the need thrumming under my skin. My longing for something—be it comfort, reassurance, or maybe just a human connection uncomplicated by fear and suspicion—overrode everything else.

Inching nearer, I could almost taste the coffee on his lips and yearned for him to close the distance. The long-ago premonition of the two of us in his bed would finally come to pass, and with that vision in mind, my surrender was complete.

Jessie dropped his arms and took a step back. His body shuddered with the effort to maintain control, and I bit my lip to hold back a cry of frustration. I sensed the tenuous grip he had on his hunger, reveling in the knowledge it was within my power to shatter his self-control, but my conscience held me at bay. Who was I that even now I couldn't stop imagining what it would be like to strip away his last shred of resistance?

He cleared his throat. "Give me a sec to grab a shirt."

With his absence, the hum of paranormal energy no longer pounded through my body, but it didn't erase how easily I would have betrayed Nicholas's trust. Was it because I couldn't stop thinking about how he may have betrayed mine with lies and pretense?

It took Jessie a few minutes to return, time I used to reign in the impulse to do something I'd likely regret. He resumed his position on the other side of the counter, and I wondered if keeping a physical barrier between us was for his sake or mine.

"Did you and Amani make up?" I had to know where we stood.

He heaved a sigh. "She is not an easy woman, but then again," he said, his eyes cutting to me, "you know I like 'em complicated."

I chose my next words carefully. "What if she's even more complicated than you think?"

He took a sip of his lukewarm coffee and grimaced. "Now you're beginning to sound like Harper."

Marie had said the teen spirit planned to hang out with me for a bit, and I fervently hoped she'd been there earlier in the day when we'd visited the Sinclair building site. I really didn't want to be the one to deliver the thankless news about his girlfriend's connection to Matthias Montoya.

"Have you talked with her today?" I ventured. "Harper, that is."

His face clouded over. "No. After Amani left yesterday, Harper had to put her two cents in, but why are we talking about them instead of what we can do to find your friend? What's going on, Blake?"

I paced a few steps, suddenly unsure. My only thought in coming here was to point out that Amani had come to Santa Carla under false pretenses, but what if he didn't see it that way? I had no proof she'd actually done anything wrong, and it wasn't a crime to be acquainted with another Nine, no matter that he might hold a grudge against me.

With a sigh, I turned around. "You have to understand that sitting around and waiting for news of Scarlett is killing me. We can't involve the police, and the person who has her seems to enjoy making me suffer—I had to do something."

He shifted on his feet. "Why do I get the feeling this is leading someplace I'm not gonna like?"

"Please don't be mad at me, Jessie," I pleaded, "but I went to see Sutton Sinclair today. To ask how and why he hired Amani."

He drew back. "Why would you do that?" The warmth between us was all but forgotten.

"All I know is an enchanter came to Jitters last week and used an innocent guy to threaten me. Then there was the near miss with a Palmarium ball before the two of us almost got flattened on a LA sidewalk. Now, a darkhaired woman, working with another Nine, drove the car that followed us yesterday right before we were attacked. None of this proves anything, but I thought it couldn't hurt to look into her background."

My chest tightened as I sensed his rising anger.

"Let me get this straight. You, a voyant who hasn't been shy about telling us what she thinks of The Nine's prehistoric traditions, gets picked on by an enchanter, of which there are dozens in our sanctuary city as well as at To The Nines, and you immediately think my girlfriend is to blame?" His voice was incredulous, and when he put it that way, I wondered why I'd suspected her.

"There's more." Even I heard the lack of conviction in my voice.

"I'm not sure I want to hear it."

It was sink or swim time. "Sutton hired Amani on the say-so of Matthias Montoya. The same Matthias Montoya—a materialist—who blames me and Nicholas for his brother's death during the regent's challenge."

He stared at me a long moment. "I thought I knew you, Blake. Amani told me you were jealous of her, but I refused to believe it. I'm real sorry about your friend, but this has nothing to do with Amani." He let that sit for a few beats before adding, "Or me."

Taking our mugs to the sink, he presented his back as he took his time rinsing them and stowing them in the dishwasher. His manners were such that he'd never ask me to leave, but I could read the room. I got to my feet and retrieved my bag from the counter. He stood motionless at the sink as I passed.

"I'm sorry, Jessie," I said in a small voice. "I shouldn't have come."

I let myself out. The birds still nattered in a nearby tree, but now their chirps fell on my ears like shards of ice in a world gone cold.

Villain or Monster

Another text came from the anonymous burner phone while I sat in my car outside Jitters. I'd fixed my makeup in the rearview mirror, but there was no hope for my red-rimmed eyes. Grabbing my cell, I read the message.

Hey, working girl, the text read. The hair rose on the back of my neck. Was I being followed? People and cars were coming and going in the parking lot, but no one seemed to be looking my way.

Keeping one eye on my surroundings, I typed out a response. *Scarlett's done nothing to you.*

True…but YOU have!

A car door next to me slammed, and I almost jumped out of my skin. Shaking off my twitchiness, I sent back, *Tell me what I did.*

I stared at the blank screen in growing frustration as the seconds stretched into minutes. Was the game on hold or were they just waiting for me to get out of the car? I could drive home to the protection of Nicholas and Marcel, but that wouldn't help Scarlett. With my heart in my throat, I waited for a lull in traffic before leaping out of my car and dashing into Jitters.

"A little help here, Blake?" Cindy called out from behind the counter the moment she laid eyes on me. The noon rush was more like midday madness, which was probably for the best. If I dwelled any longer on how messed up everything was, I'd dissolve into a puddle of nothingness.

Defying Al's directive not to have our phones on us during shifts, I pocketed my cell, grabbed an apron (this one read *The Most Dangerous Drinking Game Is Seeing How Long I Can Go Without Coffee*), and got to work. I didn't realize a scowl had worked its way onto my face until an old man whose wispy white hair matched the pallor of his skin approached the counter and told me to smile.

"Don't tell me what to do," I snarled in response. Two women in line behind him applauded, which sent him stomping out the door muttering that today's generation was doomed. Since Al didn't pay me to scare off business, I tried my best to maintain a pleasant expression after that, but it didn't stop Cindy from darting concerned glances my way.

I'd managed to slip into the rhythm of taking and filling orders when Detective Bree Navarro appeared on the other side of the counter, and fear for Scarlett rippled up my spine.

"What's happened?" I gasped out.

Her relaxed stance instantly shifted into overdrive, like a hunting dog catching the scent of easy prey. "Your name came up as a potential witness in an LAPD homicide this past weekend. Care to explain?"

Her unexpected response filled me with relief. Steadying myself against the counter, I took in her tightly coiled hair, light brown skin, and generic pantsuit. More importantly, a read of her emotions seemed to convey anticipation at a fishing expedition turning up a prize catch.

"I wasn't a witness," I said. "Only a friend of the victim. Is there anything else?"

She stared at me long enough to cause the customer behind her, a young guy with slicked back hair and a red tie to set off his power suit, to peer over her shoulder. "It's a coffeehouse, lady, not a wax museum."

Navarro snapped the police badge off her belt and shoved it into the man's face, which quickly lost its smirk. He bumped into the people behind him in his haste to put some space between him and the detective.

She clipped her badge back in place. "One of these days, Miss Wilder, you and Mr. McCabe are going to run out of convenient excuses, and I plan on being there."

"Good luck with that," I called as she departed.

When the lull between lunch hour and the three o'clock stampede finally came, Cindy and I used the time to restock supplies.

"Whatever's going on, I'm a good listener if you want to talk," she said, refilling the cappuccino machines with fresh coffee beans. "There's probably nothing you could say that I haven't lived through already. Gosh, did I ever tell you about the time Todd forgot we'd gone to Target together, and he left without me?"

She blithely launched into yet another story of her ex-boyfriend's ill treatment—the guy had gone home and taken a nap, for God's sake—but the sudden tingling of my skin shut out all other thoughts. Another Nine was close by, and from the way the unfamiliar energy prickled, it wasn't anyone I knew well.

Whirling around as the front door of the coffeehouse opened, my gaze locked on a pair of cold, dark eyes set above a sculpted nose. Full lips curled into a gratified smile.

Matthias Montoya had finally come for me.

"Jeepers," Cindy murmured, having followed the direction of my stare. "You always seem to know all the hot guys, but that one looks like he wants to eat you with a cherry on top."

Some distant part of my brain appreciated my co-worker had finally developed a sense of self-preservation when it came to men. If only we lived long enough to put her new discernment to good use.

Nicholas warned me not to invite a public showdown, but desperation to find Scarlett had led me to wave off his concern with careless indifference. Now a handful of people just going about their day, who'd stopped in to chug some caffeine and log onto Wi-Fi, stood between me and a man who'd murdered the former telekinetic regent, assuming he didn't simply use his powers as a materialist to kill me where I stood.

How could I have been so reckless to offer myself up like a human sacrifice with no plan for defending myself? Getting myself killed didn't come with any guarantee Scarlett would be released, nor that the people surrounding me at Jitters would be unharmed.

Matthias wound his way across the room. I'd imagined him as the spoiled son of a Greek shipping magnate the first time we'd crossed paths, his tan skin and athletic build likely byproducts of endless games of tennis played on the French Riviera. Now the softness was gone, his face a series of sharp angles, his body ground down to sinew and bone. Even his black curls had been razed to stubble.

I thought fleetingly of Sutton, and how grief had aged him, yet the same emotion had pared Matthias down to the quick. He walked with an economy of movement, expending no unnecessary energy as he closed in.

In desperation I reached for a pot of freshly made Americano drip. The collection of small scars on the back of my hands bore testament to its scalding heat. Cindy tracked my every move.

"What's going on, Blake?" she whispered.

"Go in the back," I said, not taking my eyes off the materialist. At least one of us would be safe.

"Fat chance of that." With a casualness that belied her trembling hands, she felt under the counter for the panic button, putting her faith in a device that would summon police. If only she knew it would be like bringing a toothpick to a gunfight.

"Not yet," I murmured, wanting to spare more innocent lives becoming entangled in whatever the man had planned.

Matthias reached the counter. He studied me a moment, taking in my defiant if terrified stance, before a mocking smile flitted across his lips at the sight of Cindy—her blue and white polka dot dress topped with a Peter Pan collar made her look like she'd stepped out of a mid-century copy of *Good Housekeeping*—hovering protectively at my side.

"You do inspire a legion of the most unique followers," he wryly observed in his thick Spanish accent.

"What do you want?" I hissed.

He lifted his gaze to the drink menu posted overhead. "A pistachio latte sounds intriguing. I'll have that."

I nudged Cindy, who shot me a disbelieving glance before abandoning her post to whip up his drink order.

"Why so tense?" he taunted. "Problems at home?"

"Where is Scarlett?" I demanded in an undertone. "I swear if you hurt her—"

"Scarlett?" he cut in, his features blank. "I do not know this person."

"Did an enchanter wipe that memory from you too?" My fingers tightened around the handle of the coffee pot, ready to burn all pretense—and a significant amount of skin—from his handsome face.

"Believe what you like," he said with a slight lift of his shoulders. "I'm here because I agreed to meet the Prime in California, but when that was no longer possible, my only thought was to drop by Santa Carla to see how the pretty little voyant fared."

"You expect me to believe you had nothing to do with my friend's disappearance?" I asked in a low growl, fury diminishing my fear.

His eyes glittered. "You mean in the same way you expect me to believe you aren't responsible for my brother's death?"

He leaned in, but I held my ground. No one waited in line, and the blast of the steam wand frothing his order would make it impossible for Cindy to overhear whatever he had to say.

"Our time will come, little voyant, you can be sure of that, but not today. I may be a villain, but I'm not a monster." My stomach clenched at the anticipation oozing from his pores. He had plans for me, but I detected no urgency, no satisfaction that he would be carrying them out anytime soon.

"What about Amani Falah?" I asked, registering his surprise that I'd made the connection.

He tipped his head in a gesture of indifference. "I may have suggested her to Sinclair as a potential consultant, but that is all."

Cindy returned and banged his beverage down in front of him, milk foam splattering on the counter.

"Oops," she said with a glare.

Smirking, Matthias pulled a twenty from his pocket and dropped it on the counter. Ignoring the coffee, he strolled out the door as if he hadn't a care in the world.

36

A Spark of Joy

Another taunting message came before the end of my shift—*Would you trade your life for hers?*—but since my pleading responses were ignored, they seemed to be sent for perverse fun rather than to actually open a dialogue.

I went through the motions of clocking out, getting my purse, and emerging into the night air with a numbness that left no room for fear. Maybe that's why I barely reacted to the tall figure standing in the shadows near my car. I'd already imagined the worst outcomes for Scarlett's disappearance, Nicholas's hidden agenda, and Jessie's scorn. Reality couldn't be any worse, and no matter how each scenario played out, at least the torture of not knowing would finally be over.

The silhouette moved into the light, and I let out a cry. It was my dad. Closing the distance at a run, I hurled myself against the solidness of him. He stroked my hair and made soothing noises while I cried, even managing to dig some lint-speckled tissues out of his jacket pocket. Little feet tapping on my shins conveyed Chico's joy at our reunion—or at least the dog's insistence not to be left out.

"What are you doing here?" I asked through hiccups.

"I thought you and Scarlett might need me." He rubbed the gooseflesh on my arms, making me aware how the temperature had fallen.

What remained unspoken was how Scarlett's own parents—a father who'd disappeared years ago and a mother who wasn't much better—had pretty much abandoned their daughter to raise herself. She'd grown up in our house and essentially become his third child.

He must have dropped everything to be here for us. Even if he couldn't do anything that wasn't already being done, having him there made it all slightly less terrible. The reality of what living at Alder House would be like, six thousand miles away from my family, blew through me like a chill wind.

"Did you come alone?" Part of me wanted Mom and Jordan waiting at my apartment, but foreboding burbled up at the thought of more people I loved being in proximity to whoever had taken Scarlett.

"I didn't want to worry your mom and sister. I told them Chico and I needed a road trip before the new semester starts next week. We'll follow you back to your apartment."

"Nicholas is there," I warned him.

"Good. I want to meet him." He leaned down and picked up the dog. "Chico's a very good judge of character. If Nicholas's face is still intact ten minutes after we meet, we'll know he's okay."

I snorted at my father's test of honor while he puzzled over my vehicle, the only Tesla in the parking lot. "Why did I think your car was white?"

Food waited for us when we came in. Chico conducted a cursory inspection of Nicholas, Marcel, and Warren before turning to gaze longingly at the containers from the local BBQ joint lined up on the counter.

I sensed Nicholas's relief at seeing me as he extended a hand to my father. "It's good to meet you, sir." The handshake was polite if not overly warm.

"I wish we were meeting under different circumstances, but I'm glad you're here to help find Scarlett," he responded.

I gestured to Warren. "This is her boyfriend, Warren."

My dad shook his hand as well. "An elementalist, I see. It looks like you're almost Class Two."

Warren perked up. "Really? I've been able to light candles pretty regularly lately, but I thought it was because I'd been practicing."

I had more pressing concerns. "What did the temp agency say, Warren?"

His face fell. "They won't talk to me. It took six phone calls and most of the day, but I finally got Adeline James, the agency's owner, on the phone. She gave me a line of BS about how their fancy pants clients expect confidentiality and told me to piss off."

My father's gaze narrowed. "Did you tell her Scarlett was missing?"

He nodded. "She said to call the police because it wasn't her problem."

Scarlett hadn't returned after meeting one their clients, and the agency's owner had the audacity to shrug it off? Worse, they had chosen to protect the guy with the money rather than the broke college student.

My hands balled into fists. "Do you have an address for this place?" I'd be having a chat with that woman first thing in the morning.

As Warren pulled out his phone to text me the information, I noticed Marcel observing my father with the same fascination as a kid spotting Santa at the mall. Maybe it was a sentinel thing.

I waved him over. "Marcel, come meet my dad."

"It… it's a great pleasure to meet you, Mr. Wilder, sir," he said, stumbling over his words as he pumped my father's hand. "Are you who I think you are?"

Color crept into my dad's cheeks. "Perhaps, but I haven't been that person for a long time."

Nicholas glanced between them, his eyes telegraphing confusion. "Do you two know each other?"

"You're the missing Prime, aren't you?" Marcel enthusiastically inquired of my dad. "Not even Mr. Silver could channel this much power."

Without waiting for confirmation, Marcel turned to Nicholas. "Every sentinel knows the story of the day Chancellor Hayashi died and the Prime disappeared, never to be seen again. He was one of the strongest Primes we've ever had, so it's this big mystery, right? He was totally devoted to her, so the story goes it was a broken heart that drove him away." He turned back to my dad, sheepish to have blurted out so much. "At least now we know where Blake gets her power."

My senses picked up Nicholas's shock at being blindsided before he even spoke.

"Did you know this about your father?" he asked in a voice heavy with accusation.

Marcel went still at the sudden chill in the room. My father crossed his arms in a stance that clearly communicated Nicholas had better take it down a notch. Warren wisely took a plate of food and retreated to the sofa.

Though my heart picked up in tempo, I met my boyfriend's accusing glare unflinchingly. The moment I'd once dreaded— the one where Nicholas learned his father had cheated and murdered his way into the chancellorship—had arrived, but now I didn't think he'd be all that surprised. From Henry Thorne sending Nicholas to find me before anyone else could, to urging his son to use the gold coin to shift blame for any potential misdeed onto the New Order, Nicholas had to be clear-eyed about his father's ruthlessness—and had perhaps inherited the trait as well.

"Yes," I said. "My dad was Prime up until the day Henry became chancellor. He invited me into his past after I came back from Alder House, and I saw how it all went down."

"And how exactly," he ground out, not sparing a glance at my dad, "did it all go down?"

I lifted my chin in defiance. "Henry murdered the former chancellor, and then blackmailed my dad to keep his secret."

Marcel's gasp was nothing compared to the outrage marring Nicholas's face. "My father has devoted his life to The Nine. He'd never do something so underhanded."

"Until the tower fell on Francesca last night, I would have said the same of you."

He gaped at me in stunned disbelief. For a moment I wished my empathic senses away, because then I wouldn't feel how deeply my accusation stung, but there was no going back.

"You really think me capable of such a thing?" he asked with a disbelieving shake of his head.

"A week ago, my father told Mr. Silver the truth about the day Henry became chancellor. Now Mr. Silver is dead, and the woman who carried out his death sentence died by telekinesis right in front us. You tell me—what am I supposed to think?"

"You've known about this… this supposed act of betrayal by Henry for days—"

"There's nothing supposed about it," I argued. "Your uncle ignored every warning and ended up dying in the challenge. Henry took his revenge, the chancellorship, and wrecked my father's life all in one move."

"And it all slipped your mind until now?" he asked, incredulous. "When you found out I knew your dad was a Nine before you did, you practically took my head off, but apparently it's okay for you to keep secrets. Thanks for clearing that up."

"I wouldn't have to keep secrets if you weren't so freaking protective," I lashed back.

His mocking tone took an abrasive turn. "Is that what McCabe whispers in your ear? That you don't need anyone but him?"

"Time out," my dad said, stepping between us and tapping his fingers against an open palm in the time-honored gesture of a football referee. "You two obviously have a lot to sort through, but none of this is helping Scarlett."

Nicholas and I glared at each other, our combined emotions swirling around me like a dark cloud, but my dad was right. Nicholas was the first to break eye contact.

"I'm taking the Tesla," he muttered as he flung open the front door.

Marcel moved with haste to catch up, tossing an apologetic glance behind him as he raced out after the regent.

What Fools These Mortals Be

There was no point lying in bed any longer and pretending I might actually sleep, so when my father started to move around the apartment at sunrise, I got up and joined him. He stood by the door, buckling the dog into his harness as the coffeemaker gurgled out the first pot of the day.

He glanced up. "We're going to take a walk while the coffee brews. Care to join us?"

Throwing a jacket and boots on over my sweats, I ventured out into the cold morning. We walked in companionable silence, my hands buried deep in my pockets, while Chico marked multiple spots with evident satisfaction.

"I know what you're doing," I said at last.

He paused to let the dog sniff one particular tree to his heart's content. "Oh? And what might that be?"

"You're not going to say anything about Nicholas and what happened last night until I bring it up."

He shrugged. "It's not really any of my business."

I shot him a look. This was another trick in the Dad book, one designed to pry as much information out of me without asking a single question. As usual, it worked.

"Everything was fine before the regent's challenge. Suddenly everyone knew who I was, and Nicholas had a whole new life to deal with. There's all this pressure now to define who we are and what we are, and now I don't even know if I can trust him. Why can't we just figure it out day by day like everyone else on the planet?"

"You're not like everyone else," he countered, tactful enough not to bring up how Nicholas had ghosted me—for my own safety—prior to the challenge. "Being with Nicholas makes a statement about who you are and what you believe. You better be sure your feelings for him can stand up to that."

Our next stop was a neighbor's lawn dotted with cement garden statues about the same size as Chico, much to the dog's delight. We could be there a while.

"You gave up everything for Mom. Do you ever wish you'd made a different choice?"

He smiled at the mention of his wife, as he often did. "Never, but we were also a lot older than you and Nicholas. Your voyancy made you grow up fast in a lot of ways, but I don't think anyone truly knows their own heart at eighteen. Give yourself time."

He'd forgotten what it was like to live in the eye of the storm that was The Nine, particularly for someone as visible as I'd become. Change was coming, and I didn't have the luxury of ignoring reality while everyone around me forged alliances or jockeyed for position.

Chico had moved on to a fence post before Dad spoke again.

"Are you happy?" he asked.

"I care about Nicholas," I replied.

He gave me a penetrating look. "That wasn't the question."

The Tesla was in its parking spot when we rounded the corner. Nicholas and Marcel waited on the doorstep of my apartment. When Nicholas spied me on the street, his tight expression remained unchanged. It was almost as if I were facing the regent and not my boyfriend, but I wasn't sorry to have things out in the open between us.

When I unlocked the front door, Marcel was reluctant to follow my father inside.

"No one is going to jump out of the bushes," Nicholas assured the sentinel. "Go grab some coffee."

When we were alone, he rested his forearms on the porch railing and observed the stirrings of my neighbors across the street as curtains opened and porch lights winked out. A curious mixture of hope, sadness, and determination swirled around him.

"Do you ever feel like an actor who's come on in the middle of a play without knowing how the story started?" he asked.

I moved next to him, mirroring his stance. "If you had known about our fathers' history, would it have changed anything?"

An elderly lady in a pink quilted bathrobe lumbered down her driveway to retrieve a newspaper. She stared suspiciously at us, prompting Nicholas to flutter a hand in greeting, but she ignored him and returned to her house.

"I took my father's lectures about loyalty, duty, and sacrifice at face value, never doubting it was all in service to the people of The Nine. What you said—what you accused me of last night—makes me question what master I serve."

"You believe me then?" It was so unexpected it took a minute for my emotions to catch up. Could a few magic words fully restore the faith and trust I'd begun to feel for him? Or was he just saying what he thought I needed to hear?

"Yes." He reached over and took my hand. As always, a spark flared between us, but the wanting was no longer enough.

"You challenge me, infuriate me, and scare me half to death, but you tell the truth, even when it's painful to hear."

"What about you?" I withdrew my hand. "Will you tell me the truth?"

He remained silent.

I turned to face him, and he did the same. "Did you kill Francesca?"

His mouth twisted with exasperation. "She arranged the death of Mr. Silver, killed his assassin to cover up her crime, and left a poor young sentinel to die on the flagstones outside Alder House. I do not grieve her." Righteousness and disgust roiled underneath his indignation, but nowhere in the mix was guilt. Still, I had to know.

"That wasn't my question."

His eyes shuttered, and he returned his gaze to the street. "No." I regarded his stony profile, wanting to trust him but not knowing if I could.

After a long, tense moment, I nodded. "Okay. I believe you." I could extend the same trust he was offering me, even if that meant shoving aside my doubts for the time being. I leaned into his side, resting my head against his shoulder. "Feel like helping me rattle the cage of a certain temp agency owner?"

"Can't think of anything I'd rather do," he replied.

People Mover was located on a milelong stretch of road in central Santa Carla known as the Boulevard. Numerous restaurants, coffeehouses, mom-and-pop businesses, and assorted retail stores populated both sides of the street, but parking hadn't yet become a fight to the death when Nicholas and I, with Marcel in tow, arrived at the time the agency's website said they opened.

Dad had stayed back at the apartment, muttering something about emails and research before waving us out the door.

"What's the plan?" Nicholas asked as we got out of the car.

"We're not leaving until we know everything they've got on the person who hired Scarlett," I said flatly.

A bell chimed as we pushed through the agency's front door and entered a cramped lobby. The vaguely claustrophobic air was compounded by walls painted chartreuse, a shade that never did anyone's complexion a favor.

A young woman in cheap career wear a size too small lounged behind the reception desk. She looked up expectantly, her gaze flicking over me dismissively in favor of admiring my male companions. Normally her rudeness wouldn't have bothered me, but between my desperation to find Scarlett and these people refusing to help, my tolerance had run dry.

"We're here to see Adeline James," I said, the name Warren provided sounding like a character on a daytime drama.

Dragging her attention to me, the receptionist offered an insincere smile. "Do you have an appointment?"

"No, but it's important we see her." I crossed my arms to make it clear we weren't budging until the agency's owner agreed to speak with us.

She drew a talon of a fingernail down her computer screen as she pretended to consult the day's schedule. "No can do," she responded, enjoying a little thrill at flexing her power. "If you'd like to fill out an application—"

Leaning over the desk, I let my fingers graze the back of her hand. She drew back as if stung, but it didn't matter. I had what I needed.

"Listen, Kristy," I said in a low growl. "If you don't take us to your boss this instant, I will find her myself. When I do, I'm going to tell her all about what you and her husband like to do on the blue sofa in her office. She's especially not going to like what you two get up to with her expensive throw pillows."

Kristy's mouth gaped while Marcel coughed to smother a laugh.

"He promised he wouldn't tell," she whined, all smugness gone. "I really need this job."

"Adeline James?" I reminded her.

"Down the hall, second door on the right." She bolted from the desk and dashed in that direction. I assumed she planned to warn her boss, but she veered to the left instead, running through a doorway marked as the bathroom.

"Throw pillows, huh?" Marcel mused as she went. Nicholas's scowl ended that line of inquiry.

The three of us made our way to the designated door.

"Knock or no knock?" I debated aloud.

"You decide," Nicholas said, his lips twitching as if he were enjoying himself.

"Eff it," I muttered.

Adeline James stood pensively at the window, but she whipped around in surprise as I barged in, my companions flanking me on either side. She was one of those middle-aged women my mom would call well preserved, from her expertly made up face pulled so tight her eyebrows arched in permanent surprise, to her youthful, Pilates-toned figure.

"Who are you?" she demanded. Against one wall was the blue velvet sofa that had starred so vividly in my vision, a stack of elegant silk throw pillows neatly arranged at either end.

"Kristy!" she yelled.

"Your assistant is in the bathroom," I informed her, which gave the receptionist some cover. I wasn't completely heartless. "Tell me the name of the client who hired Scarlett Sloan."

She stalked to a large desk topped with a handful of carefully curated items including a miniature bonsai tree sprouting in a moss and pebble garden, a gold fountain pen held upright in a slab of black marble, and a silver-framed photo of her and the man I'd seen with Kristy flashing blindingly white veneers.

There was also a hardback copy of Stephen King's *Demon Keepers*.

"I'm calling security." She snatched up her phone. "You have sixty seconds to get out before I have you thrown out."

Nicholas took a step in her direction, but I held up a hand. Focusing all my energy, I silently willed it to do my bidding.

The phone ripped from Adeline's hand, leaving her dumb-struck. Then with a flick of my wrist, the office door slammed shut. I tried not to feel too satisfied at sensing her shock turn to terror, but it wouldn't hurt to give her a taste of what Scarlett must be going through.

I braced my hands on her desk. "Now give me everything you have on the person who employed Scarlett Sloan, or I will tell you the date and manner of your death."

Nicholas managed not to react, but Marcel couldn't hold back his snort of amusement. Staying in character, I leveled my gaze at him. "Careful, sentinel, or you're next."

He immediately sobered and lowered his head submissive-ly, probably to hide his smirk. "Yes, mistress."

Satisfied my henchman had been properly chastised, I turned back to Adeline.

"Well, Ms. James?" I stared her down. "What's it to be?"

The woman nodded vigorously before clumsily lowering herself into her chair. With trembling fingers, she struck a few keys on her computer. I came around the desk to view the screen, causing her to squeak and shrink away.

"You won't be harmed if you give me what I want," I promised, gentling my tone. Despite taking zero responsibility for the people she profited from, she didn't deserve a coronary.

A document opened with Scarlett's name at the top. I scanned the page, expelling a relieved breath at finding the in-formation we sought. Reading the name of her employer without surprise—Max Amleth—I took a screenshot with my phone. With that accomplished, there was only one thing left to do. Rotating her chair to face me, I rested my hand on her shoulder, causing her to flinch.

I locked eyes with her. "We are going to leave now, Adeline, but I would advise against calling the police and making up a story about being assaulted."

Her face blanched with genuine horror at how I could possibly know what she intended to do the moment we left, but the premonition I'd picked from her mind had spelled it out.

"How… how did you know that?" she asked. "Who are you?"

Her choice of reading material had given me an idea too tempting to resist.

"We walk the earth, Adeline James, saving innocents and damning those who would do them harm. Your name is on the damnation list, but it's not too late to change that. Be kinder to those who walk through your door, for you are their keeper. Are we clear?"

She began to weep. "I will do better. I swear."

"You might also want to rethink your husband," I advised. "He's definitely on the damnation list."

Welcome to the Nine

I was astonished to pull up in front of the address Max Amleth had given People Mover to discover it actually existed. The two-story, U-shaped apartment building had about two dozen units opening directly onto a cement courtyard with a fenced-in pool, though no one lounged on any of the slated chairs on this January day. I'd called Warren to give him the address, and we parked next to his Honda in a space designated for visitors.

As we gathered on the sidewalk, Warren tugged a frustrated hand through his tight curls. Since his normally tame hair now looked as if he'd stuck his head in a blender, it was obviously not the first time.

"Do you have an apartment number?" he asked.

I shook my head. "To be honest, I'm surprised the address didn't send us to a dry cleaners or an empty lot."

Nicholas nodded at Marcel. "See if there are any Nines here. That should narrow it down."

The sentinel quickly moved to obey. He began walking a loop around the complex while I stared morosely at how closely the neighbors were packed together. There'd be no way you could hold someone hostage there unless you kept them sedated so they couldn't scream for help. Scarlett didn't even like taking Tylenol.

A silver pickup truck pulled in and parked before Marcel had made it halfway around the pool. Jessie hopped out, and an undeniable rush of warmth swept through me, but I refused to give into it. We were both with other people, and he'd saved us both by not making things more complicated than they already were. I ducked my head and prayed my hair would hide my flushed cheeks.

Nicholas bristled. "What the hell is he doing here?"

"Harper." I suddenly dared to hope. There could be no other reason for Jessie to even know where I was, especially considering how we'd left things.

The phantomist didn't spare a glance at Nicholas as he approached, and I fleetingly wondered what else the young spirit had told him of the past twenty-four hours of my life. My empathic skills were of no use because the air was so fraught with strong emotions I couldn't tell where mine ended and the others began.

"Harper was mighty impressed with how you handled yourself this morning, Blake," Jessie said, his gaze lingering a beat too long on my face. "She wants to help."

"I just best she does," Nicholas sniped.

Jessie skewered him with a glare. "What's your fucking problem, Thorne?"

"We have an address but not an apartment number," I cut in. "There's no telling if it's real or not."

Jessie turned to the empty air beside him. "Go, Harper. See what you can find out."

Marcel soon returned with lips drawn tight. "There aren't any Nines here."

Jessie cocked his head. "Maybe not, but Harper's found something."

My breath caught in my throat. "Where?"

He shot off a text before answering. "Upstairs. Apartment 204. She says the place is divided by lead walls."

"Lead walls?" Warren questioned as we crossed the courtyard and pounded up a stairwell open to the elements. "Why would anyone have that?"

"We have a couple of lead-lined panic rooms at Alder House," Nicholas said, taking in the numerous cracks in the building's stucco, "but I don't think anyone who lives here could afford one."

"There's a much more simple explanation. Anyone who's done their homework on Blake knows how close we are, and that I would do anything to help her, including asking my spirits to look for her missing friend." The superior note in Jessie's voice hit the intended target, and a surge of resentment hovered about Nicholas like a swarm of angry bees.

Warren glanced at the phantomist. "I don't understand. What does that have to do with a lead-lined room?"

"Ghosts can't penetrate lead," Jessie said. "The metal's too dense."

Heavy curtains were drawn over the windows on either side of the front door with brass numbers spelling out 204. I knocked, but no sounds of movement came from within. It didn't matter. We weren't leaving until I knew what was inside. I glared at the lock and willed it to turn.

"C'mon," I ground out, resisting the urge to kick the door. My telekinesis had obeyed me at the employment agency when my blood practically sang with adrenaline, but with a cooler head my wishes seemed to go unanswered.

"Allow me, sweetheart." Nicholas rarely used endearments, and after what had recently passed between us, I knew it wasn't meant for me. He eyed Jessie smugly as the door popped open.

A partition a few feet past the front door did its best to create an entry way, but there was no hiding the dining room table and narrow kitchen just beyond, which then fed into a living room with barely enough space for a sofa and a few chairs. The odor of stale garbage made my nose wrinkle, and a quick peek at the overflowing kitchen bin revealed whoever stayed there was on a steady diet of Chinese takeout.

We all turned to face the smooth, gunmetal grey wall opposite the kitchen. It was devoid of a door or any other means of access. I pressed my palms against the dull, unyielding surface.

"Scarlett!" Warren yelled, banging with both fists. When he stopped to listen, faint thuds came back in answer.

Overwhelming gratitude and relief made me want to laugh and cry at the same time. "We're here! We're coming!"

Warren raised his hands so they were a few inches from the wall's surface before glancing around self-consciously. "Don't laugh, but this really helps."

Before I could ask, he screwed his face up in concentration and said, "Abracadabra."

A small fire began to burn. After a minute or so, when he dropped his arms, the wall was scorched but otherwise undamaged.

"Stand back." Nicholas took a few deep breaths as if preparing to lift a heavy weight. The entire apartment began to rattle as if a small earthquake were building up steam. I stood at his shoulder and added my own energy. Thin cracks started to snake up the living room walls, and dust from the ceiling plaster rained down on our hair, but the metal wall held fast.

"Stop," I urged, wilting from the strain. "It's not working."

Marcel's head snapped up. "Another Nine is here." He took up position between the door and his regent. "It's a materialist."

"Get behind me, Blake," Nicholas ordered tersely. "Marcel, contain him."

The door banged open.

"Stop!" I said again, recognizing the figure backlit by winter light. Gustav, The Lower 8's house materialist, stepped over the threshold, and the tension in the room deflated.

"You got here fast," Jessie observed.

Gustav scowled. "You didn't give me much choice. 'Get here in five minutes or you're fired.'"

Nicholas glared at the phantomist. "It didn't occur to you to tell us you sent for him?"

"Now why would I rise up from the gutter to tell you that?" Jessie offered up a lazy smile as he echoed Nicholas's own words from the night the Texan lost his bid for regent.

"Over here, Gustav," I said. "We think Scarlett's trapped behind that wall. Can you do something about it?"

Gustav's annoyance turned into a show of boredom at being asked to do something so obviously beneath his talents. With a careless wave of his hand, a doorway opened in the wall. As I rushed into the room beyond, a wave of fury crashed over me that wasn't mine. Instinct made me retreat a few steps, saving me from the table lamp that would have fractured my skull instead of harmlessly slashing the air in front of my face. Stunned, I stared mutely at Scarlett, whose own face was blank with shock.

"Blake?" she asked, almost in disbelief. The truth of her rescue dawned, and she barreled into me. I braced for rage, blame, and words that would scar me for life, but she threw her arms around me and began to sob. Tears spilled down my cheeks as I clung to the girl who'd given more for our friendship than I could ever repay.

She let out a cry when she spotted Warren. I stepped aside as he wrapped his arms around her. It was his turn to weep, and she comforted him as if their positions were reversed. It was such a Scarlett move. A sketchy homelife as a kid had honed her inner strength to a fine edge.

"I'm fine." She cradled his face in her hands. "Other than being force fed really bad Chinese take-out, which should be against the Geneva Convention, they didn't hurt me."

They spoke quietly for a few moments while I took in the details of Scarlett's lead-lined prison. An air vent in the ceiling was the sole source of fresh air. Other than the ill-fated lamp, the only other furniture was a bed and dresser, with no television or reading material in sight. She'd committed no crime, and yet she'd been sentenced to solitary confinement.

Warren finally calmed enough to seek out the connecting bathroom to splash cold water on his overheated face.

"You really are okay?" I asked.

She took a fortifying breath and nodded. "It's you he wants, not me."

"Then let's get you home and—"

"No." Her indignant expression brooked no argument. "I'm not going to sit at home anymore. Maybe I can't move things with my mind or set things on fire with a hard stare, but that doesn't mean I'm helpless. I'm not a victim, okay?" A rush of defiance accompanied her last few words. Whatever she'd gone through, her essence had survived intact.

She gazed about the windowless room. "We have a lot to talk about, but for the love of Pete, can we do it somewhere else?"

"Maybe at The Lower 8 over the best macaroni and cheese outside of Texas?" Jessie asked, drawing Scarlett's attention to the doorway where he and Nicholas pointedly ignored each other. "I'm Jessie McCabe, and I'm mighty pleased to meet you."

She took in his ridiculously handsome features and sinuous form before her eyes slid back to me with a look that said we'd be talking about this later.

"You know I'm not a Nine, right?" she asked him.

He grinned, lightening the mood. "With all that our people have put you through, I think you've earned an honorary membership, don't you?"

Out for Revenge

Scarlett blinked owlishly as we stepped into daylight. Marcel had remained outside to warn of any approaching Nines, and Nicholas told him of our plan to reconvene at The Lower 8.

"I need you to stay here and watch the place," he added.

"Who's going to shield you?" Marcel protested. "You heard the acting Prime. I'll be the door sentinel in hell if anything happens to you." He stiffened, as if suddenly realizing his words painted him as the opportunist he was, despite his newly adopted humility. "Ah, what I meant to say, Regent, is your life is of the utmost—"

"I'll call Blake's dad as soon as we leave here to explain things," Nicholas said dryly. "Right now, our best chance at finding the man responsible for taking Scarlett is by waiting for him to come back. If he has a sentinel with him, you are the only one of us who can fly under the radar."

"It's two people," Scarlett clarified. "The man is the one who makes walls appear and disappear. I don't know what the woman does."

"And when they return?" Marcel directed the question at his boss.

"Call me immediately," he replied. "Take pictures of them if you—"

"Follow them," Scarlett interjected, her tone steely. "You can't let these people get away. They aren't done with Blake—not by a long shot."

I handed the sentinel the plastic card that served as the Tesla's spare key. "A red car is pretty noticeable, so try not to let them see you."

Scarlett cast me a confused glance. "I thought our car was white."

Rather than ask Warren to let go of Scarlett's hand long enough to take the wheel, Nicholas volunteered to drive the four of us to The Lower 8 in the Honda. The reunited couple huddled together into the back while I took the front passenger seat.

"Are you sure about bringing my dad into this?" I asked Nicholas. I couldn't help thinking about the anonymous phone call warning my father not to stir up the past.

"Try keeping him out of it. I called him as soon as we found Scarlett, and it was all I could do to convince him not to rush right over."

"Mr. Wilder is here?" Scarlett piped up from the back.

"He came as soon as he heard you'd disappeared," I tossed over my shoulder.

Scarlett's warmth and gratitude sweetened the air. It made texting my dad with the address of the club a little easier.

The vast parking lot in front of The Lower 8 was deserted and would be until the place opened in the early evening, but the handful of cars parked near the employee entrance was evidence the prep cooks were already hard at work. As we passed through the kitchen, Scarlett slowed to breathe in the scent of roasting meats and bubbling cheeses, sighing with anticipation. It was the main room of the club, however, that made her stop in her tracks.

Gustav had been in the process of converting the space into a fantasy from the Arabian Nights when he'd been called away to aid in her liberation. The Austrian's injured artistic sensibilities were soothed by my friend's astonished reaction to the rich carpets, brightly tiled walls, velvet divans, and golden pillars supporting arches through which one must pass to get to the bar, kitchen, and dance floor. By the time she joined the rest of us at a large table, the materialist gallantly informed her that participating in her rescue had been his honor.

"You need a job?" Jessie joked, eyeing his prickly employee's retreating back. "I'll make you head Gustav wrangler."

"I'm done with temping, that's for damn sure," she said.

The kitchen door swung open. My dad strode in with Chico tucked under one arm, and the sense of my worlds colliding was complete. Never did I think to see both him and Scarlett gathered at The Lower 8 with the likes of Jessie and Nicholas.

Dad's gaze went right to her, and she sprang out of her chair. He enveloped her in a wordless hug, the dog's frantically wagging tail conveying enough happiness for all three of them. Jessie rose next and introduced himself to my father with a handshake and his customary charm before everyone got down to business.

"It was all a ploy," Scarlett said, offering Warren a brief smile when he returned from the bar with her diet soda. "The job, the running around, getting me to drop my guard… it was all to get revenge on Blake."

"Revenge for what?" Dad asked. He may have been there in his capacity as a sentinel, but that would always take second place to being a parent.

She directed her answer at me. "Do you remember someone named Luna?" My gaze flew to Jessie, knowing he too would recall the showdown at the abandoned warehouse that ended in the enchanter's death. The memory of her cruelty still haunted my dreams.

"She's the one who tried to make Jordan kill me," I said.

Scarlett nodded, confirming she remembered the story. "The man who took me is her cousin. He says you murdered Luna in cold blood."

I bit back words of denial, resisting the urge to defend myself when everyone at the table knew it had been self-defense.

"What does this person look like?" Nicholas had his phone out, ready to take notes.

Her mouth pursed as if being asked to recall a bad date. "I'd cast him as a scumbag stockbroker who makes just enough money to support a bad drug habit." It was such a Scarlett thing to say it gave me hope she truly was as unaffected by the experience as she professed to be, but Nicholas had yet to type a word.

She caught his bemusement and sighed. "Brown hair, kinda cute, mid-twenties, around five foot eleven, a hundred and fifty pounds, desperately in need of a better skin care routine because he has—" She waved her fingers about her own face. "The kind of skin you get from powdering your nose, if you know what I mean." No one at the table believed she referred to makeup.

The kitchen door flapped open again, and this time a man wearing a clean white apron bore a large tray into the room. Jessie must have requested an assortment of dishes because the cook set down plates of burgers, salads, and fries. Scarlett lit up when he placed the promised platter of macaroni and cheese directly in front of her.

"His girlfriend called him Cosmo." She eagerly spooned a heap of the steaming dish onto her plate. "I never heard her use his last name."

My dad perked up at the name and reached for his phone.

"You know something, Dad?" I asked.

"Do you have the number for the acting Prime?" He was so distracted I sent him Dev's contact without further question.

"Did you see her?" Nicholas asked. "The girlfriend?"

She nodded, taking a bite and closing her eyes in ecstasy. "This is heaven."

"I keep my promises." Jessie's eyes slid over me before he grabbed one of the burgers, and I wondered which promise he meant. To always have my back?

"Girlfriend?" Nicholas prodded again.

She swallowed another bite before answering. "Pretty, thin—I bet she didn't get stuck eating endless orange chicken—long dark hair, and about the same age as him."

The description fit Amani, but I didn't dare glance at Jessie. He took matters into his own hands and scrolled through his phone. Once he found what he was looking for, he flashed the screen at Scarlett. On it was a picture of Amani in the pink dress she'd worn at To The Nines.

"Is this her?" His expression remained neutral, but his emotions betrayed his pensiveness.

Scarlett narrowed her eyes, taking a long moment to inspect the photo. "No."

This time I did look at Jessie and hoped he could read the apology in my eyes. Our gazes held for a few moments before he nodded his acceptance. Another knot loosened in my chest.

"Does anyone have my phone?" It had taken Scarlett longer than expected to ask about it.

"It's at your place," Warren said, "but it may be time for a new one. It got kind of wet."

Her brows knit together. "Wet? How?"

I glanced at my dad, who didn't yet know about my watery run in with the materialist, and I suppressed a groan. Keeping secrets had begun in the name of protecting those around me, but somehow it had simply become easier to stay quiet than to argue or defend my choices.

I'd come to realize withholding the news from Nicholas about the Nines harassing me at work had less to do with easing his worry and more to do with my own need for independence. Not telling my dad about the Tesla being transformed into a goldfish bowl let me avoid lectures and attempts at control that were doomed to fail. On the flipside, didn't I expect those I cared about to be honest with me? And if I was truly ready to stand on my own, was it really that difficult to defend my choices?

Nicholas's ringing phone postponed having to explain how Scarlett's phone drowned in the middle of a busy street.

"It's Marcel," he said before answering. "You're on speaker."

"They're back," the sentinel reported. "It's a materialist and a telepath."

Scarlett was the first to jump to her feet. "Let's go."

Warren hurried to stand beside her. "You've already been through a lot. Maybe we let the others handle it."

"Don't you dare try to sideline me." She glared at her boyfriend. "I was stuck in that room without a phone, television, or even a stupid magazine, and it gave me a lot of time to think. Do you know what came up again and again? That every single Nine in my life—you, Blake, even Mr. Wilder over there—has kept me out of everything *for my own good*." She put a mocking spin on the last few words.

"Nines can be dangerous," Warren said, foolishly wading in while my dad and I had the good sense not to interrupt when Scarlett had something to say.

"You think I don't know that? I was just kidnapped and held hostage for the past—" she paused in her tirade and pinned me with a look. "How long was I gone?"

"You disappeared Saturday night, it's now Tuesday around noon," I responded.

"Three days! Did I mention there wasn't a clock in my prison? I couldn't tell day from night." She picked at the Cal State

Santa Carla sweatshirt she wore over a pair of leggings. "And I'm still wearing the same clothes, the same *underwear*, I put on Saturday morning."

She may have strayed from her point, but none of us dared to interrupt. She deserved a few minutes to release the pent-up fright and rage of the last several days.

"If you people are going to be in my life, then guess what?" She turned her glare on the table as a whole. "I'm going to be in yours. No more 'you can't go where we go' or crap like that. Now the asshole who conned me and wants to hurt Blake is about to figure out I'm gone, and I don't want him to get away."

"Scarlett, wait," Nicholas said when she would have charged from the room. He held up his phone so we could all view the screen. A mugshot of a nice looking, brown-haired man beamed from the display. He looked familiar, but I couldn't place him.

"Is this the man who took you?" he asked.

Despite almost shaking with the need to hunt down and punish the people who'd held her captive, she paused to view the image. Her expression hardened. "That's him."

"Dev says he's Cosmo D'Onofrio, a Class Two materialist. We know who he is, Scarlett. He's not getting away."

"Uh, Regent?" Marcel's voice piped up through the phone's speaker. I'd forgotten he was still there. "They're coming back out, and the guy doesn't look happy. What do you want me to do?"

Nicholas and Scarlett locked gazes, her desperate determination obvious even to those who weren't empaths.

"Follow them," he said.

Unexpected Company

"They're circling Blake's apartment building," Marcel said, Nicholas's phone still on speaker. Scarlett's abductors were almost certainly checking to see if my latest car was in its designated spot, which meant the sentinel had so far done a good job of going undetected. "They're leaving. It looks like they're going to that coffee place where Blake works."

I pulled up the Tesla app on my phone and tracked the car's red icon travel the familiar route to Jitters.

"They're hunting you," Jessie murmured, putting words to my own disturbing thoughts.

"The telepath has gone inside," the sentinel reported from the Jitters parking lot. "Wait—she's coming back out." The woman had stayed inside only long enough to discover the staff behind the counter didn't include me. "We're moving again."

While we waited to hear where they went next, I asked my dad the question that had been bugging me for the past few minutes. "How did you figure out who the guy was so quickly?"

"Cosmo isn't exactly the most common name," he said. "In fact, the first known use of the name was by a Christian martyr in the third century, but it doesn't appear again until Italy's brutal Medici family. Grand Duke Cosmo wreaked havoc on Tuscany in the late fifteenth, early sixteenth centuries, although he did commission Donatello's *David*, so he wasn't a complete despot. After that—"

"Dad," I cut in, knowing we'd be there all day if he had free reign to recount all the Cosmos of the past five hundred years. "Can you fast forward to the twenty-first century please?"

"Ah, of course. As it happens, I'd just received a response to my inquiry into that dead enchanter, Luna, and at the top it listed the Nines in her family tree, which included Cosmo D'Onofrio. I simply sent the name to the acting Prime, and he did the rest."

Nicholas opened his cell again, and the image on screen was still the photo of Cosmo D'Onofrio he'd shown Scarlett. This time, something clicked.

"He was here last week, at The Lower 8," I said. "He tried to stop me from leaving."

"Why would he do that?" he asked with that protective edge in his voice, but I couldn't very well say the materialist had blocked my path as I attempted to flee from Jessie and his new girlfriend.

"I thought he was hitting on me, so I kinda blew him off," I said, not untruthfully, "but now I wonder what he really had in mind."

"They're going into a parking garage," Marcel broke in. "I think it belongs to the apartments overhead that look like tall, connected houses."

"Condos," Scarlett murmured.

"Text me the address," Nicholas said. "We're on our way." We all rose from the table, including Jessie.

"I got this, McCabe," Nicholas said dismissively.

Jessie appeared distracted for a moment before a slow smile slid across his face. "Harper wants to help. Who am I to deny an eager, young spirit?"

The phantomist followed in his truck while the rest of us piled into my dad's SUV.

We traced Marcel to a part of town Scarlett and I scouted when we were apartment hunting last fall. She'd rhapsodized over the beautiful old pepper trees fronting rows of pretty condos, but it had taken us less than five minutes to discover the only way we could afford to live there was if we gave up the luxuries in life, like eating, electricity, and running water.

"The least the guy could have done was hold me prisoner here," Scarlett griped.

We pulled up behind the Tesla with Jessie on our tail. Marcel and Jessie got out of their cars and congregated at my front passenger window, keeping a low profile in case the couple we pursued should happen to glance out at the street.

"They went down that driveway," the sentinel said, pointing across the road to the entrance of an underground parking garage at the other end of the block. Above it was a tri-level development painted in buttery shades of yellow with top floor Juliet balconies jutting over the street. Each of the six units had its own entrance, their front doors set back from a wide sidewalk.

My dad unbuckled his seatbelt. "You all wait here while I go check it out."

"I'll go with you," Marcel volunteered, but my dad shook his head.

"One of them might recognize you from some of the places you've worked." He cracked a sardonic smile. "At least one good thing will come from spending the last twenty years of my life as a mild-mannered professor."

"Harper's going too," Jessie said. "She thinks she'd recognize the materialist who hassled Blake if she saw him again."

Snapping on Chico's leash, Dad strolled toward the building with purpose, and I realized he was enjoying himself. With Scarlett safe, he could flex long dormant muscles that had once been finely tuned in his role as the Prime. He slowed once he reached the building, meandering past each door with his phone in his hand as if searching for a particular address. The dog was more than happy to sniff every shrub and potted plant along the way, lifting his leg and leaving his calling card in several places. It was a convincing enough performance that it was a shame no one but us was around to notice.

"There are two Nines in number 748, second door in from the left," he reported when they returned to the car. "A telepath and a materialist."

Scarlett leaned up from the backseat. "You can tell that just by walking by?"

There was a touch of pride in Dad's smile. "Almost any sentinel worth their salt can pick up a Nine's signature if they're relatively close by, and a Class One can identify what powers they possess."

"It's the same guy Harper saw last week," Jessie confirmed. "She doesn't know the woman he's with."

"The question now is what we do about it," I said.

"I'll tell you what we do about it," Scarlett said. "You and Nicholas use your telekinesis to pull that condo down around their ears."

I turned in my seat to face her. She didn't suffer fools and would be the first to stand against any injustice, but when she'd learned how Sutton Sinclair had served as judge, jury, and executioner after his son had confessed to murder, she'd condemned The Nine for their biblical and bloodthirsty approach to crime and punishment.

"Are you sure that's what you really want?" I gently inquired.

Her lips clamped together in frustration, her justifiable rage clashing with the more sensible side of her nature.

"Okay, maybe I don't want to bring a house down on their heads," she allowed, "but they need to pay for what they did to me and be stopped from doing whatever it is they plan to do to you."

"We're walking a fine line here," Dad counseled. "Other than possibly harassing Blake a few times, they haven't committed any offenses against a Nine. If we move against them, it is us who will be in the wrong, at least in the eyes of The Nine."

"So they're going to get away with it?" Scarlett's eyes shone with angry tears.

"No, they're not," I said firmly, shooting Nicholas a beseeching glance, but he was focused on his phone screen, his thumbs flying across the keyboard.

"Someone's here," Warren said, drawing all eyes to the pretty little Mercedes coup pulling up in front of the second condo from the left. The car door opened, and a fashionably trendy boot stepped onto the pavement.

Standing at my open window, Jessie's face lost all color as Amani emerged from the car with keys in hand, which she used to open the door to 748 Hudson Street.

An Unlikely Alliance

My mind raced to sort through the implications of Amani's arrival. There was no denying she'd used a key to enter the residence where Cosmo D'Onofrio and an unknown telepath sought refuge. At best, the telepath was her sister or a close friend, and she was unaware of the woman's agenda in Santa Carla. At worst, Amani had come to town to help orchestrate my downfall, and she'd used Jessie to get close to me.

The phantomist hadn't budged from his position outside my open car window, and the air around him crackled with outrage and pain.

"I'm so sorry," I said just loud enough for him to hear.

He glanced at me, his expression strained. "Me too."

Nicholas finally looked up from his phone. "We have the authority to detain the materialist."

"What does that mean?" Scarlett asked.

"I explained the situation to the chancellor and the acting Prime, and they've agreed he should be brought in for questioning," he explained.

"By us?" Warren didn't seem thrilled by the idea.

"We can wait for Dev and a few of his deputies," Nicholas said, "but if I'd kidnapped the best friend of a powerful Nine who'd then escaped, I'd be packing my bags and leaving town right about now."

"Oh no, they're not," Scarlett vowed, unbuckling her seatbelt and making to climb over Warren.

"Wait," her boyfriend urged. "We won't let them get away. I promise. But let's at least have a plan before taking on a materialist and an enchanter, okay?"

"An enchanter who's also a sentinel," I said for those who hadn't gotten the memo.

"Are you saying she can prevent Mr. Wilder or Marcel from containing her power or shielding us?" Warren's voice rose higher with each word.

My dad's face was grim. "Possibly both, but there's no way of knowing until we try."

"We're running out of time," Jessie warned. "Harper says they'll be walking out the front door in just a couple of minutes."

Nicholas charged out of the car. "We're going in. We need to keep this contained."

"Fine by me," Scarlett said, sliding across the backseat.

Warren moved to block his girlfriend's exit. "Please stay here. It's too dangerous for you."

Dad and I glanced at each other, his dubious expression a mirror of my own thoughts. Good luck telling Scarlett to do anything she didn't want to do.

"Don't take this the wrong way, Warren," she bit out, "but get the fuck out of my way."

My dad came to Warren's rescue. "Jordan's softball bag is in the trunk. How 'bout we arm her with a nice titanium bat? Packs quite a wallop, you know."

Within moments, our unlikely posse—one sentinel, a former Prime, a telekinetic, a phantomist, a baby elementalist, one pissed off woman wielding a bat, a dog, and me—gathered on the sidewalk. Jessie and Nicholas regarded one another stiffly. They were on the same side of the argument for a change, but it didn't mean either of them had to like it.

"Can we count on you to get us in the front door?" Jessie asked him.

Nicholas snorted dismissively. "Considering I could open a digital bank vault at seventeen, I think I can handle it."

Jessie regarded the rest of us. "Harper says they're on the second floor."

"The sentinels should go in first and focus on neutralizing the materialist and the enchanter," Nicholas said.

The phantomist squared his shoulders. "*I'll* deal with Amani."

It was less of a plan and more like a reckless outline. My blood chilled at the thought of Jessie throwing himself into the line of fire, but he didn't seem to care. If Amani regarded him as nothing more than a means to an end, there was no telling what she might do when he confronted her.

"Try to keep your thoughts on what you're having for dinner, or what you're bingeing on Netflix right now," my dad instructed as we crossed the street. "If the telepath is on alert, the less hostility you emit, the easier it'll be for Marcel and me to mask your intentions and retain the element of surprise."

I caught up with my dad. "Are you sure about this?"

He shrugged, but the grin tugging at the corners of his mouth betrayed his excitement. "Two sentinels against three Nines? Hardly seems like a fair fight."

We reached the front door, and Jessie shifted on his feet like a boxer about to enter the ring. "Ready?"

Nicholas started forward, but I put a hand on his arm. He tensed, a reminder of yet another battle to come.

"Keep an eye on my dad," I murmured. "Please. He seems to have forgotten he hasn't been the Prime in twenty years."

"I thought you'd be more concerned for your friend McCabe." He shook off my hand and joined Jessie at the door. With an effortless flick of his fingers, the door silently popped open.

Dad and Marcel padded inside like a pair of cats on the prowl with Jessie right behind. Warren hovered protectively about Scarlett, despite her determination not to be sidelined, while Nicholas and I followed. Thick carpeting muted the click of Chico's nails.

To the right of the front door, a stairway rose to the upper levels. Terse voices from above trailed down the steps, and fear danced up my spine. I'd been forced to defend myself a number of times since The Nine entered my life, but going on the attack felt frighteningly medieval. We might lack broadswords and armor—although Scarlett gripped the bat as if she anticipated bringing home the winning run—but lives were at stake, particularly ones I cared about.

We'd crept halfway up the stairs when a gasp sounded from above and the conversation stilled. Everyone froze, barely daring to even breathe.

"What is it, Sybil?" a brusque male voice demanded.

"I don't know," said a woman, her answer shaded with uncertainty, "but we need to leave."

My father turned to us and held up three fingers. We stood poised as he put each finger down in quick succession.

"Now!" he commanded, and we all charged up the stairs.

42

The Meaning of Love

The blank expressions on the three people standing in a living room with tall windows and vaulted ceilings would have been comical if we'd had more than a split second to prevent a bloodbath. To his credit, Marcel didn't hesitate as he flew across the room to tackle the lone man before the materialist could gather his wits. An unfamiliar woman—the telepathic Sybil, no doubt—shrieked as a side chair in a pretty shade of blue upended, and the men landed in a heap.

They were evenly matched in size, which probably inspired Cosmo not to give up without a fight. The sentinel could block the materialist's powers, but there was nothing wrong with his fists. I winced as Marcel took a punch to the face, but he took his revenge by smashing his opponent's head against the floor, barely missing a glass coffee table.

Sybil, a dark-haired young woman whose pointed chin and close-set eyes added a hint of slyness to her otherwise pleasant face, picked up a heavy crystal vase filled with a beautiful bouquet and raised it over her head. She avidly followed the brawl, likely waiting for Marcel to gain the advantage so she'd have a clear shot at crowning his skull. Seeing her opening, Scarlett sliced the air with her bat, and the vase exploded in a colorful spray of flowers. Sybil shrieked as water and shattered crystal flew in every direction.

"Don't move," Scarlett ordered the telepath, "or you'll be the only girl in your Pilates class without knees."

The woman must have heard the fearless intention behind Scarlett's words because she raised her hands in surrender.

Marcel continued his assault on the materialist. The desperation seeping from Cosmo's pores made me think he relied on his paranormal power to bully his way through life and couldn't best the sentinel without it. Seizing an opening, the materialist lunged toward the fireplace and snatched a poker hanging from a hook. With a triumphant sneer, he leveled the metal spear at his opponent and charged.

I had to disarm him. Putting every ounce of energy into that one thought, the poker flew from his hand and rocketed through the air—and straight at Warren. With reflexes honed through hours of surfing and skateboarding, he dropped to his knees as it zinged overhead and imbedded itself into the wall. We both stared at the quivering rod as the close call sunk in.

"Sorry," I said weakly.

"Don't mention it," he said, getting shakily to his feet.

Chico began barking wildly, and I whipped around to find another bizarre tableau. Nicholas had my father's arm twisted behind his back, grimacing each time the small dog nipped at his legs. Next to them Jessie struggled as if his feet had been nailed to the floor.

Immune to a sentinel's influence, Amani had overpowered them all.

The crack of a fist against bone echoed like a gunshot, and Cosmo collapsed limply on the floor. Marcel climbed to his feet, face and knuckles bloodied and panting for breath, before he too turned to stare at the unfolding drama.

Amani's allies were lost and she was dramatically outnumbered, but her confidence remained undimmed, and rightly so. An enchanter who could restrain three people without breaking a sweat could probably do the same to the rest of us. Her gaze narrowed as she regarded the noisy dog.

"Quiet, mutt," she commanded.

Chico's mouth snapped shut. A few whines escaped as he cast a baleful eye at my dad before flopping down on the floor in defeat.

I glared at her. "Why are you doing this?"

A sweet floral sheath in some filmy fabric floated about her, completely at odds with the fire in her eyes. "I was Luna's patron, and you murdered her in cold blood.'"

"Don't know how I missed that detail," my dad muttered.

"I was there the night she died," Jessie said, leaping to my defense. "What happened is no one's fault but her own."

Amani took an angry step forward. "You lie! You're so wrapped up in that voyant she couldn't even take a walk down the street without you rushing out to watch over her."

"It *was* you!" The SUV coming at me full speed flashed through my mind. "You tried to run me down."

Her smirk confirmed the accuracy of my accusation. "I wouldn't have needed to if the Palmarium ball had done its job." She glanced between me and her one-time boyfriend. "However, they do say third time's the charm."

Without warning, Jessie lunged at me. His hands wrapped around my throat and squeezed.

"No!" he howled, his tortured expression much like my sister's when Luna had tried to force her into being my executioner. The absurd thought that Amani must have taught this murderous technique to her protégé flashed through my mind.

"Let her go," my dad pleaded, the terror in his voice frightening me more than anything else. After everything The Nine had taken from him, he didn't deserve to lose me as well.

Suddenly another pair of hands were there, slowly prying the phantomist's fingers off my neck. Stars shot across my field of vision when at last I could draw breath, and I coughed with relief.

"I got you, buddy," Warren said with great effort, gradually pulling Jessie's arms behind him as if the both of them were moving through glue. The phantomist closed his eyes in gratitude, his chest heaving.

"What's your plan, enchanter?" Nicholas challenged. He nodded at Jessie and Warren. "It looks like you've reached your limit. How much longer do you think you can hold us off before your strength completely gives out?"

"You broke in here and attacked me," she said with feigned innocence. "I'm just protecting myself. It's Luna's cousin who wants Blake dead."

"You lying bitch!" Huddled in a corner, Sybil had apparently decided she chose the wrong side. "*You* put Cosmo up to this. We were only supposed to frighten her. No one said anything about murder!"

Amani glanced at Scarlett, and a look of terror distorted the telepath's features at whatever crossed the enchanter's mind.

"No!" Sybil said in a terrified whine.

"Finish the job," Amani commanded, and Scarlett's face went blank even as her body was in motion. She took a swing at Sybil, who dove to the floor and scrambled behind a sofa.

I couldn't let my best friend kill someone against her will, no matter how hellbent on vengeance she might be. Nicholas had said breaking a Nine's concentration could loosen their hold, so we needed a distraction.

"Warren," I whispered with a tilt of my head in Amani's direction. "Abracadabra."

His eyes widened as he understood my meaning. He stared hard at the enchanter and whispered the magic word.

The wispy fabric at the hem of Amani's dress sparked and glowed. She squealed in pain and surprise, and the room erupted. Nicholas dropped my father's arm while she slapped out the small flames. A split-second later, her body flew skyward. Nicholas stood with his palm raised, keeping her pinned to the ceiling twenty feet overhead.

Dad pulled me into a trembling hug as Chico barked and danced at our feet. After inspecting my neck and being satisfied the damage was only skin deep, he bent down to offer the dog the same reassurance he'd needed himself.

"Get me down, Regent, or I promise you will regret what happens next," Amani fumed.

"I'd be very careful if I were you," Nicholas called up to her. "Use your power on any of us, and I *will* let you fall. The acting Prime will determine what's to be done with you when he arrives."

My attention snagged on the heavy glass coffee table. With so much emotion racing through my veins, sending it sliding telekinetically across the room and directly underneath the enchanter proved to be no big deal.

I grinned up at Amani. "Just in case you're thinking a little fall is no big deal, I wanted to make sure you have a really good story to tell the doctors at the ER." She unleashed a string of threats and profanity, but I ignored her in favor of placing my hand on Nicholas's shoulder, adding my telekinetic strength to his.

A glance around the room revealed Warren and Scarlett standing vigil over the cowed telepath, Jessie with his back to us as he stared out one of the tall windows, Cosmo D'Onofrio sleeping peacefully on the blood-spattered living room rug, and Marcel splayed on the sofa, his handsome face almost unrecognizable beneath swollen and bruised flesh.

With Chico contentedly tucked under one arm, my father took stock of the situation.

"Don't let the telepath say a word," he said to Warren and Scarlett. "And sit on that materialist, Marcel," he ordered, slipping easily into the once familiar role of Prime. "I don't want him waking up without us knowing about it. I'll get some ice for your…" He took in the extent of sentinel's injuries, from his face to his bloodied knuckles to a bite mark on his arm. "For everything," he concluded.

After Dad left to find the kitchen, a heavy silence hung over the room. I sensed Jessie's resolve before he turned back to regard the woman he'd come to care for, but she refused to meet his accusing stare.

"Was any of it ever real?" The emotions flowing from him were a bitter mix of hope and heartbreak.

His question broke through the ice of her reserve. "You were just supposed to be some player who could get me close to the voyant, so I figured we'd both get something out of the deal. Why couldn't you stick to the plan?"

His jaw clenched. "Were you really going to kill Blake?"

"Not at first," she admitted. "I only wanted to make her suffer for what she did to Luna, but then I thought: why should she get to have everything when she's taken so much from me?"

"You had me," he said quietly. "Why couldn't you let that be enough?"

The question seemed to bring home what she'd had—and what she'd lost. "I don't know." She closed her eyes for a long moment. "I think I could have loved you. Maybe I already do."

Jessie drew in a ragged breath. "You know nothing about love. Love is risking everything to be open and honest, even if the other person questions your motives. Love is apologizing, even when you're right, because that's what the other person needs to hear. Love is being who that person wants you to be, even if you can't have that in return." He shook his head. "You will never understand."

Amani lifted her chin, gathering her pride about her like a tattered coat. "You're not talking about us anymore, are you?"

Over in her corner, the telepath let out a little gasp and gaped at me.

My dad returned with several baggies full of ice and a dishtowel, oblivious to the new tension in the room.

"I texted the acting Prime to confirm he's coming with a healing evanescent," he told Marcel, eying the other man's blackening eye. "We'll get you fixed right up."

Signposts

Dev arrived with enough sentinels to keep Amani in line while she, Cosmo, and Sybil were delivered to Alder House. Despite the enchanter's declaration of innocence, and Cosmo groggily protesting he'd committed no crime against another Nine—filling the Tesla with water had been nothing more than a prank, he claimed—the board of regents would hear the evidence and decide if their crimes deserved punishment.

Betty Goldberg, a local senior citizen who happened to be a powerful healing evanescent, trotted up the stairs. With unruly hair resembling steel wool in both style and color and a wardrobe that could best be described as garage sale chic, she left an indelible impression every time we met.

"Mr. Trivedi thought I might be needed," she said with a touch of self-importance, her knowing gaze scrutinizing the two battered men. "I see he was right."

I led her over to Marcel, who had baggies of ice covering a variety of body parts. Betty gently removed the one atop his right hand and tsked at the sight of his bloody knuckles swollen to disconcerting proportions.

"What about me?" Cosmo sullenly demanded, one hand bracing his chin as if it might otherwise fall off. "I think that bastard broke my bloody jaw."

When he'd come round, my father had forced him and Sybil into seated positions against the wall. Along with the newly arrived Jane Cassidy, who stood proudly at Dad's side, he watched over the pair while three other sentinels guarded Amani.

"Wait your turn," Marcel told the materialist with a glare, which would have been more effective if his eyes hadn't swollen to mere slits.

"Oh my," Betty said with a girlish giggle. "How exciting to have two handsome young men fighting over me."

Cosmo's attempt at a rude scoff turned into a sob as he cradled his jaw with both hands.

Scarlett trudged over with one of Warren's arms slung around her waist, his free hand gripping her elbow as if he feared she might keel over. Considering what she'd endured over the last few days, his concerns were valid.

"Can we go home now?" she asked, swaying on her feet with the bat still gripped firmly in her fist.

Nicholas was tied up with Dev, Jessie had departed soon after the cavalry's arrival without saying a word, and Dad was enjoying the rare company of fellow Nines far too much to be interrupted, so I slipped away without fanfare. By the time we reached our apartment, Scarlett and Warren were slumped together in the back seat of the Tesla, both dead to the world. They roused long enough to stagger into her room, but after the door closed behind them, silence reigned.

Two cardboard boxes had been left on the doorstep while we were out, the slightly larger one for Scarlett and the smaller one for me. The sender on hers was listed as a fulfillment center in town while mine appeared to have been hand delivered with nothing more than my name scrawled across the top. Grabbing a pair of scissors, I took my package to the coffee table and sliced it open. On top of the mysterious contents was a handwritten note from Jessie.

In case of emergency, break glass xo

Pushing aside a wad of brown paper revealed a black object about five inches long that fit neatly in my hand. A metal point protruded at one end, and pressing a button on the side unsheathed a serrated blade. I smiled as its purpose became clear. He'd sent me a tool to break a window or slice open a seatbelt if I ever found myself trapped in a car again. Despite my accusations against his girlfriend—which turned out to be spot on, though there was little satisfaction in being proven right—he'd still cared enough to make sure I could escape if the incident with the Tesla was ever repeated.

My heart ached for the Texan. Regular people could nurse their pain in private if they wished, but the first curious telepath who crossed his path would pluck the story of Amani's duplicity from his mind. His only defense would be to not think about it, but it was almost impossible to lockdown your mind, especially when raw emotions were added to the mix.

I reached for my phone to give Layla a heads up, but a missed text notification from Julia Martin brought me up short. Had she broken into Henry's safe? Were any of the twenty-eight gold coins missing, and if so, how many? What I most feared, now that the answer was likely at my fingertips, was that only one coin was gone. It wouldn't prove the one in Nicholas's possession had been used to muddy the waters around Francesca's death, but it wouldn't rule it out either.

Not giving myself time to dwell on the uncertainty any longer, I opened my phone and read the text.

There are 27 coins in the safe. How did you know one was missing?

Curled up on the sofa and lost in thought, I hadn't noticed the arrival of late afternoon shadows. By the time a knock came at the door, darkness had fully claimed the room. Switching on a few lights, I glanced out the window to see Nicholas, Marcel, and my dad standing on the front porch.

A black SUV with its lights on waited at the curb. Of course it did. Scarlett was safe, the people harassing me were in custody, so Henry had snapped his fingers and summoned Nicholas back to Alder House. I yanked open the door, and they filed in with Chico trotting at their heels.

"What a day," Dad said, his eyes shining. "Are Scarlett and Warren okay?"

I nodded. "They're sleeping."

"Can we talk for a minute?" Nicholas cut in. Without waiting for an answer, he went straight to my room and flicked on the light. My dad nodded, so I dutifully followed, closing the bedroom door and leaning my back against it. He glanced up from folding a shirt into his suitcase.

"You're leaving," I said, stating the obvious.

"I have to," he said, quickly gathering his things. "Dev is flying to Alder House tonight with the others, and in a few days he'll announce he's no longer willing to serve as acting Prime. The regents will then convene to decide his punishment for a lapse in duty, and I can't let him face the firing squad alone. We must also choose a new Prime, and since it's a ten-year term, it's important I weigh in. Then there are the deaths of Silver, Francesca, and the assassin she hired to be further investigated, and I've been asked to deal with what we suspect are a couple of bank robbing telekinetics in Warsaw."

Nowhere in his speech was regret at our parting, that we would find a way to make things work between us, or even a pat on the back for my role in taking down Cosmo and Amani.

I studied him for a long moment. "What about us, Nicholas?"

He zipped up his bag and crossed the room until we were toe to toe. His affection and admiration engulfed me, tempered with a sense of duty and determination.

"I choose you, Blake, and I want you to choose me. Give us time at Alder House to learn who we can be together, to prove I'm worthy of your love and trust." He leaned in and gave me the most gentle and exquisite kiss I'd ever known. "What we know about Henry changes everything. Our future is right there in front of us. All we have to do is take it."

My eyes fluttered open. "Are you happy?"

It took him a few moments to respond. "I believe in us."

A knock came at my back.

"Regent?" Marcel called through the door. "It's time."

As the rumble of Nicholas's SUV faded in the distance, I realized he hadn't answered my question.

Ally or Enemy

I was alone at the kitchen table the next morning when my father came by to say his farewells. Having refused an invitation to sleep in my room while I bunked down on the sofa, he and Chico had spent the night at a local hotel.

"They had a halfway decent breakfast buffet," he said, accepting the offer of coffee but declining eggs or toast. "Chico gave the sausage two paws up."

"Nothing but the best for your favorite child," I joked.

He asked about Scarlett, who had yet to stumble from her room, and he talked about the warm reception the group of sentinels had given him yesterday. Once or twice, he lost the conversational thread, and I was reminded once again of how much I'd come to depend on my growing empathic abilities to read between the lines. Something was on his mind, but I'd have to ferret it out the way normal people did.

I narrowed my gaze. "What aren't you telling me, Dad?"

He let the silence settle for a few moments before dropping his bombshell.

"I'm going to Alder House."

Dumbfounded, it took me a moment to find my tongue. "But… you can't. If Mr. Silver was killed because of what you told him, how do you think you're going to get past the front door?"

He paused to pick up Chico and settle him on his lap. "Devraj Trivedi will be waiting for me."

I sat back in my chair as my thoughts spun. When Dev met my dad and learned who he was, he must have realized he'd found the perfect spark to ignite his rebellion. If the rest of the sentinels reacted to the reappearance of the legendary missing Prime as Marcel had, Dev could transform their admiration to outrage with the tale of how their most powerful member had been betrayed by the chancellor himself. Maybe Ashwin, his own father, would be willing to provide the proof.

"No," I breathed. "Let the other sentinels deal with this. You can't go."

"If my phone call to Mr. Silver is what led to his death, I've set something in motion that won't stop until no one is alive to tell my story." His eyes traveled over my face as if he could etch the curves and planes on his heart. "This is my battle. I'll drive home, pack a bag, and fly out tomorrow."

Dev planned to wait a few days before announcing his resignation, and now I understood the delay. He wanted the missing Prime at his side when all hell broke loose.

I tasted tears on the back of my tongue. "What are you going to tell Mom?"

"That I'm going to finish what I started twenty years ago." He stroked Chico's ears as he deliberated his next words. "Whatever happens, I'll make sure the three of you are safe."

"I'm going with you." I rose from my chair.

He too got to his feet, setting Chico down in the process. "I would do anything if I could go back in time and make The Nine a safer place for you, but now I've got a second chance to do the right thing. You must let me see this through without endangering anyone else."

I came around the table, and he opened his arms to me. "What about your students? Who's going to drive Jordan to practice? How can you leave Chico?"

He stroked my hair, seeing my delaying tactic for what it was. "Everyone will keep until I get back."

Drawing back, I gazed up into the beloved face of my dad, my teacher, the cornerstone of my life. "Then why does it feel like you're saying goodbye?"

"No matter what happens, your eyes are open now. It's time to forge your own path, whatever that might be. Join forces with Nicholas if you wish, and you'll become a powerful ally in your own right." Nicholas had said as much last night.

I wiped at the moisture on my cheeks. "And if I'm not with Nicholas?"

His eyes flickered with both pride and trepidation. "Then step carefully, for you could become what Henry Thorne fears most—a daunting enemy."

He gave me a final squeeze and kissed my forehead. "Give my love to Scarlett when she wakes up."

Scarlett slept well past noon while I drank prodigious amounts of coffee. It gave me something to do other than think about all the things that could go wrong with my dad showing up at Alder House unannounced, but as a result, I practically vibrated in my chair.

Warren passed through at one point, grabbing his own cup on the way out the door.

"I have a timeslot at the student store this morning," he said, gulping it down.

We both understood the importance of keeping that appointment. With classes starting in a few days, students were given windows when textbooks could be purchased without standing in a massive line. Miss your date and a simple errand turned into an hours-long endeavor.

"Do you want me to bring you anything?" he asked, eyeing my jiggling leg. "A set of pens? A new calculator? An elephant tranquilizer?"

When Scarlett finally woke, she went straight into the bathroom. The shower ran long enough for me to wonder if the building's hot water would run dry, and when she finally emerged swathed in a thick robe, her face glowed a bright shade of pink.

"First coffee, and then we're going to burn my clothes," she cheerfully announced.

"I'll bring the lighter," I offered, not letting the fact we didn't have any place to carry out such a thing put a damper on her enthusiasm.

She poured a cup from the third pot of the day. It was mostly decaf at that point, but I'd kept it fresh so she could easily slip into her usual—and hopefully comforting—routine.

"Warren was here until about an hour ago," I said, joining her at the kitchen table.

"Please say he wasn't watching me sleep," she said with a mock shudder. "I always thought that part of the vampire book was creepy."

I laughed, mostly from the joy of having my best friend home safe. "Don't worry, he was exhausted too. I don't think he slept much the whole time you were gone." That evoked a pleased smile.

"By the way," she said, "do you know someone named Layla?"

"Head of the waitstaff at The Lower 8 Layla?" Not that I knew any others by that name.

She pulled a scrap of paper out of the pocket of her robe. "Warren left this note for me. She called his phone to invite me to come in for a job interview."

"At the club?" My face must have reflected my shock. "But you're not a Nine."

"I guess they know true talent when they see it." She flicked a wet strand of hair out of her face with a certain amount of satisfaction before spotting the package addressed to her. "What's that?"

Before I could explain it had arrived yesterday, she ripped it open. Inside was a brand new smartphone at least two generations more recent than her waterlogged one, but no note or receipt to indicate who had sent it.

She regarded me with a sage smile. "Is this your way of telling me my old phone has passed the point of no return?"

I shrugged, as nonplussed as she was. "I wish I'd thought that far ahead because your phone is probably dead, but it didn't come from me."

Turning it over in her hands, she mulled that for a moment before happily yanking off the overly excessive packaging and turning it on. She was thrilled to see it already programmed with her number and apps, which meant it must have come from The Nine. Other than the CIA, they were the only ones I knew who could remotely clone a dead phone and have it delivered so quickly.

As she dialed the number jotted across Warren's note, I wondered why a non-Nine was receiving such special treatment, not that I minded.

"I have an interview at The Lower 8 at four," Scarlett chirped, breaking into my thoughts. "I better go dry my hair." She jumped up from the chair with a level of happy excitement I hadn't expected so soon after her recent experience, but a rush of gratitude for Jessie's kindness, whatever the reason, made my heart swell.

With the drone of the blow dryer humming in the background, I called The Lower 8. When the call went to voicemail, I picked up the note Scarlett had left on the table and dialed Layla.

"Hey Blake," she said after the first ring.

"Hey, are you at the club?"

"I'm driving there now." The honk of a car horn underscored her words. "What's up?"

"How's Jessie?"

She expelled a breath, as if I'd asked a weighty question. "He didn't come into work last night, which never happens. In fact, the two nights he was in Los Angeles was the first time I think he's taken time off since the club opened."

"Did he tell you what happened with Amani?"

"I haven't talked to him, but Marie called last night. His spirit, Harper, saw that witch's betrayal and apparently couldn't wait to crow about it." Her disapproving tone conveyed what she thought of the dead girl. "It's a good thing that ghost is going to hang out with Marie for a while because she's got a lot to learn about being a phantomist's companion."

"Speaking of friends, you know my roommate Scarlett isn't a Nine, right?"

"Yeah, but hiring a family member or close friend of a Nine to work in a sanctuary club isn't unheard of. It'll just be a first for us."

"I think you'll like her. She's got a good aura." I didn't know if that was true or not, but Layla put great stock in such things.

Warren returned before Scarlett had to leave for her interview, so he volunteered to drive her to the club. That left the Tesla free for me to get it charged before heading off to work an evening shift. A text I'd sent to our landlord asking if she'd consider installing a charging station had been answered with an unequivocal no, but if I left soon, I could juice up at one of the chargers in the nearby Target parking lot, do a little shopping, and still get to work on time.

It was hard to pinpoint the exact cause of my downcast mood because so many things in my life seemed to be in flux, but the thought of buying something I didn't yet know I needed helped brighten my spirits.

The World Be Damned

No one got possessed and nothing morphed into a dangerous creature during my uneventful closing shift at Jitters. This was despite the apron I wore—*Like My Coffee, I'm Sweet, Strong, And Hot*—which, interestingly, provoked more smiles from women than men.

Cindy had hit the costume sale at the local playhouse and bought most everything from their recent production of *Grease*. From her Pink Ladies satin jacket to black kitten heels, she looked ready to burst into song.

At ten o'clock on the dot, I followed the last customer to the front door, intent on locking up before anyone could beg to come in for a double espresso to get through a late-night cram session, or an emergency cappuccino to help them finish a quarterly report. Before I could slide the key into the lock, Mr. Silver's face loomed out of the darkness and stared at me through the glass door. I stumbled back a few steps, my brain frantically trying to make sense of the impossible. The door swung open.

"Blake Wilder?" he asked.

As the thrumming in my chest slowed, I realized that while the tawny skin, full lips, and athletic build were the same, his cheek lacked the scar Silver had worn as a badge of honor, and this man's straight nose showed no signs of ever having been broken. In fact, the stranger wore a black hoodie, jeans, and scuffed trainers, clothing the Prime would have disdained.

"Rafe Silver," I whispered, feeling his internal sadness weighing him down like an ocean current. He was an evanescent who'd discovered he was also telekinetic when he was barely out of elementary school, and I wondered if his multi status had progressed even further since then.

He glanced at Cindy, who had her back to us as she cleaned the row of cappuccino machines and hadn't noticed his presence. "Can we talk outside?"

"I'll be right back," I called to her.

Except for the Tesla and my co-worker's old Camry, the parking lot was deserted. I followed Rafe Silver to the relative privacy of the stucco wall separating Jitters and Tony's Express Dry Cleaning next door. The occasional tourist would laugh to see locals wearing parkas in sixty degree temperatures, but the goosebumps breaking out on my exposed arms said it was definitely jacket weather.

"I'm so, so sorry about your brother." The words were inadequate to convey my sense of loss, but nothing better came to mind.

He nodded his appreciation. "He was coming to talk to you about the day Henry Thorne became chancellor."

The heartburn from too much coffee suddenly sharpened. "How do you know?"

"I've been Akim's personal Shadow since he became Prime eight years ago. After speaking with your father, Akim gave me a list of people who'd played roles in the challenge and asked me to find them."

Rafe stilled as a lone car traveled down the quiet road in front of the strip mall, but it drove on without slowing. Santa Carla was now considered a college town, but it still had one foot firmly planted in its bedroom community past.

"Couldn't he just look them up in The Nine's database?" I asked.

His gaze remained on the road. "Those searches are tracked. If Akim had looked up those names, it would have been reported to Henry Thorne. He'd figure out pretty quick what my brother was investigating."

What about a singular Shadow Nine search from Nicholas's computer? Would it pique Henry's interest enough for him to want to know more? My teeth started to chatter, but it wasn't solely from the cold.

"I've only been able to learn the whereabouts of three people so far. An enchanter named Solenn da Silva, a materialist called Danila Kovalenko, and a second materialist, Beatriz Santos." The latter had been one of Mitsuko's defenders, but the other two had sided with Henry. "And the first two died under suspicious circumstances almost twenty years ago."

I stared at him, horrified. If what I suspected was true, Solenn had been aware of the plan to distract my father with a rogue voyant; had Henry taken measures to ensure she never used that information against him? Danila's only crime, as far as I knew, was failing to act in time to save his brother, but maybe that was enough for Henry to sign her death warrant. Of course, this was all guesswork; I had no proof.

"Are you saying those women were murdered?" I asked.

Light brown eyes, so similar to his brother's, focused on me. "I'm only telling you what I've learned because Akim said you could be trusted. It was his job to put the information I gave him into context, not mine."

The door to Jitters swung open, and Cindy popped her head out. "You doing okay, Blake?" Though a bit of side work had to be done before we could clock out, I sensed it was genuine concern rather than impatience that prompted her check on me.

"Yeah, I'll be right in." I turned to Rafe to ask if we could continue this conversation when I got off work, but his receding form was already at the other end of the mall. Another moment, and true to his designation, he became one with the shadows.

My dad didn't answer when I called a few minutes later from the comfort of my car, but he was likely exhausted from his long drive home. Rafe's visit had left me scared and unsettled, and I needed someone who could help me make sense of it all. I left a message saying I'd hoped he'd made it home safely before dialing a second number from my favorites list.

"The Lower 8," Suki answered sulkily. Strangely upbeat music blared in the background.

"It's Blake. Everything okay?"

"Fine," she huffed. "Jessie didn't come in tonight, so Gustav chose Oktoberfest for tonight's theme. It's a beer festival they celebrate in Austria or Germany or wherever, but do you know how many people have demanded their cover charge back after being forced to listen to polka music for an hour?"

I smiled to myself. "Sounds, uh, interesting."

"Kill me now," she said with a groan. "Someone just started to yodel."

"Sorry to miss all the fun." I said goodbye and hung up, having got what I needed.

Traffic was light at this time of night, so I arrived at Jessie's place before I could fully think through why it was a good idea to appear on his doorstep unannounced. Warm light filtered through the multipaned windows just under the loft's roofline, but the street was so quiet I could hear the whisper of my sneakers on pavement as I padded to the door.

Would he be happy to see me or would the memory of the warning I'd delivered last time I was there cause him to slam the door? There was only one way to find out.

I rapped on the front door and waited. A light breeze kicked up and rattled the leaves of the nearby tree. Across the street the glow of a big screen seeped through a set of window blinds, and the yip of a small dog trailed down from a second-floor balcony. After a minute or two of standing there with no sign of movement from the other side, I started back to my car. The metallic click of a deadbolt rolling over made me turn back.

Jessie stood in the open doorway, the light from behind transforming his unbound hair into a golden halo but rendering the terrain of his face into a valley of shadows. The only emotion I picked up was sadness, making it impossible to gauge my welcome. I became even less certain as the silence between us stretched into awkwardness.

"I'm sorry," I finally blurted. He had his own troubles. The last thing he needed was to hear about mine. "I shouldn't have come."

"Wait." He retreated a few steps, and the ambient light revealed eyes darkened to the color of storm clouds, a mouth pinched with dejection, and a chin that hadn't seen a razor since the last time we'd met. "Come in."

After closing the door, he made his way to the couch. On the coffee table, a cut-glass tumbler and an open bottle of Jack Daniels stood at the ready, though the liquor had barely been tapped. He flopped down and raised a half-filled glass in my direction.

"Help yourself to one if you want," he offered.

I took the other end of the sofa. "I don't drink, and neither do you."

That wasn't exactly true. While he always seemed to be nursing a glass of Coke when I visited the club, he'd sipped from a glass of amber liquid, presumably whiskey or bourbon, the night he'd lost his bid to become regent.

"It's not for lack of trying." He took a nip and grimaced. "I just hate the taste of the stuff."

I scooted closer and reached for his glass. "Then don't torture yourself." He allowed me to take it from his hand.

"Use a coaster," he urged when I would have set it directly on the table. He might have a broken heart, but his exacting nature was fully intact.

"Where's Thorne?" he asked. "He always seems to be around when I'm at my lowest."

"Gone." I leaned back on the sofa and sighed. "He only seems to be around when I'm at my most desperate."

He settled in beside me and propped his bare feet on the coffee table. I kicked off my shoes and did the same, showing off socks covered with cute drawings of cats that I'd liberated from Scarlett's drawer. Doing laundry had been way down on my list of priorities lately.

"Why are you with him then?" he ventured after we'd both spent a minute admiring my feet.

"How many girlfriends have you had?" I countered.

"A few," he admitted.

"And each time you met one, did it turn out like you thought it would?"

He gave the question some thought. "Sometimes yes, sometime no. The more interesting the woman, the more likely I was to be surprised by the direction things went. God knows I didn't see Amani coming."

He reached for his glass and took another vile sip. "Why do you ask?"

I should be offering sympathy and a shoulder to cry on, but for some reason all my questions and doubts of the last few weeks surfaced instead.

"How do you know if you can trust someone?" I asked.

His laugh was tinged with bitterness. "You're asking *me*?"

"Sorry. It's just that I've had visions of all sorts of betrayals—within families, between lovers, between best friends—and each time, the person being stabbed in the back was *so* surprised." I wiggled my toes, making a couple of the cats undulate. "Do you think it's made me too cynical? Or is it like paranoia, in that just because you're paranoid doesn't mean you're not being followed?"

He sat back again, and this time our shoulders touched. I did my best not to react to the flare of energy our slight contact generated.

"When we first met," he said, "do you remember me telling you not to trust anyone?"

I snickered at the memory. "You said that included you."

"I don't think you can trust anyone, really," he said, his voice reflective. "They're always going to do what's best for them, no matter how it affects you."

I turned my head towards him. "Now who's being cynical?"

He glanced at me, our faces inches apart. Neither of us said anything as our hearts ticked away the seconds. The depths of his gray eyes appeared fathomless, and I wondered if that would change if he looked at me with the same passion he'd shown toward Amani in the vision that had so stirred my blood. Since learning she was also a sentinel, I'd realized it must have come from him. Perhaps my thoughts were too transparent because he abruptly turned away and pushed up from the sofa.

"Have you eaten?" He crossed to the kitchen, giving me a moment to regain my composure.

"Have you?" It was late, but he probably had no idea of the time.

"I haven't been hungry 'til now." By the time I joined him, he had a variety of cheeses, olives, and cured meats on the counter. Half a baguette came out of a drawer.

I started to unwrap a wedge of brie. "You just happened to have all this lying around?"

He opened a chilled bottle of near beer and took a swallow before handing it to me. I took a tentative sip and found the yeasty taste not all bad.

"You never know when someone will drop by to discuss doomed relationships." His tone was light, but the sentiment gave me pause. I set the brie on a bamboo platter he'd produced for the purpose.

"Do you think Nicholas and I are doomed?" I echoed his casual manner.

He stopped what he was doing to study my face. At last he said, quietly and simply, "Yes."

I gasped slightly at his answer. "Why?"

"My guess is he sees you as a worthy partner in his quest to unify The Nine, and that together the two of you would save the world as we know it."

My mouth twisted in confusion. "Is that such a bad thing?"

Neither of us had yet looked away, and it left me feeling oddly exposed. He took a few moments to answer, as if measuring his words.

"I think you'd rather have someone more interested in saving you."

I stared at him, suddenly aware of the intense feelings filling the space between us, drumming against my skin like a soft summer rain. Desire pulsed through me, but I didn't know if it was mine or his. The intensity was the same as it often was with Nicholas, but there was a depth of emotion enveloping me I had never experienced before. I trembled with the sweetness of it.

"What if I don't need saving?" I asked, almost breathless from the onslaught.

"I didn't say you did." He stepped closer, our bodies very nearly touching. "But wouldn't it be nice to be with someone who would save you first and let the rest of the world be damned?"

Despite so many unanswered questions, I was still with Nicholas. Jessie was an opportunistic player who would likely use me the moment I dropped my guard, especially after having been so recently burned. Yet stepping away from him was unthinkable as I savored the anticipation of what might come next until it became almost unbearable.

Never taking his eyes from mine, his hands rode up my hips and slowly encircled my waist. He pulled me against him, and I shivered as his muscular length pressed against my gentle curves. He lowered his face to mine until our breath mingled.

"Don't kick a man when he's down, darlin'." His hungry gaze dropped to my lips as if he could almost taste them. "If this is going to happen, you can't tell me later it meant nothing."

His words shredded the last of my resistance. The truth I'd been denying for so long filled my soul with an exquisite vulnerability that demanded to be seen. My feelings for Jessie were tangled and confusing, but indifference was nowhere among them.

My hands found the back of his neck. "If I ever said that, it would be a lie."

I pulled his face down to mine, and our lips met.

The Nine:
Book 4
COMING SOON

Follow Owl Hollow Press on social media or subscribe to our newsletter at OwlHollowPress.com for the latest news and updates on The Nine, a nine-book series by Kes Trester.

Or find out more about Kes Trester and her other books at KesTrester.com

ACKNOWLEDGEMENTS

I will be forever grateful to Emma Nelson and Hannah Smith of Owl Hollow Press for reading the first book in The Nine series and wanting more. Having the opportunity to develop and grow a cast of characters over multiple books is an author's dream, and I hope you're enjoying the evolution of Blake Wilder as much as I am.

Thank you to my incredibly supportive husband, family, and friends, and to my editor Olivia Swenson. Also, much appreciation to my agents, Kim Lindman of Stonesong Literary, and Addison Duffy of UTA.

Most importantly, I am grateful to the readers who picked up my debut novel, *A Dangerous Year*, and have stuck with me ever since. Your enthusiasm and words of encouragement have meant the world to me.

A native of Los Angeles, Kes Trester's first job out of college was on a film set, though the movie's title will remain nameless because it was a really bad film. Really.

As a feature film development executive, she worked on a variety of independent films, from gritty dramas (guns and hotties) to steamy vampire love stories (fangs and hotties) to teens-in-peril genre movies (blood and hotties).

Kes produced a couple of independent films, both award-winners on the festival circuit, before segueing into television commercials. As head of production for a Hollywood-based film company, she supervised the budgeting and production of nationally broadcast commercials (celebrities, aliens, talking animals!) and award-winning music videos for artists such as Radiohead, Coldplay, and OKGO (more celebrities, aliens, and talking animals!).

Kes' contemporary novels are cinematic, fast-paced, and above all, fun. Her well-received debut novel, the young adult boarding school thriller A DANGEROUS YEAR, has been optioned for film/television. She is a four-time Pitch Wars mentor and an SCBWI Susan Alexander Grant award winner. When she's not writing, she can usually be found in the company of an understanding husband, a couple of college-age kids, and a pack of much-loved rescue dogs.

Find Kes online at KesTrester.com

#THENINE #TOTHENINES

www.ingramcontent.com/pod-product-compliance
Lightning Source LLC
Chambersburg PA
CBHW060654190726

48289CB00002B/406